Snow Roses

By Taryn Tyler

For Hallel Tyler
Thank you for all the support

Thank you to my patrons Kimberly and kickass author J.J. Elliot for your continued support. I cannot thank you enough for believing in the value of my words.

SNOW ROSES

In the Dark

What is out there in the dark?
Teeth and claws and endless shadow
What is out there in the dark?
Winds that bite and beasts that swallow

But I am safe here in these walls
Cradled away from light that blisters
Smothered, I cannot hear the calls,
The howling shrieks and crying whispers

Here I spin an endless thread
Of powers I cannot hope to reach
My heart bleeds in an endless red
With songs I must not try to breach

What is out there in the dark?
The pain of loss, the screams of sorrow
What is out there in the dark?
Too much past, too much tomorrow

I am locked behind these walls
Cowering inside a memory
I am bound by soundless calls,
By fears that screech to be set free

Forbidden thoughts frost with ice,
Melting in a heap unspoken
Silence is life's sacrifice
If you want your mind unbroken

I am trapped here in the dark
Without a friend, without a vision
I am trapped here in the dark
Within these walls, within this prison

Whatever horrors lurk out there
I know that they could never be
As treacherous as this black hole
Twisted deep inside of me

SNOW ROSES

I am lost here in the dark
Blind to hope, unmasked of purpose
I am lost here in the dark
Lost to thought, alone with madness

SNOW ROSES

SNOW

I grew used to papa's death the way summer dwindles into winter. Silently. Laboriously. Without hope.

I do not know when the funeral was held. I do not know how many foreign dignitaries attended or how the common folk mourned the loss of their ruler. I imagine I was invited --expected to attend in somber black silk, suffering silently by my stepmother's side. I imagine that my handmaidens pleaded with me to allow them to dress me but I never heard them. I paced across the intricate weave of my chamber's rug, losing myself in its elaborate swirls, trying to conceive some kind of consistent pattern. My eyes grew raw and tender around the rims. I slept little and ate only when coerced. My already slight form and pale skin became a rattle of bones and a ghostly pallor.

When I did sleep I dreamt that I was drowning. Ice cold water poured into my lungs, filling them until I thought my chest would burst. Other nights —or days; I had long since stopped keeping track of time —thick, thorny vines wound their way around me, squeezing until I bled. I woke, screaming, only to realize that the reality was worse than any nightmare.

I woke one day, blinking up at the ceiling above my bed. It took me a moment to realize that the big-eyed, bat-like creatures engraved on it were not trying to eat me. I remembered that Papa was and always would be dead. He would never tell me another story riddled with indecipherable morals again. He would never look up from mounds of records with a fond,

1

preoccupied smile and tell me that he was going to be king for the afternoon and my questions would have to wait until dinner. He would never press his hand against mine and tell me how strong I was, making the statement true with the deep strength of his voice.

My chest burned with an inner sinking I thought would never end. My limbs felt dead and leaden as they sank into my down mattress. It was a familiar feeling that I had begun to accept along with the damp of the cooling season.

Through the haze of despair I suddenly realized that I was hungry.

Hunger. I'd almost forgotten the sensation curdling in my stomach, gurgling around like a boiling pot until it almost seemed to hiss at me. I lay there for a moment beneath the heaviness of my comforter, remembering the sensation now that I had given it a name.

I sat up. I rolled the comforter off and walked across my chamber floor. The door creaked as I pushed against the iron handles. It felt heavier than it had the last time I had opened it. My thin arms shook under the weight. I poked my head out into the antechamber.

Brightness streamed in from the windows, blinding me. I squeezed my eyes shut. "Elise." The sound came out a whisper. My throat felt hoarse and scratchy. I cleared it and tried again. "Elise." Louder this time but still not quite clear. "Elise."

"Elise is gone." The voice was tight, short and irritated as if I had interrupted some great and all important thought. I pried my eyes open to see the shadow of a tall, dark haired woman in mourning clothes sitting on Elise's embroidered chair. She scowled at me.

"When will she be back?" I asked. I had thought it was still morning but perhaps I'd slept longer than I'd thought. "Is Dana--"

"Elise and Dana are both gone." Her voice grew tighter. "They will not be back. I am Constanze." She seemed to think that a sufficient explanation for why both my handmaidens, who had been with me since they were my nurses, had suddenly abandoned me.

Gone. Just like Papa. My throat swelled but I didn't want to cry in front this strange, stone faced woman. I squinted at her, trying to decide if I'd seen her before but I couldn't remember. The last days had danced by in a whirl of pain and whispers. I raised my head in the best lady-of-the-manor stance I could manage with red eyes and a wet nose. "Constanze, I am hungry. Bring me some breakfast."

Constanze bowed her head. At least I think she did. The motion was so slight it might have been a shadow shifting outside the window. Her long, black gown rippled around her ankles as she slipped out into the corridor. The whole household must have been wearing black now. Except for me. I'd been up here in the same thin, white night shift for I didn't know how long.

I let the heavy ebony doors slam shut and slunk down against the wall. My body ached with exhaustion. The tears started again. By the time Constanze brought me my breakfast my eyes were swollen once more, my nose red and tender. I stirred the simple oat porridge around, nibbling only a little at the unbuttered bread she had brought with it.

When I was finished Constanze returned to fetch the half empty bowl and crumbled bits of bread away. She looked down at me. I didn't look very much like the lady of the manner crumpled against the wall with my night shift stretched around my feet. She curled her lip and raised an eyebrow in a mocking query. "Will you be dining with the queen tonight, your ladyship?"

The queen? Oh, she meant Lucille. The last thing I wanted was to sit beneath my stepmother's scrutiny while she waited for me to use the wrong fork or spill gravy on my chin. I never did but that didn't stop her from watching me with more intensity than any of my tutors ever had. Papa had laughed when I'd complained. 'You make her as nervous as she makes you.' I hadn't wanted to be the one to smooth the laugh lines out of his forehead so I hadn't argued but Papa was gone now. There was no longer a reason to pretend I liked her.

Gone. The aching feeling in my chest deepened. I struggled to remind myself that Constanze was still staring down at me, waiting for an answer. I forced myself to meet her gaze. I shook my head then looked back down at my fingers, limp in my lap. I didn't see or hear Constanze leave but she must have. The next time I looked over at the patterns on my rug she was gone. So was the porridge and the bread.

I couldn't sleep that night. I squirmed and rolled beneath my comforter and the gaze of the bat-like carvings overhead but not even nightmares would overtake me. I rose out of bed and went to the window. The pane was caked with dust and frosted over with ice. I leaned forward and breathed onto the glass. Tiny icicles melted away, drizzling down the pane onto the black ebony windowsill. I pressed my palm against the glass and smeared away the dust with my fingers. The ice bit through my skin into my bones.

The courtyard was dark but for a few lanterns pacing back and forth near the gate. The fire in the forge was on and I could make out the shadows of Lucille's men working in the yard. The window was closed but I could imagine the rhythmic hammering of iron wares being made. I shuddered, remembering the burn of hot iron from my dreams.

If it had been a dream. I shut my eyes, trying to blot out the memory with darkness.

I climbed back into bed. Soon I was asleep, dreaming the worst of all the dreams. Papa, tossing in his bed, unable to recognize me through the fog of fever in his eyes. Me, gripping his hand as if I could make him stay if I held on tight enough. His eyes, gray and lifeless as Lucille stooped over him and rolled them shut with her pale, soft hands.

It was still dark when I woke. The quiet, thin dark of early morning, not the busy, thick dark of night. I drew myself out of bed and went to the window again. Squinting, I could see only one of Lucille's men in the yard, chopping wood outside the stable. His work was quick and meticulous as he piled log after log onto the wood pile. It was late for such work. Or early. Not even the cooks and scullery maids were up yet. He stopped suddenly and looked up toward my window as if he could feel my gaze.

I stepped back. The silver-spun drapes dropped over the window, blocking me from sight. I clenched my fists. My breath tightened. Why had my heartbeat quickened? Why had my blood gone so cold, heavy as if it were being drained down into the ground? Had it been so long since the world outside had acknowledged my existence? I laid my palm against the top of my breast where the pain was the deepest. How long had it been? Days? Weeks?

I glanced at the heavy ebony door across my chamber. Only a few steps away. I dropped my hand to my side, edging my way toward it. I pressed my ear against the wood and listened. Constanze acted more like a jailer than a handmaid. I wasn't certain she would let me out if I asked. I breathed deep, clenching my fingers tight around my hand. Nothing stirred in the antechamber. I unhooked the latch and pressed the door open, inch by inch to keep the hinges from creaking. I peeked out.

Constanze lay across the handmaids' sofa, her legs dangling over the side, her head rolled back. The dark, somber fabric of her gown looked strange against the embroidered silk of the sofa even in the shadows. Snores filtered out of her mouth in a series of short starts like my first attempts at notes before I convinced Papa I wasn't meant to play the flute.

I crept past her, balancing my bare feet against the carpeted floor. I pressed my hand against the door handle and held my breath. Constanze stirred, rolling her head amongst the pillows. The snoring stopped. I bit my lip to hold back a gasp. A stinging drop of blood rolled down the corner of my mouth.

The half-hearted whistle of Constanze's snores returned. I breathed again and pressed against the door, bracing myself for the pull of a latch chain.

The door opened. I caught my balance as I stumbled out into the corridor. The long hall was eerie. Strange. Nothing like the safe labyrinth I had memorized as a child. The candelabras were unlit. The dark threaded tapestries draped toward the ground like heavy spider's webs. I glanced back at Constanze to be sure that she was still asleep and clicked the door shut.

The corridor was empty. No one stopped me as I pattered through the twists and turns, quiet and sightless like a blind rat, until I reached the manor's side door. I hung back just outside of the shadow of the door's pale wooden planks and tarnished silver hinges. A pair of night guards dozed against the wall on either side of it, catching what few minutes of sleep they could before the morning guards relieved them and sent them back to the day's training.

I crept past the guards on the balls of my feet. The deep scratch of their breaths echoed through the dark, interrupted only by the irregular thump and clatter of ax and wood. Once outside, I shivered. The stone was cold against my bare feet, sending chills up through my soles. A scullery maid knelt next to the well, fetching the morning's water. She gathered up her bucket and scurried past me.

I approached the woodcutter, still working next to the stable. I had seen him before. He had been among the first to arrive with Lucille, always lurking in her shadow, whispering in her ear. Her other men called him the Hunter since he wasn't a part of their ranks and regiments. No one knew quite what his function was except that he often returned from long trips into the forest with a deer or a swan for Lucille's dinner table. I glanced at the long knife thrust into his belt, the bear fur lining his tunic. Whatever his function he didn't look like a man who would hesitate to kill.

The Hunter looked up at me, letting his ax head fall to the ground. He scowled.

I stared, wondering if I should speak. If he would ask me what I was doing out in the yard so early. If I had any kind of answer for him. "I can help." I said "With the wood."

He pressed his lips together. His scowl deepened beneath his wild mat of black hair. He glanced up at my chamber window. "I suppose Constanze isn't much for company." He lifted his ax, turning the handle out towards me. "Be careful. It's heavy. Half your weight I reckon. Hasn't the queen been feeding you?"

The queen again. Papa had never called Lucille that even after he'd made her his wife. "I . . . haven't been feeding myself." I took the ax. Its weight pulled at my arm sockets and I almost dropped it. I tightened my fingers around the handle. It was worn but free of splintering slivers.

The Hunter nodded. "It takes you that way sometimes. The sadness."

"How long?" I asked "Since . . ."

He pointed up at the pale sliver of moon above us. It glowed faintly through the drifting veil of clouds. "The night the king died there was no moon." He said. "Tomorrow there will be no moon."

My grip on the ax slackened. A month. Twenty nine days. It was a long time to be shut up in my chamber.

He nodded toward the unchopped logs. "Get on with it then. Work makes you hungry."

I lifted the ax. My arms shook. It had been so long since I had lifted even a hairbrush. I aimed for the wood laid out on the chopping block and swung downward. The ax fell. Fast.

The Hunter put out his hand, catching the ax before the blade swung into my shins. "Steady. Swing, don't drop. Stay in control. Go slow if you have to."

I lifted the ax again and swung downward. This time I brought the sharp edge down onto the chopping block, missing the wood by at least three inches. Another try and I tapped the wood but didn't swing hard enough to slice it. Again and again and again I tried until I'd lost track of how many times. My shoulders grew sore then warm then numb, my breath short, then strained, then long and controlled, as I concentrated on guiding the ax blade. The Hunter stood beside me, watching, interfering only when the blade came near my shin or toes.

Finally I swung the blade down, hard and direct, onto the wood. It splintered beneath the blow, falling away with a heavy thud.

"Good." The Hunter held his hand out for the ax. I handed it to him. My fingers and palms ached as I let go, red and scratched from gripping so hard.

The Hunter resumed his work without a word, grim and determined as if nothing else in the world existed. I sat on the ground with my back against the stable wall and watched him work, lifting the tool up over his head, then letting it swing down onto the wood. Pieces of log clattered onto the ground and he stooped to stack them against the stable wall.

Winter was on its way but the woodpile was already high enough to keep the manor warm for months. I wondered why the Hunter needed to work in the early hours of the morning, why he needed work to make him hungry. My eyes drooped as I listened to the splintering, uneven fall of iron against the chopping block.

I started at the touch of the Hunter's hand against my wrist. The chopping had stopped. I opened my eyes, blinking up at him. It was almost dawn. I hadn't meant to fall asleep.

"You'd better go." He said "The queen won't like me taking you up."

I nodded and rose to my feet, shivering. My feet were wet and numb from the morning frost. The hem off my night shift was drenched where it had draped over the ground. I turned and trudged back toward the manor.

"Snow."

I turned around, startled. He had called me by my name as if I were any other child on the manor. As if I weren't the king's daughter. I should have been angry but I wasn't.

"Next time bring a pair of shoes. You don't want to get frost bite."

I nodded.

Every morning after that I rose before dawn and joined the Hunter ---Hans he told me to call him--- in the yard next to the stable. We didn't speak much. We just chopped wood. My arms grew stronger, my aim steadier. When I could split almost as many logs as he could he showed me how to throw knives and make animal traps then taught me where to slice a man's throat for the cleanest, quickest death. I watched him kill first a rabbit then a lamb for Lucille's dinner table.

The moon reappeared and grew full again. The morning frost began to harden and remain throughout the day as the season grew colder and colder. I never told Constanze about my lessons. As far as she knew I didn't wake until late morning when I poked my head out of my chamber to ask for breakfast. I never went out when it was light. I didn't want hundreds of eyes prying at me, wondering where I had been the last weeks when I should have been taking up papa's duties to the villages.

"Does she miss him?" I asked Hans one morning. I pulled the silver knife he had given me to practice with out of the molding straw doll he had set up against the stable wall. I blew a piece of straw off it, trying not to wheeze on the spores of mold.

Hans blinked. He fixed his eyes on me, searching for my meaning.

"Lucille." I said. "Does she miss Papa?" I hadn't seen her since the night she had rolled his eyes shut. The night she had had my hands pried from his and had me dragged to my chamber, squealing like a pig before slaughter.

Hans shrugged.

"You would know." I gripped my hand tight around the silver knife handle. I could feel the grooves marking their pattern of vines and oak leaves into my skin. "If she missed him you would know."

I stepped away from the straw doll. I balanced myself on both feet then drew the knife back behind my ears. It was difficult to see in the dark but not impossible. The waxing moon was bright overhead. I aimed upward and just a little to the right since my throwing hand was on the left, then flung my arm forward. The blade reached the center of my vision. I released it. It tumbled through the air in an uneven whir, then plodded into the straw doll's faceless head.

"He didn't marry her for love." I said "He married her because he knew he could never win a war against her."

"You are wrong. " Hans said "Your father did marry Lucille for love."

I turned towards him, pivoting on my heels in the chill of early morning. It wasn't true. I had seen no fondness between them. No snatched whispers or lingering glances. Papa had spent more time with me than he ever had with Lucille and more time with his kingdom than the two of us together. There was nothing wrong in it. Only people in stories married for love.

"It was your father's idea to marry Lucille." Hans said. "When she

7

first came she wanted him to give you to Prince Boris in exchange for peace. Your father married her instead."

I opened my mouth but nothing came out. The morning chill settled around me, soaking into the sudden stillness. I stared at Hans, trying not to imagine myself far away in Lucille and Boris's big castle in the north. The one all her soldiers and servants had come from. I tried not to imagine Boris as my husband, hungrily watching me undress for my wedding night.

For me. Papa had married for love of me and the marriage contract had been his death warrant.

No. That wasn't fair. Papa had held no love for Lucille. I held no love for her. That didn't make her a murderess.

Small, soft hands, rolling lifeless eyes shut. How had she been so calm?

"It doesn't matter anymore." I said. "He's gone." Nothing mattered. I walked over to the straw doll and pulled the knife out, fighting back a wave of nausea, of darkness, of my whole being sinking down into the ground. I bit my lip, tasting the rust flavor of my blood, as I walked back to Hans. I held my hand out and unfurled my fingers around the knife, waiting for him to take it.

Hans closed my fingers back over the hilt. "Keep it."

"Thank you." I gripped my hand around the handle, taking comfort in the solidity of the engraved silver against my palms.

It wasn't until later that morning, while I was looking for a place to keep the knife, that I realized that every other sharp object had been removed from my chamber. Even my embroidery needles and Mama's silver comb. I touched my matted tangles. They had refused to come unwound even after a full day of brush strokes.

If only I had a pair of sheers. I looked at the blade still in my hand. Sharp. Elegant.

A few moments later the tangles were in a pile of black shreds around my feet. The remaining threads bounced clean and light around my ears. The edges prickled my neck.

Constanze looked horrified when I gave her the shreds of hair to dispose of but she said nothing. She seldom spoke except to ask me if I would be dining with the queen each day in her harsh, mocking tone.

The next day I asked her for a bath as well as my breakfast. The day after that I picked up a book and tried to read. The Latin hymns were hard to concentrate on. The love poems were worse. I took out a quill and paper and wrote what I could remember of one of Papa's tales. Tears prickled in my eyes and dripped down my nose, soaking into the crisp paper along with the ink. I wrote until the light was too gray to see by then laid the pages out on the table to dry. I changed back into my night shift and sat on my bed, watching the sky darken.

I must have fallen asleep. I woke from a long, twisting stream of nightmares to the scent of wheat porridge and honey. The bright light of late morning streamed in through the window, dancing with the dust that permeated from my drapes and tapestries. I bolted upright. Hans was supposed to show me how to skin an animal pelt that morning.

It would have to wait. The still of early morning was past. The yard would be full of drilling soldiers.

I pulled myself out of bed and examined the breakfast already waiting for me on the table next to the pages of papa's story. The bread was still warm. I ate all three pieces, smothered in honey, while I stacked the pages and read through what I'd written. It wasn't much like papa's stories at all. I'd forgotten the part where the princess confessed her deception to the cook and added a crow who kept trying to peck out her eyes. I'd ran out of light before I'd gotten her out of the castle dungeons.

I finished my breakfast and set the story aside. I didn't know how to get the princess out without the cook as her ally. When Constanze returned to take my dishes away I was already dressed, my feathery crop of hair brushed as neatly as I could manage. She placed her hand the the dishes to take them away and paused. She arched an eyebrow. "Mourning clothes?"

"Of course." I looked down at my long black gown laced tightly around my shift. It hung over the toes of my boots, dragging the hem against the carpet. It hadn't been three months yet since papa's death. Surely everyone in the castle was still in mourning. Constanze herself wore the same plain black wool gown I'd seen her in everyday since I'd met her.

Constanze curled her lips. She lifted the tray and turned toward the door.

"Wait." I said. This was when she usually asked me if I would be dining with the queen. With Lucille.

Constanze turned back. Her small eyes sharpened like a cornered rodent's. What could she possibly be frightened of?

"I will be dining with the queen tonight." I said.

Constanze bowed her head. A real bow. The crown of her head drooped from her shoulders with an unaccustomed weight. "As you wish, your ladyship."

I watched her go. The door clicked shut. My belly swirled with nausea. Why had I said that? To vex her? To frighten her?

No. I sank down onto my mattress and stared up at the iron bat-like creatures frozen onto the ceiling. I almost wished they would come to life and devour me the way they did in my nightmares. I'd said it to find out why Constanze no longer wished me to dine with Lucille -- why she had ever suggested it at all. The last thing I wanted to do was spend the evening making polite remarks to Boris and his mother. Especially after . . .

The sickness in my stomach tightened. I breathed deep, hating myself for being glad for the first time that papa had married Lucille. Not even a prince could take his own sister even if she were only a stepsister.

I closed my eyes, resisting the urge to leap off my bed, pound my fists against the door, and scream to Constanze that I had changed my mind. I wasn't sure I could stomach the whispering gaze of the servants, wondering what I had been doing shut up in my chamber all this time.

Nothing. I had been doing nothing.

I couldn't concentrate on transcribing any more of papa's story. It was insufficient. A vacant copy using only some of his words without the vibrancy of his laughter and wit as he had told it. I stared at the pages of the philosophy and romance books that cluttered my chamber, scanning my eyes across the words but registering none of it. The thoughts and images each scrawl was meant to unlock in my mind remained hidden to me as I stared, uncomprehending, at the ink and paper.

At last I gave up. I took the knife Hans had given me out of my jewelry box and practiced thrusting it into one of my pillows. My nerves were beyond calming but at least the repetitive motion gave my hands something to do. My fist clenched tight around the knife hilt as if it would give me some of its steadiness.

When there was nothing left of the pillow I dumped the feathers and shreds of silk into the bottom of my chest so Constanze wouldn't ask questions when she came to dress me for dinner. The pale white flakes floated out of my hand and settled among my colored stockings and gowns like winter's first falling of snow. I slammed the lid shut.

Constanze came earlier than I expected. The sky hadn't even started to gray when three even knocks sounded against my chamber door. I jumped up off my bed and fumbled with the latch to let her in.

Constanze stepped inside. Her lips pulled even more tightly together than usual as she glanced at the black velvet gown I had already laid out across the chair behind me. "Mourning is over." She said "The queen will expect color." She brushed past me, snatched the gown off the cushion, and popped my clothing chest open. If she saw the feathers and silk shreds inside it she said nothing. She rummaged through my clothes until she found a deep purple gown embroidered with silver leaves around the wrists and bodice line. The chemise she chose for it was cream white with wide, flamboyant sleeves.

Constanze helped me out of my daytime clothes and into the silk gown. Her hands were quick and firm as she pulled the laces tight around the bodice. She gave me a pair of silk stockings to put on then slipped a pair of deep purple slippers to match the gown over my feet. She stood up and eyed the hacked threads of my hair sticking up around my ears with disapproval. It was too short for any of the ribbons or hair pins crowded together in my jewelry box. She flattened what she could down with my brush and left the chamber. When she returned she had Mama's silver comb in her hand. She pressed it into the side of my hair and stood back, examining her work with pursed lips. "That will have to do."

I glanced toward the window, trying to see my reflection in it, but it hadn't grown dark enough yet. I counted back the days again in my head. It couldn't have been three months. It hadn't even been two. Perhaps they didn't mourn as long in the north.

"Hurry." Constanze said "Or you'll be late."

My heart hiccuped in my chest as I made my way through the corridors towards the dining hall. I hadn't been down these corridors since . . . since Papa was waiting for me at the end of them. I had taken my suppers with him in his chamber after he'd taken ill. I breathed deep, struggling to keep my footsteps slow and steady. He hadn't been ill for long. A day at most.

The corridors were quiet. My slippers clicked against the stone floor in the fading light. Lucille never burned oil or coal if she could avoid it. I could barely make out the shadows of the footmen as I passed them. A draft howled past me from an open window. I shivered.

At last I saw a flicker of torchlight. The thick savory scents of apples and cinnamon and sausages filtered through my nostrils, sharpening my hunger. I quickened my pace and stepped into the dining hall.

I stopped, unable to move.

Lucille turned toward me from Papa's seat at the head of the table. Her green eyes glittered in the torchlight. Nut brown curls rippled down her back. She smiled. It was the first smile I had seen in weeks and it chilled me to the marrow.

"The mad princess emerges from her tower at last." Her son Boris fixed me with a smile of his own from his seat beside her. It was a clever, amiable smile that almost made me like him until I remembered how many villages he and his men had ransacked. How many settlements he had burned and women he had taken against their will.

I moved my gaze from him back to Lucille. The table was spread with sweet breads and candied nuts, pears, apple strudels, roast swans, and platter after platter of sausages. My belly heaved with sickness.

"Well." Lucille said. "Are you going to sit down?"

I shook my head, unable to speak. Lucille. Boris. The six footmen lined up and down the walls on either side of the table. They were all dressed in a plain, somber, unmistakable black. Even Lucille's thick, abundant hair was held back in a simple braid. She wore no jewelry.

Constanze had lied. Mourning wasn't over at all.

I stepped back, wilting in my draping silk sleeves and deep purple gown. Mama's comb, engraved with deep, elaborate vines, stabbed into my hair like a knife. I should have known. I should have stopped Constanze instead of stampeding over Papa's memory as if he had been nothing.

11

"She looks like she's going to be ill." Boris said.

I turned and ran. My feet flailed against the stone floor, pounding as if I could crush the deep leaden feeling out of my chest. I gulped air into my chest but it didn't quell the dizziness swarming my mind, pelting it with memories. I rushed through the corridors until I reached my chamber. I darted across the antechamber without glancing at Constanze and flung the doors of my bedchamber open. I slammed them shut behind me and leaned against the ebony splinters, pressing my forehead into the ironwork.

I closed my eyes, waiting for the tears to come but I was given no such relief. Papa's laughter turned to a scream inside my head. Soft delicate hands rolled his round eyes shut. Lucille's lyrical voice grew harsh as she ordered me to be taken from him. A strange curl edged itself into the corner of her lips as she turned away. Could it have been a smile

ROSE

The sky lit up with the brightness of the full moon but Greta kept the windows draped. "To keep the spirits out" she said but I never saw any spirits. Only the hypnotic turn of Greta's spinning wheel as we sat in the almost dark of a single candle, waiting for the night to pass. Greta kept her eyes on her wheel, pulling the thread through her fingers while it spun with the familiar thumping rhythm I had heard every day for as long as I could remember. Some days the sound almost put me to sleep. Tonight it made me restless and jumpy. The wind howled outside, beating against the draped windowpanes.

I carded a tuft of wool in my hands, pulling the rough material apart with a comb until it was smooth between my fingers. The house was cluttered with baskets of wool and pile after pile of spools wound with spiderweb-thin threads. A pot sat over the fire, bubbling with our supper as we worked. The scent of onions, carrots, and thick rabbit gravy filled the room. My stomach growled but we weren't to touch a bite until Gran arrived.

"Rose." Greta looked up from the steady whir of her wheel. It kept spinning. Her fingers knew what to do even without the aid of her eyes. "The miller's wife wants her thread next week not next year."

I gripped the wool in my hands, feeling the rough texture between my fingers. My stomach wasn't growling anymore. It was snarling. "Gran is late."

Greta looked back down at her wheel. The thread spun around and around, never stopping for a moment. "Perhaps she's seen sense and decided a walk after dark on a full moon is madness. Especially in that wood."

"Not Gran." I said "She isn't afraid of anything."

"Then she's a fool."

I sighed. Gran came every full moon no matter how many times Greta told her not to risk the long, cold walk on such a night. No matter how many times she begged and pleaded with her to come and live with us instead of among the wild dangers of the wood. I hated nights like this when we sat together, never knowing if Gran would arrive or not. Greta was dour in her best moods. On full moons she was like the living dead.

I stifled a giggle, imagining Greta haunting the forest with the rest of the spirits. I doubted she would have enough life in her even to moan. A spiritless spirit. Maybe it wasn't so amusing after all.

The wind beat harder against the window, groaning against the glass. A razor sharp gust leaked through the cracks in the door. I shivered.

"Add some logs to the fire, Rose." Greta said "And fill those cracks."

I stood, glad for the excuse to put down the wool and carding comb. I lingered over the fire, letting its warmth scorch the surface of my skin as I piled logs onto it. Embers scattered. A spark flew up toward my chin. I jumped back. It landed on my shawl and burned its way into the plain gray fabric. Wool of course. Everything in our house was made of wool. The curtains. The blankets. I sometimes wondered why Greta didn't insist we eat it.

I reluctantly stepped away from the fire and pulled a heap of scraps out of the scrap basket. The wind whistled at me as I moved toward the door. I knelt next to it, shivering. The moaning wind grew louder. A long howl pierced through the night, sending chills into my blood. I gasped, pulling back from the door. "Weres." There had been rumors of them in the village but no one had seen them for certain.

"Pay them no mind." Greta kept her head bent over her work. "They won't come near the fire."

"Gran is out there." I said.

For the flicker of a second I thought I saw Greta's tiny calloused hands go still but then the shadow in her eyes disappeared and thread was whirring through her fingers once more. The rhythm of her spinning wheel hadn't stopped turning. "We don't know that."

"She comes every--"

"And every moon I tell her she is a fool for it. She knows what dangers are out there better than any of us. If she comes to grief it is through her own choice and more importantly" She closed her eyes and let out a sigh, small and faint as if she her lungs had no air left to empty out. "More importantly, Rose, there is nothing we can do about it." She opened her eyes and looked down at me where I was still crouched on the floor. "We can't fight weres. We can't fight ghosts or storms or hobgoblins or kings or witches. The best we can do is stay out of their way."

I wrinkled my forehead. "Witches?"

The wool on Greta's wheel came to an end. She spun the last inch, then stopped the wheel with the palm of her hand. She wrapped the last bit of thread around the spool and tucked it so that it would hold. Her fingers moved quickly, done almost in the blink of an eye. "Pour the stew, Rose." She said "We can't wait any longer."

I stuffed the wool scraps into the cracks of the door with trembling hands. The howling released again outside, long and shrill. I couldn't decide if it sounded more like a battle cry or a call for help. I stood and poured stew into two wooden bowls but I wasn't hungry anymore. I stirred the gravy and vegetables around while Greta swallowed bite after bite in silence. The wind whistled, rattling against the door. I stared at the gray wooden planks, willing Gran to step through with her jaunty tired gait and gap toothed smile, boiling over with unspoken wisdom. Maybe she would bring us dyed wool to spin for her again.

Last time she had brought red. I had spun it myself, admiring the bright color as it ran across my fingers like a soft trickle of blood. Gran had taken the finished threads away and returned the next month with a blood red cloak. The wooden clasp was carved with a single rose.

"Like your name." Her honey colored eyes had wrinkled around the corners as she had draped the cloak around the plain gray of my skirt and bodice, covering the worn, heavy boots on my feet that had once been Greta's.

"You won't wear it of course." Greta had said almost the moment Gran had gone. "It's asking for trouble, brazen finery like that. The weres and hobgoblins will swallow you alive. Not to mention the village boys. Now there's a kettle I don't need boiling yet."

I had glared at her. It was a kettle she would never be ready for no matter how old I got. If Greta had her way I'd end up a spinster like her, condemned forever to drab grays and browns or whatever other rustic tone the wool was when the goat herders sold it to us. She'd taken the cloak and locked it away in the cupboard as if the bright hues would come to life and devour us.

Greta finished her supper. She put out the fire while I washed the dishes then we both climbed the rickety ladder up onto the loft. I laid next to her in the pile of straw with our quilt tucked beneath my chin. The wind moaned and howled outside. Unless it was the ghosts and weres. For all I knew they were the same thing.

I tried to sleep. At least I think I tried. My mind flooded with the image of Gran wandering alone in the darkness of the storm. I gritted my teeth and tightened my fingers into fists, willing myself to hold still. Soon Greta was snoring beside me.

I peeled back my half of the quilt and rolled out from underneath it, careful not to let cold air sidle through to the straw and wake Greta. I bit back a yelp as the chill of the night poured into my skin, harsher than ever now that the fire was gone. I smoothed my palm over the quilt, pressing it back down over the straw. My breath held, suspended in my chest. I made my way down the ladder, convinced that Greta would wake at any moment.

At last my feet touched the damp earthen floor, cold like ice. I turned and scurried around the room for my boots, my extra bodice, my shawl, and my gray cloak. Once I had them on my teeth stopped chattering. A fresh gust swept through the crack beneath the door. The wool scattered across the floor along with a flaky sprinkling of fresh snow. The howl sounded again outside. The sound vibrated through me, chilling me to the bone.

I snatched a basket full of thread off the floor and took out the spools, setting them silently onto the floor. If I found Gran she would need food, herbs, bandages perhaps. I wished I knew what exactly she would need. She was the one who knew the herbs. She had to, living alone in the wood. I took the cheese from the food cupboard along with what was left of the morning's bread. It was hard and dry but I could soften it with the stew Gran had never come for. I ladled the cold gravy and vegetables into a bowl and wrapped it in a piece of wool at the bottom of the basket. I scanned Greta's collection of herbs. The bottles winked at me with a flicker of moonlight from the window but I couldn't see what the ground powders inside were. Tarragon. Lavender. Sage. Greta kept mostly cooking herbs. I piled them all into the basket and turned toward the door.

I stopped. Without quite knowing why I pivoted. The locked cupboard in the corner cast a long mysterious shadow across the floor. My eyes strayed to the lock.

My cloak. The red one Gran had made me. It was only the first snow. Greta hadn't lined my gray cloak yet for winter. I would need them both to keep me warm out there in the chill of night.

I took Greta's cloak off the hook next to the door and fumbled in the pockets for her key. I felt nothing but the familiar course flop of wool and Greta's tight, tiny stitches.

The night howled again outside. Shivers leapt through me. "I'm coming Gran." I threw the cloak down and looked around the room. Where else would Greta keep the key? It could be in any basket. In any chest. Did she sleep with it hidden between her bosoms so that I would have no hope of finding it?

But that wasn't Greta. She might put something where I was least likely to look for it but she would also put it somewhere that made sense.

Somewhere practical for her. I pressed my lips together. Where would make sense inside Greta's neat, ordered mind?

The spinning wheel. She had her hand on it almost every moment of the day and I never touched it without her eyes on me from behind as she commented on my work. I stepped toward it and examined the spokes on the wheel, ran my fingers over the needle in the dark, felt underneath the foot treadle. I sighed. Nothing.

I sank down onto Greta's chair with more force than I should have with Greta only a few feet above me. She didn't stir. Something clinked against the ground beneath me. I bent over and peered between my ankles, letting my bushy mess of hair drape against the ground. A tiny shadow lay beneath the chair. A tiny key shaped shadow.

I snatched it up and swept toward the locked cupboard. It took a few tries but the lock finally snapped apart. The door creaked as I pulled it open. A single board lay across the middle. The top shelf was empty but below the board sat a lump of fabric, magnificent even in the dark. It smelled sweet and frothy and soft. Just like Gran.

I whisked the cloak into my arms and held it up to my nose, soaking in the scent. Like laughter. Like stillness. I unclasped the clasp and flung the wool over my shoulders. It settled over my other cloak, draping over me like a protective fog. Warmth spread through me. One side of the cloak weighed down more heavily than the other, pulling tight against the carved wooden clasp.

I slid my hand inside the right pocket and touched a lump of cold, smooth metal. The shape was familiar. I ran my finger along the long sharp tip, pressed my palm against the knobby head. A spindle. I lifted it out of my pocket. Its smooth surface almost seemed to gleam in the dark. I held it up to the moonlight to get a better look.

I gasped. Gold. Solid gold. But that wasn't all. On the head, right below the needle, was the engraving of a single rose. The petals twirled around the center exactly the way they did on the cloak's clasp.

"Like your name." Gran had said when she'd fastened the clasp beneath my chin.

An uneasy feeling swept through me. A kind of queasiness as if I'd seen the spindle before in some kind of nightmare. I shook myself. Ridiculous of course. I'd never seen anything gold before in my life. For all I knew it wasn't even real gold. There were other minerals, weren't there, that looked like gold?

I didn't have time for mysteries. Gran needed me. I thrust the spindle back into my pocket and headed for the door. I glanced at the flint and candles by the fireplace. This wind would smother any flame I tried to bring out into it but the moon was bright. I would have to trust that it would be enough.

It was cold inside. It was colder outside. A gust greeted me as I stepped through the door. I gripped the basket in my hands and closed the latch behind me, shivering. The wind gnawed at my nose and chin with icicle teeth. The night howled again, strong and wild. Hungry. The cold lessened as the call stirred fire through my veins.

I stepped forward, leaving a trail of foot shaped shadows in the virgin snow behind me. The tall gray specters of the other village houses slipped past me, one after the other under the bright pool of moonlight as I followed the road toward the wood. The village slept. I passed the bakery, the ovens heated with nothing but ash. I passed the mill, still like a corpse.

Asleep? The village might have been dead for its stillness. How could I ever have feared waking Greta? The fires of hell itself could never rouse anyone who lived here, just outside the cusp of the wood, afraid to enter it, afraid to remember how close it loomed.

At last I reached the edge of the wood. Tall oaks and laurels towered above me, binding their leaves and branches around each other in a tight embrace. I looked up at the swirl of clouds overhead. It would be the last I would see of the sky that night. The last I would see of the sky at all if the ghosts or hobgoblins found me. Or the weres. Even the moonlight would have trouble squeezing through once I was locked under the canopy of the tree branches.

Something stirred from inside the darkness. Shadow moved against shadow. A fox or a badger. A wolf or a hobgoblin.

A shiver crawled its way up my spine beneath my layers of clothing, turning itself into an unfamiliar tingle in my belly. My pulse and breath quickened. I stepped forward.

There. I'd done it. I'd stepped out of the village. Farther from home than I'd ever been before. Farther than any of the villagers had gone.

Any of the live ones that is.

I moved forward. The jitters fluttering through my chest dissolved as I turned the constant steps, one after the other, into a kind of rhythmic dance. My fingers and nose turned numb with cold. Straight up the road. Gran had once said I would know I was close to her cottage when I came to a creek. I listened for the sound of water but all I could hear was the shrill howl of the wind.

No. That was the animal call again. The howl that was neither ghost nor wind. Every time I heard it it seemed to come from deeper and deeper inside the woods and yet it sounded louder, almost as if it were vibrating from inside my own being.

The branches rustled. Animals scurried around my ankles. The air moaned with a voice that was almost human. I could almost catch words, short and monosyllabic, brushing past my ears in chilling song notes. "Lost" "Run" "Gone" "Hide". Imagined or heard, the threats trickled into my mind.

I shook my head, trying to hold them out with thoughts that were my own. Thoughts of Gran. Thoughts of her cottage. What it might look like when I found her and brought her to it. She had told me once that roses climbed over the walls and fence like icing. Greta thought flowers were silly but Gran didn't. She had never been much like the villagers. She didn't talk as much. She didn't work as much. And she laughed. Even when she wobbled and shook with cold and hunger she still laughed. I'd never even seen her inside the village except when she came to visit Greta and I on full moons.

The wind shrieked, pounding against me from every side. I pulled my cloak up around my neck, feeling the soft warmth of the wool with my frost stiffened fingers. The path twisted and swirled around bushes and tree trunks. When I entered the forest I had known I was heading north. Now I didn't know what direction I was going, only that I was following the only path available to me, not much wider than a deer trail. It was rough and narrow and full of more twists than I could count. Rustles and growls and chirps penetrated through the constant whir of the wind.

"Lost." It was unmistakably a child's moan, cold and fragile like ice. "Gone." A hiss like when a kettle of tea was ready.

The voices of the dead. If I listened they would lead me into a ditch or at the very least a painful tree branch. I hummed to myself, trying to shut them out. The song was Gran's, slow, monotone but melodious. I surrendered my voice to it, letting it carry me away in the swell of the music, but the voices only grew louder.

"Lost." "Go." "Gone." They could have been flesh children hissing like snakes in my ear, they were so loud.

Crunch.

Footsteps now. Close. I took a deep breath, forcing myself to keep a steady pace. All the ghosts could do was frighten me. Everyone knew they couldn't touch you. Only scare you into hurting yourself.

Everyone knew. That had never stopped it from working before.

I hummed louder, letting Gran's song whistle out of my lungs, soaring over the fury of the wind with the force of my breath. A shadow floated past me.

Only it wasn't a shadow. It was too pale. Too still. Where the moonlight shone I could see her features as clearly as if she had been alive. A tiny nose. One wide blinking eye. Trees and ferns filled the darkness where the rest of her face should have been.

I closed my eyes then forced myself to open them. The ghost child's face was gone. I listened, rooted to the earth, my heart pounding in my chest. Silence.

I resumed Gran's song. The sweet, haunting melody filled my lungs, calming me. It had no words and yet its meaning rooted itself in my mind, changing as it wound through me like Greta's threads around a spool. Tight and quick and clean.

I stepped forward. The footsteps moved behind me. Closer this time. I could hear breathing. A heavy heave, deep inside a broad chest. Too big to be a ghost child's. Too alive.

"Lost." The ghost voices swirled through my ears, mingling into a single breath. I could taste their warning. Despair tangled with their moans like too much thread on a wheel, tightening itself through my chest in a messy tangle. Their hunger consumed me until I wanted to cry out from the pain of the cramps. The emptiness.

I clamped my hands over my ears, turning toward the sound of the footsteps.

Crunch. The footsteps turned too. An echo of my own.

"Go" "Gone." "Lost." The wispish tones grew louder. The number of speakers grew. A multitude of whispers inside my head, pelting me with word after word.

I turned again.

Crunch. The footsteps followed.

The threads of despair in my chest tightened into naked fear. Any minute and I would bolt to my death.

Steady, Rose. They can't hurt you.

"Lost." "Gone."

Crunch.

"Go."

Another fragment of a face drifted past me. I could barely see it through the curly strands of my hair, caked to my face by the push of the wind. A parched bleeding mouth. The red swollen puff of a cheek. An eye still wet from tears. I could feel her terror, her shock as she realized she was going to die.

A shadow moved toward me from behind, blocking the light. The bits of face disappeared. I turned around toward the shadow.

Crunch.

I saw nothing but more trees in the darkness.

"Lost." "Gone."

I shook my head, dizzy from turning. I was trapped in some kind of sick harvest dance. Icy chills vibrated through my veins, my stomach, my head. Thoughts wouldn't form inside my mind. My mouth grew dry.

"Stop it." I screamed so loud that it hurt my throat. "Go away. Go away and leave me alone."

The moans stopped. The first ghost child blinked at me with a single visible eye, then her pale gray skin vanished like a vapor into the moonlight. Their fear, their sorrow, their hunger, all vanished.

The ghosts were gone but I was not alone. I could feel a presence still lurking in the darkness behind me.

Crunch. The steps moved toward me. The breathing was close enough for me to feel its warmth in the cold winter air.

"Who are you?" I demanded without turning.

"My name is Boris." A young man's voice said. "You appear to be lost."

I turned around. I could just make out a head of curly brown hair flaked with snow and a long green hunting cloak. Boris flashed me a crooked smile, illuminated perfectly by the light of the moon.

I breathed deep, holding back a sigh of relief. Just because he wasn't a monster didn't mean he was safe. "I'm not lost." I said "Ghosts were talking to me." I knew where the path led. What I didn't know was what lay between me and Gran's cottage. Or what waited for me once I reached it.

Boris stood still, silent for a moment. The wind filtered through the trees in a soft whisper. "There are quite a lot of ghosts around here." He said.

"I know." I stepped closer to get a better look at him. Striking cheekbones gleamed in the moonlight. His eyes were a warm, deep amber. His smile deepened into a grin that made me like him immediately and fear him even quicker. I knew what kind of creatures roamed these woods on a full moon and I had never seen him in the village. I would have remembered.

"You shouldn't be out here alone. At all actually." Boris tilted his head. The amber in his eyes glinted a mischievous gold. "Danger lurks behind every tree. Weres. Hobgoblins . . . Ghosts."

"And witches." I said, remembering Greta's warning before I'd left the house.

Boris laughed. "Yes. Witches too. Perhaps I ought to take you somewhere they can't hex you."

"I must find my Gran." I said. "She . . . she was supposed to come to supper but she never arrived."

Boris shrugged. "It's a cold night. Perhaps she decided her own hearth would be better than a long walk through the wood."

I shook my head. "Not Gran." My throat caught on the words. I bit my lip to keep from crying.

Boris's smile softened. "There now. Let's not make your lovely eyes as red as your hair. We'll just have to find her won't we?"

I blinked up at him. "You'll help me?"

He laughed. "Of course. There we are. There's a smile. Promise me you won't let the overly talkative ghosts float off with it again. These woods are cold and dreary without it."

We walked together. The trees thickened. The pools of light pouring in through the forest canopy became more sparse. So much darkness engulfed us that I felt almost blind. Boris didn't speak. Neither of us did. We were too absorbed in the stillness of the night, listening for signs of Gran in the absence of light to see by. But at least the ghosts didn't return and it was good to know that someone made of flesh and blood walked beside me even if I was still miles away from trusting him.

What would Greta say if she knew I was walking through the wood on the arm of a young man on a full moon? I tried to imagine her quiet serene face twisted into shock but I couldn't imagine more than a dour downward curve of the lips as she told me how dangerous it was.

No amount of pressed lips could stop me from finding Gran. The somber village life already seemed so far away. Out here the world was alive. I felt the dangerous pulse of the woodland course through me even in the silence. If I could choose a place to die I would be honored to rest beneath the tall trunks of the trees and let my soul sink like a root into the ground. It would be better than shriveling into an old woman with a carding comb in my hand.

The gentle trickle of water washed over my ears. I started and let go of Boris's arm. "We're close to the cottage." My heartbeat quickened. "Perhaps she never left after all." I sprinted forward, unable to make my feet move fast enough.

Crunch. Boris strode beside me. I brushed past the trees, all but guessing where the path lay. I reached the creek. The thin planks of the footbridge clattered beneath my feet. "

Gran." If the cottage were nearby either she hadn't left or I had missed her somewhere in the dark. "Gran."

"Run." "Go."

Specter voices fluttered through me, drenching me in chills, but I didn't care. I pushed each of their stories back with the forward movement of my feet. I could see streams of moonlight where the trees opened into a clearing up ahead.

"Stop."

A hand of pale, silvery fingers whisked past my ear in the moonlight. I waved my hand to shoo it away. My toe hit the edge of the footbridge. It caught in the woodwork and I tumbled forward.

I smashed into the forest floor. My knee hit a rock. My palms scraped against the earth. The spindle in my cloak pocket bounced against my hip bone as my basket skidded forward and sank into the dark of the water. I bit back a cry and sat up, opening and closing my fingers over stinging prickles of blood. I shivered. My cloaks and skirts were soaked through with snow.

I picked myself up, turning to flash an embarrassed smile at Boris, but he was gone. "Boris?" I must have lost him in my hurry.

Never matter. I didn't need him to defy the spirits. Not when Gran could be in danger.

I bit my lip and stepped forward once again. I went at a slower pace this time. The ghosts wouldn't trip me more than once. My feet crunched against the untouched snow. The water slithered behind me in a quiet trickle.

That howl again. Hungry and as exciting as it was frightening.

The clearing dipped down into a tiny valley. The long logs of a fence cast shadows over the ground as I neared. I hadn't realized how much protection the trees gave from the wind until I stepped out of their sanctuary. Ice cold air shivered through my damp clothes. I clenched my teeth to keep them from chattering.

The moon glowed overhead, a perfect sphere. The path was blocked by ragged fragments of wood that had once been a gate. I climbed over them, avoiding the splintered edges where they had been ripped from the hinges. Thorny plants twisted up and down the path, pulling at the fence and cottage like greedy fingers. Chopped logs lay cluttered over the ground in dark lumpy silhouettes.

My heart pounded as I moved forward. I didn't like the silence. I had always imagined Gran's cottage would be filled with sound. The singing of winter birds. The roaring of a fire. The warm gentle hum of Gran's voice as she sung the whole earth to sleep. But all was still. Not even the faintest thread of smoke trailed from the chimney.

"Gran." It came out a breath more than a word. A prayer I was afraid to give voice to.

I reached the cottage door. It was cracked open so that I could see the pitch black inside. I pressed my palm against the worn wood and pushed it all the way open. A stream of moonlight poured over the floor, lighting my way as I stepped inside.

"Gran." It was a real word this time. Just barely. "Gran, it's me."

My eyes adjusted slowly to the darkness of the room. Everything was exactly as it should have been. A stool and chair next to the fireplace –a real fireplace not an iron stove like Greta had. A warm, thick rug. A cluttered china cabinet. A wardrobe with the door swung open, shifts and linens hanging from the wrong side. A large featherbed beneath the loft because, of course, she couldn't climb the ladder every night at her age. Everything was right except . . .

I wished I could close my eyes and shut the sight out of my mind but my eyes were stretched open as if by force.

There, on the bed, lay Gran. Her eyes bulged wide. Her mouth hung open, unmoving, as saliva dripped down her chin into the blood blackened gash in her throat. Claw marks ran down the side of her head. The top half of her ear dangled over her jaw. My stomach wrung at the sight of the carnage but I couldn't move.

SNOW

I didn't sleep that night. I ripped off the purple silks Constanze had decorated me in and put on the first black gown I could find. The laces running up the back were too complex to tie without Constanze's help but it didn't matter with only me in my chamber. I let the dark velvet sleeves slide over the shoulders of my chemise.

Dusk blurred my vision with a smoky gray. I looked for a candle and flint to light it with. The flint was in the usual drawer but there were no candles. That was odd. The servants had always been so diligent at keeping the stores filled. I surveyed my chamber. Weeks worth of laundry draped across the furniture. Dust coated the shelves and cupboards. Grime smudged across the window glass. How long had it been since the servants had been up here?

I shook my head. As if it mattered. I had probably sent them all away in my fog of grief. I would have sent Constanze away too if I hadn't been hungry.

I used some writing paper for kindling and re-lit the half charred log Constanze had left in the fireplace when she had dressed me for dinner. It gave off a sick red glow, all but impossible to see by, but at least it offered me some warmth.

I wouldn't lie down and let oblivion take me. Not tonight. I pulled the knife Hans had given me out from under one of the pillows I hadn't mutilated and sat on my bed, waiting for dawn to arrive.

The night seemed to go on forever. A deep black void filling itself with every nightmare I'd ever had. Thorns tightening around my breast. My chest swelling with ice. My dreams crawled over my skin, seeping through to my lungs but even they were better than my memories.

Eventually morning would come. Hans would greet me in the courtyard and . . . and we would throw knives. Not even the coldest memories mattered when I had a target to concentrate on. The focus kept my limbs steady even when they wanted to shake like shattering glass.

I listened. Footsteps in my antechamber. Slippers shuffling across the carpeted stone. Probably Constanze, flopping herself onto the sofa for the night. The sound stopped next to my door then scuffled away, leaving the chill of silence in its place.

The night wore on. The fire's dark glow sank moment by moment until all that remained was a lingering splattering of embers. I watched them cool, one by one, until even they were gone. Shadows stirred on my ceiling overhead but the ones in my mind were stronger, playing over and over inside my mind.

Soft, delicate hands rolling round eyes shut. The velvet curling of Lucille's lips as my eyes met hers.

Papa had told me that the tonic the physicians had given him tasted like Christmas, rich and tingling against his tongue. Lucille had laughed at him and asked the physicians to bring him another to toast the coming of winter —and the improvement of the king's health.

I shivered inside my room. A draft rushed through the fireplace, filling the chamber with icy air. Winter had come that night, almost as if Lucile had summoned it with her toast. A frost had settled over the land. It burrowed deeper than a simple season's chill.

I rose and went to the window, gripping my knife by the hilt. The manor's courtyard rippled with the pale gray of moonlight. Empty. Silent.

Lucille's smile had been welcoming as I had entered the hall to dine with her and her son tonight. Warm. Almost sweet. Why, then, had it turned my stomach like a roasting sow when I had been the one to defile Papa's memory with ribbons and color?

My breath shortened. I turned and paced back and forth over my chamber's rug, examining the inky black and white swirls. I studied the creatures embedded into the ceiling overhead. Their teeth seemed to gnash at me. Their coiling limbs seemed to reach for me with open claws. I almost wished they could. At least then I would be spared the relentless rhythm of my feet pattering against the carpet.

At last dawn spread over the sky. The clouds oozed a pale red around the edges, casting a haze of gold over the courtyard. The season's first sprinkling of snow lay scattered across the ground. Untouched. Unscathed.

I laced my boots quickly and threw my cloak over my shoulders. Almost shaking, I placed my hand over the iron door handle and pushed. The door stood still, solid against the pressure of my palms. I bit back a scream and pushed again, harder this time. The ebony wood rattled against the lock but the door didn't budge.

Soft hands rolling amber eyes shut. The lifting corners of her mouth. What could they have been but a smile?

No. I shut my eyes and shook my head as if I could rattle the memory away.

Soft hands. Amber eyes. She knew what I saw. She knew and she had smiled, sealing the secret forever. She knew everything that I had seen.

I pushed against the door a third time, pressing hard against the wood with my hip and shoulder. It didn't move.

A toast to winter? No. Lucile had toasted to tears. To sorrow and pain and grief. I should have drunk it with him. I should have thrown it in Lucille's face rather than let a drop of it touch his lips. I had known what she was. Why hadn't I spoken?

I held back a scream and sank onto the floor. Tears streamed down my face in a hot salty rush. They burned the surface of my skin, scorching themselves into my being like molten iron. They poured down my nose and cheeks onto my wrists and the palms of my hands as Lucile's smile tightened around my memory.

I should have drunk the tonic with him. I should have died in Papa's place.

I do not know how long I crouched there, my spine pressed against the door, my head held in my hands. When I moved again my bones ached. I rose unsteadily to my feet and turned toward the door. I didn't realize why until light poured in through the crack. A moment later it was open. A thin pale woman stared at me with a disapproving gaze.

"Constanze?" I squinted at her but it was not Constanze. This woman was shorter with pale gold hair and tiny wrists that looked too thin for her hands.

"Constanze is gone." The woman said.

Gone. Like Papa. Like Elise and Dana. Where was it that they all went?

The pale woman held out a platter of cold fruit and sausages. I recognized them from last night's supper. "Your breakfast M'lady."

"I'm not hungry." I mouthed. My lips and tongue were too swollen with snot and tears for speech.

"You may change your mind." The pale woman placed the tray on the ground next to my feet and left. The lock clicked into place behind her with such force that I wondered how I had managed not to hear it in the night.

I turned and stared at the platter. I had lied. I was hungry but it wasn't the kind of hunger that fruit and sausages could cure. Unless . . .

Would they taste like Christmas?

I sat down, examining the food more closely. The fruit and sausages were from last night's supper, I was sure of it. I imagined the rich savory spices and sweet juices breaking apart inside my mouth. They wouldn't last long but perhaps they would quiet the battle raging like a bubbling cauldron inside my belly. Perhaps they would quiet the memories in my head, leaving Lucille's secrets forever unspoken.

Quiet. Silence. That was what the queen wanted. It was what I wanted.

I lifted a grape between my fingers, squeezing it just enough to rupture the skin and expose the naked flesh inside. The juice dripped onto my hand, thick and saturated like blood.

Gone. I could be gone too. It would only take a moment. A sweet treat followed by a sweeter oblivion. Just like Papa.

No. I drew my hand away. Not like Papa at all. It hadn't been his choice. He hadn't known. I shoved the tray away.

I spent the rest of the day in my chamber. I watched the soldiers drill in the courtyard, careful not to be seen from my grime covered window. They stomped out the first thin layer of snow with their heavy boots. Tiny remnants of ice glittered unnoticed beneath the shadow of the well.

At last the sky began to fade to a pale gray. It burst into a brilliant splattering of golds and purples, then faded until there was nothing but darkness. The manor yard emptied itself as the last of the scullery maids and errand boys scurried inside and all was quiet. I knelt at my door, bundled in layers of cloaks I couldn't remember putting on, and listened through the crack for the pale woman's light, pattering footsteps.

Nothing.

I climbed back to my feet and placed my hand on the iron handle.

It was foolish to hope but somehow it seemed more likely in the dark silence. Perhaps the pale woman had forgotten to lock it when she left. Perhaps . . .

I nudged at the heavy ebony. The wood creaked. I winced at the sound, sinking my teeth into my lip. A thin trickle of light leaked through the crack.

I choked back a gasp and pushed the door open wide enough to peer out.

The anteroom was empty. There was no sign of Constanze. No sign of the pale woman. Why . . .

But I wasn't about to squander my chance with questions. I snatched Hans' knife off the ground where I had left it and slipped through the door.

The corridors were empty. I had never seen the manor so quiet. Silent. Like a tomb. Papa's night guards had always hummed to themselves as they kept watch. I had gone to sleep as a child listening to them laugh amongst themselves in quiet whispers. But tonight I had to strain to hear the deep flow of my own breathing.

The glow of torchlight flickered up ahead. The silhouettes of a pair of guards danced against the wall like Papa's shadow puppets before bed. One guard kicked his toe against the ground. The other spat next to his boot, his hands thrust in his pockets.

I turned down a different corridor. There wasn't much chance the main door would be unguarded but I wasn't going to fail for want of trying. Not this time. I quickened my pace. My pulse swelled through my limbs. At last I could see the high wooden beams of the manor's main doorway.

No guards. Don't question the impossible. Not when it meant freedom was only a few steps away. My feet scuffled against the stone floor. I almost tripped in my hurry.

A moment later I stood in the courtyard. The cold winter air bit through my cloak with the frightening teeth of freedom. My breath rose like smoke in the air. Hans stood waiting for me, leaning against the stable across the yard. I moved toward him, crunching bits of snow with my feet.

What was he doing up so late? How had he known I would come? The questions formed in my throat but made no sound. I stopped when I reached him and blinked up at his dark familiar beard and fierce eyes. So much like Papa. So different.

His jaw tensed. "You've stopped eating again."

"Only since last night." It couldn't have been long enough to make me thinner.

Hans grunted. "Come with me then." He uncrossed his arms and started up the ladder leaning against the stable wall.

I slid my knife into my cloak's pocket and scrambled up after him. The staves were wide apart and I fumbled more than once on my skirts. Hans held the ladder steady once he reached the top and waited for me to catch up to him. I pulled myself up onto the roof, examining the shades of darkness around me.

"This way." Hans strode across the roof toward the forest edge. I followed. The manor wall had been damaged here in a siege long ago. The stone had crumbled down until it was level with the stable's roof. Papa hadn't bothered to repair it. It had been so long since we'd had a siege.

Until Lucile.

Hans stopped. He motioned for me to stay back then leapt over the deep gap of darkness, landing without a sound on the stone wall. He stood back, waiting for me to follow.

I hesitated. Hans was too far away for me to see his face in the dark.

He stood still and tall, solid like the stones the wall was made of. It was a large leap but Hans had never expected more from me than I could manage. He had always known when a knife thrust was too complex for me to try just yet or when I had been practicing as long as my body could take.

I took a deep breath and stepped back. I rocked back on my feet to find my balance then sprang forward.

My feet slammed into stone. The crown of my head crashed into Hans' chest. My knees hit his shins. I stepped back involuntarily, looking for solid ground but the soles of my feet touched air. I felt the weight of my body falling after them. My arms flailed. My heart jumped as if it thought it could keep the rest of me upright.

Hans's arms closed tight around my back. Half a second and I was securely on the wall again with my cheek pressed against his chest. I could feel his pulse beating inside him like the march of soldiers' feet. He let go and stood back, silent for a moment as we both caught our breath.

"Alright?"

I nodded.

Hans crouched next to a pile of loose stones. He lifted them one by one, revealing a long coil of rope. I watched him fasten it to the wall and fling it over the side. He tugged at it to be sure it was secure and nodded for me to make my way down.

The rough flax burned my skin as I climbed. My fingers ached from clenching. If my palms hadn't already been roughened against blisters from chopping wood I never would have made it down without letting go.

At last my feet touched solid earth. I let go of the rope. A moment later Hans dropped onto the ground beside me.

"Where are we going?" I asked.

Hans held his finger against his lips for silence. He turned and strode into the woods. I followed.

The full moon shone through the canopy of trees in tiny splotches like stars scattered across the ground. Only bits of snow dripped through. Most of it caught in the treetops, casting a thick shadow over the darkness of night. We had only walked a few paces before we were beyond sight of the manor.

I shivered in the winter cold. How long had it been since I had stepped outside those walls? Weeks? Months? Since before Lucille had come. I strode forward. Each step took me further and further from the cage my home had become.

Or had the cage become my home? I almost missed the locks and silence. Out here I felt exposed. Every tree seemed to have unknown monsters lurking behind it.

Hans stopped. He turned to face me. The lines on his forehead wrinkled into a frown. "Why haven't you run yet?"

I stared up at him. "Run?"

His frown deepened. Silence filtered between us. He raised an eyebrow. "Did you imagine I could get you out of the manor without Lucille's consent?"

I didn't answer.

"Snow," He stared down at me. "Why did you shut yourself up inside your chamber?"

The deep sinking feeling I had lived and slept and dreampt with since Papa's death clawed at my chest. "Grief." The lie echoed hollow against the chill of night, stumbling out of my lips in a rush.

Not quite a lie. A half truth.

"Constanze is dead." Hans said. "She is dead because she fed you. She is dead because she kept you from eating what the queen had prepared for you."

Dead. Gone. Because of me. Because of what I had seen.

Christmas, he'd said it tasted like, but I knew better. It had tasted like the powder Lucille had sprinkled it with. Just before she'd looked up at me, her green eyes glittering in a flawless smile that never touched her lips.

I stood still, unable to move or speak. I could hear Hans breathing less than a pace in front of me but the sound seemed far, far away. My breath tightened, wrenching what had been trapped in my chest since papa's death out like an old wash rag, rancid with soap.

Terror. Terror that had kept me in my chamber for months, hiding itself in grief. Terror that had been afraid to give itself a name, afraid to speak, to even remember the things that I had seen. So many things I didn't want to know.

"Lucille wants me dead." My words hiccuped into the night, hardly audible in the darkness.

"It was meant to look like an accident." Hans said. "The dead king's daughter taken by her own grief --but you've lasted longer than she expected. Desperation has made her bold." He drew his dagger and lifted it over my head. It dripped from his fist like a piece of stalagmite.

I stepped back. I pulled my own little knife out of my cloak pocket. Hans had given it to me himself. One quick slice across the jugular, he'd told me. One slice in the right place and he would be dead. I gripped the hilt tight in my palm but I knew I could never hurt Hans. Not after so many early mornings when his teachings had been my only comfort.

"Run." The word slithered out of his mouth, quick and hushed. "Run, Snow. As fast as you can. As far as you can. I make no promises about what will happen if I catch you."

He didn't have to tell me again. I turned and I ran. My body thumped with the rush of my blood. My feet pounded against the forest floor. I didn't know or care where I was running to. I didn't know or care how far I had to go. I only knew I had to get away. Away from Lucile. Away from nightmares and the meaningless complexities of my rug. Away from the reaching claws of the creatures carved on my ceiling. Away from Boris and the pale woman and the cold silence that infected the manor halls.

Away from Hans.

I never heard him behind me but I knew he was there, moving closer every moment. I wouldn't hear him until his knife was already singing through the air as it had on so many gray mornings of practice. Only I wasn't a straw man. I wouldn't be there to see him rip it back out of my chest.

Dark branches tangled together, blocking my path. I dodged over and under and around thick knobs and thin, stinging vines. My feet grew numb. The gauzy silk of my shift caught in a mesh of thorns. The threads ripped apart from my wrist up to my shoulder. I didn't realize the flesh beneath it had been punctured until I saw the blood drip onto the snow in front of me. The ice crunched like tiny shards of glass beneath my feet. I plummeted forward, numb of everything but the desire to keep moving.

The bushes stirred with creatures of the night. Or were those my own reckless steps? Every frightening tale my tutors had ever told me about forests screamed for attention inside my head but I paid them no mind. What did it matter if something awful jumped out of the shadows to gobble me up? I would likely freeze to death by morning anyways.

Burs clung to the edge of my gown and cloak. Branches scraped across my skin, stinging my cheeks and forehead. The trees began to thin, exposing me to the eyes of the wild as well as my hunter. A clearing loomed before me. Before I had fully comprehended it, I was standing in it. The dark shadows of a cottage stretched against the ground in the blinding glare of the moonlight.

I stopped. The night echoed around me, still and pregnant with horror. My heart pounded inside my chest, leaking pain into my neck and belly until I thought it would burst with soreness. A gust swept through my hair and gown, prickling my skin with its teeth.

How long had I been running? I looked to either side of me, listening for the signs of Hans I knew I would never hear.

A shrill cry shot through the night. It vibrated through me like the sounds scrambling to escape from inside my own soul. Grief. Horror. Anger. Helplessness. The sound screamed through my ears into my breast, my stomach, my toes.

My own lips were still, my lungs frozen stiff with fear and weariness. My side and chest ached. Past exhausted, I climbed over the shambles of a fence that surrounded the cottage and made my way through the yard.

Vines wound their way across the ground like shadowy serpents in the dark, dead or dormant for the winter. Were those footsteps pattering against the earth? Was that my own deep breathing or the panting of some forest creature? I only knew it couldn't be Hans. He would never make that much noise. I gripped my knife, ignoring the tightening itch of my own sweat that covered the hilt.

The cry sounded again. It was closer now, muffled only by the thin cottage walls. I should have been moving away from it but somehow I couldn't. Not when it had felt so much like a cry wrenched from my own being.

I stopped when I reached the cottage door. It was open, creaking back and forth on its hinges. A thick darkness loomed inside.

"Hello." My voice came out stronger than I expected. I pushed against the door. The wood groaned, opening bit by bit beneath the pressure of my hands. I stuck my head into the blackness and stepped inside.

A girl with thick red curls and a red cloak whirled around to face me from across the room. I could only just make out her face in the dim light the door let in. Round hazel eyes. A thin, curved nose. I recognized the glazed look in her eyes. The lifeless half circle her mouth made. She wanted to cry. She wanted to cry but she had forgotten how.

I wished that I could show her.

Then I saw the gore in the bed next to her. What had once been an old woman lay crumpled and lifeless among the quilts.

"Close the door." The girl's whisper was urgent. "Close it now." Her eyes were fixed on the space behind me just a little to the left. There was that heavy sound of breath again, unmistakably real and far too even to be my own.

I turned around.

Bright amber eyes blinked in the darkness outside. Moonlight gleamed against pale yellow fangs. Dark tufts of fur raised along haunches bigger than any I'd ever seen in waking life.

I stepped back into the cottage. I reached for the door. The wolf creature sprang forward. His weight pushed against mine through the splintered frame of the door, flinging me onto the floor. I landed with a crack against the wood. My back and shoulder sickened with pain.

The wolf creature stepped inside. He brushed past me, approaching the red girl. Slowly. Languidly. He released a low growl. Almost a purr. The hunger in his eyes was not the wild need of an animal. It was calculated. Patient. Infected with greed and desire. The eyes of a man.

The red girl thrust out her chin. She clenched both her hands into fists. "You killed Gran." The accusation crackled with fire.

The wolf creature paced back and forth, moving closer to her with every step. His growl deepened.

I gripped the hilt of my knife and pulled myself to my feet. The blade was small but sharp. Deadly if grazed across the right artery. I wasn't sure I could puncture the wolf creature's brain even if I did manage a thrust through his eye. Even his throat was risking too much on chance. But his belly. If he pounced on me I might have just enough time to jab upward in the right place before he did any lasting damage to my flesh.

I took a deep breath. My heart hammered in my chest. My limbs felt like a pudding boiled wrong but I forced them to move.

It happened in the fall of an ax blade. I screeched, rushing toward the wolf creature. Claws scratched against the floor. Fur blurred across the room. Teeth sank into the side of my neck, tearing pain and the salt scent of blood down into my shoulder. I fought to shove it out of my mind as I pushed the knife upward. The blade tore into the soft flesh of the wolf creature's belly but before I could twist it into his bowel tissues he leapt back.

The wolf creature released a yelp of pain followed by a long, angry howl. It wasn't until the red girl rushed to my side that I realized that I was screaming too. She grabbed me around the waist and lifted me up onto my feet. My head clouded from the motion. The room swirled like the useless weave of my chamber's rug. My knife dropped from my slackened fingers, clattering against the wooden floor, splashing into the same thick wolf's blood that dripped down my palm and wrist. My own warm blood leaked down the back of my gown, spreading into the sleeve of my chemise.

"Run." I hissed at the red girl. If she was quick she could make it to the door before he got his bearings back.

"Are you daft?" She hissed back. "Not without you." She wrapped my arm around her neck, supporting my limp, bleeding side. I scuttled with her toward the door, too weak with blood loss to protest. The door wasn't far. Only a few more steps.

The wolf sprang back to life. Fur whirred overhead. There was a creaking of wood against wood as his paws pressed against the door, slamming it shut. Streams of moonlight disappeared along with our only escape.

"The loft." The red girl whispered. "Let's hope he can't climb."

We scrambled toward the ladder in the deepened dark. The red girl lifted me onto the first stave then hoisted herself up after me. Her arm clenched tight around my stomach. I could feel her soft rapid breath against my neck, close, almost comforting even in our panicked scramble.

The wolf creature sprang again. He landed above us on the ladder. Tufts of fur from his tail flicked across my eyes. The ladder wobbled backward and fell.

China shattered. Wood groaned. A kettle rolled out of the fireplace, barely missing the tip of my fingers as it thumped past. I lay on the ground again. Broken ladder spokes pressed against my arm. My head sang from the force of the fall. The red girl sat up beside me. The wolf creature rose beside her, snarling.

My eyes rolled toward my knife, still lying on the floor in the sticky smear of blood. Mine and the wolf creature's. I tried to lift my arm but it was pinned by the weight of the ladder. I closed my eyes, fighting against a fresh rush of pain. I opened them. The lines in the room began to run together again in a smudged, leaky mess. The remaining shards of my consciousness wavered.

I slid my foot across the floor, reaching for the knife hilt, but the wolf creature was already standing over me. His hot breath bled into my lungs, seeping into my wounds like fire.

"Get away from her." The red girl jumped to her feet. She pulled something sharp and shiny out of her pocket.

The wolf creature turned toward her. He jabbed his head into her stomach, flinging her across the room. The object rolled out of her hand among the fragments of broken china.

I stretched my toes toward my knife, hooking them around the hilt while the wolf's attention was on the red girl.

He whirled back towards me. His amber eyes swarmed with fury.

I reached for the china shards scattered over the floor. My hand closed over a broken saucer. I lifted it off the ground and flung it at the creature. It slid off him, barely scraping the edge of his snout.

The wolf creature shook his head. He snarled, showing the sharp dagger points of his teeth.

I slid my foot upward, wincing at the sound the knife made against the ground. I reached for another dish. This time my fingers closed around the ragged edge of a mug. The newly broken china sliced through my skin. I flung it at the wolf creature. It crashed against the side of his snout, leaving a thin trail of blood above his nose. He moved forward, undaunted.

I turned my head to look at the red girl. My lips wouldn't move. 'Run' I tried to tell her with my eyes but she stood where she was, flinging broken dishes at the wolf, screaming for him to stop.

The wolf creature stopped just in front of me. He sank his teeth into my boot and jerked my foot away from the knife. He shook my foot back and forth in his jaw. My bones rattled. My ankle twisted. I tried to pull away but the motion only ground his teeth further into the leather of my boot and into my flesh.

The red girl screamed. The room shook with the sound, rocking up and down with the jerking movements of my leg in the wolf's jaw.

Footsteps pattered toward me. No. She was going the wrong way. Ink swirled before my eyes so that I couldn't tell one color from another. I steeled myself, determined not to give way to oblivion. Not yet.

A shout from outside. Fists pounding against the door. Another cry. Wood splintered. The floor shook with the force of a new pair of firm, determined footsteps creaking across the floor. My body moaned with nausea.

"Out. This is my job." I barely recognized the voice through the sickening haze that fogged my brain. Short and rough as tree bark.

The wolf stopped shaking my leg. He growled then sank his teeth further into my foot. He pulled them out with a sudden jerk, ripping open the flesh. My leg dropped against the floor with a sickening thud of pain.

More ink swirled above my head. Red. Black. The ground heaved beneath me. A pair of hands touched my wrist then the side of my jaw. Probably the only two places on my body that didn't ache.

The wolf creature released one final howl then paws scurried against the wood. The vibrations jostled my bones, hammering pain into my dizzy mind. I closed my eyes, waiting for them to disappear and then I was only listening to the mad babblings of my dreams

ROSE

The huntsman helped me bury Gran. He found a spade outside the cottage and dug a deep grave at the edge of the clearing where the shade of the woodland could just reach it. I worked beside him. I tried to think of the playful crinkles around Gran's eyes, the hoarse bark of her laughter, but all I could see was the carnage that had been in her bed when I'd arrived at the cottage. It might have been Gran's body but it was nothing like Gran.

By dawn the grave was finished. I helped the huntsman drag the mangled flesh out of Gran's bed. He wrapped her in her bloodied quilt. I wondered if he treated the animal carcasses of his trade with such tenderness. We lowered her into the hole and packed the earth over her.

The grave seemed to fill up quicker than it had been dug. As if the earth were still hungry. As if one life had not been enough to sate it. The winter sun drizzled overhead, bright and cool and damp. The surface of the snow melted off the tree branches, dripping the tears I couldn't shed myself onto the ground. A bitter wind swept over the clearing and I suddenly realized how fatigued I was. How it almost hurt just to stand upright.

When we were finished the huntsman looked at me from across the grave, waiting to see if I had any kind of prayer. I didn't have one. I should have at least cried but I didn't.

Greta, I remembered all at once. Greta would have to be told.

The huntsman leaned the spade against a tree trunk and turned toward me, arms crossed. I couldn't tell if the shadows under his eyes were rings or smudges of dirt like the rest of his face was covered in.

"Don't go back to the village." The huntsman said. "There is nothing for you there. It isn't safe."

I almost laughed. "Not safe? The village?" What dangers could possibly lurk in the day to day drudgery of spinning thread and buying milk? It was the forest that had killed Gran. Had almost killed me. The forest with its ghosts and weres and hobgoblins. The forest I should never have stepped foot in. I had been warned. Ever since I was a child I had been warned of the dangers of these woods. No one came here.

Only . . . Gran would have died whether I had come or not. Wasn't it better to at least know? I swallowed. My throat swelled with pain. I wasn't sure that it was.

"Stay here." The huntsman said again. "Look after Snow. She will look after you too once she heals. She's stronger than she looks." His face was still and unreadable but a smile crept into his voice right at the end. Like a master craftsman unable to hide the pride of his work.

"Snow." I repeated the name. Hardly a name at all really. Fragile, as if it would melt off my lips and disappear. The noble girl had been small but she'd looked anything but fragile facing the wolf creature with nothing but a little knife. She had held her ground with the stubbornness of a glacier.

The huntsman turned and headed into the trees.

"Wait." I limped after him. My limbs resisted speed regardless of what my mind told them to do. "The wolf. What if it comes back?"

"It won't." The huntsman didn't look behind him. He strode forward at a steady pace, moving further and further away from me.

"I can't stay here." I shouted, breathless from trying to catch up to him. "Greta will worry. She'll . . ." Kill me herself most likely once she realized I'd left without her permission. The huntsman kept moving. I tried to catch up to him but his strides were long and quick. The distance between us grew further and further. "Come back." I wasn't even sure he could still hear me. "I don't even know how to dress the girl's wounds."

"Your Gran left books." The huntsman's voice carried through the trees, surprisingly clear. I could barely see him now through the thickening trunks and branches.

How would he know what my Gran had left? He couldn't have had time to ransack her cottage last night between scaring off the wolf and cleaning up the blood and broken dishes. I stopped, unable to move another step. I could only just see his shadow as it slipped behind a great oak up ahead and then he was gone.

"I can't read." I muttered, breathless with exhaustion. I doubted even the trees could hear me.

I leaned back against a tree trunk. The bark pressed through my cloak and bodice, rough and knobbly against my spine. A cold wind rustled through my knotted mess of curls. I breathed deep, absorbing the chill of the winter morning. My eyelids fluttered closed. A soft hum rose from my lips. One of Gran's tunes. I couldn't remember when she had sung it or if it had ever had any words. It vibrated deep in my throat, filling my whole body with its sound. The earth filled with memories of Gran just as the hole the huntsman and I had dug had filled itself with her body.

For the fraction of a breath I saw her again. Warm hazel eyes. Her mouth open in the onset of a laugh. Pain welled in my chest. "Gran." I whispered, hardly able to choke out the word, but the vision was already gone, scattered like shards of light inside my head.

I opened my eyes. The wood was silent. Still but for the shiver of leaves in the wind. Was it only at night that it was filled with ghosts and monsters? I wasn't going to wait to find out. I turned and headed back toward the cottage.

The noble girl –Snow—was awake when I stepped inside. She sat straight and silent on the edge of the loft where the huntsman had moved her. She stared at me as I closed the latch on the door behind me. It wasn't just the rich black velvet of her gown that marked her as a noble. It was the poised way she held her gaze, unblinking as if her eyes were made of stone.

Or ice. Her name suited her very well.

"Where is Hans?" Her voice was quieter than I expected, small and hoarse from fever.

I blinked up at her, careful that my eyes did not stray toward the stripped and bloody bed beneath the loft. It was hard to see if her wounds had stopped bleeding through the blood already soaked to her gown. "Hans." I said. "He was the huntsman?"

Snow nodded.

"Do you trust him?" I asked.

"Yes." Her answer was quick. Fierce and certain like the thrust of a knife.

I sighed. "He's gone. I don't think he's coming back. He said . . ." A thought occurred to me. "Can you read?"

The space between her eyes crinkled. "Of course."

If the huntsman –Hans –was telling the truth we weren't entirely stranded. I strode across the floor and knelt next to the toppled cabinet. There was no sign of any books. Just some pieces of broken china I'd missed in the dark and . . .

I closed my hand over the spindle I'd found in Greta's cabinet. The gold spindle with the same markings on it as the clasp on Gran's cloak. I thrust it back into my pocket and stood, scanning the room for any other place Gran might keep a book. I'd never seen one before much less owned one. Where were they usually kept?

Under the bed? I took a deep breath and turned around to face the loft. The stripped mattress beneath it was steeped in dried blood. Wrinkled feathers poked out, crusted with brown. The deep stench hit me with a rush of sickness. The last thing I wanted to do was crawl underneath looking for books that might not even exist.

"Are these what you are looking for?"

I looked up, startled by the sharp glass sound of Snow's voice. I must have looked like a wild animal as I stared at the three hand-bound volumes in her lap. Stained, uneven pages curled around the edges of worn leather covers.

"Yes." I stepped toward the ladder and scampered up onto the loft. I had to take extra large steps to avoid the staves that had cracked when the wolf had knocked the ladder over. Snow edged out of the way as I reached the top. I sat beside her, dangling my feet over the edge.

An unexpected wave of shyness washed through me. She stared at me with her locked noble's gaze. Solid. Unreadable.

I still hadn't thanked her for saving my life. I twisted one of my curls to curb the sudden fit of jitters. "Hans said your name is Snow."

She nodded.

I attempted a smile. "I'm Rose."

The smile she returned was strained but bright and crisp for the short moment it lasted.

"Thank you." I faltered, unsure how to begin. "For last night. For -"

"Of course." She piled the books onto my lap, wincing slightly as their weight left her shoulder. "These were in the chest in the corner." She nodded toward a small wooden chest surrounded by straw. Her hand brushed against my arm as she pulled it away from the books. I shivered. Her skin was almost scorching with fever.

I looked down at the volumes in my lap, still fingering one of my curls.

I had never held a book before. They were heavier than I had expected. Like a brick or a yule log. I opened the one on top. The thin sheets inside were ink and water stained, smudged with fingerprints. Thin, dark markings stared at me. Strange lines and swirls that made me dizzy to look at. I looked up, wrinkling my nose in confusion, and thrust the open book back onto Snow's lap. "What are they? What do they say?"

Snow turned a leaf. She lowered her lashes, scanning her eyes and fingers over the markings. I bent my head next to hers to see more closely. I could still feel the warmth of her fever radiating from her skin and her breaths were slow and strained.

A pair of long lines spiraled across the page in what looked like a kind of vine. "This one looks like an herbal." Snow pointed to a collection of markings near the edge of the page. "The handwriting in the margins is the same as the bulk of the writing but smaller and messier. They were added later. What are we looking for?"

"An herbal." I repeated. That sounded promising. "Is there anything in there about dressing claw wounds? And teeth wounds." I added, remembering her foot.

"Probably. It looks very thorough." Snow fingered the pages, scanning them one at a time. Her deep red lips pressed together in concentration. A strand of her short black hair fell against her face, reaching across her cheek down to her chin. The ends were frayed and uneven like she'd cut it with a knife.

I sat back. I fingered the books still in my lap. The one on top was smaller than the other two. The leather cover was so worn and cracked it felt like dry leaves.

"Here." Snow tapped a finger against a page toward the middle of the book. Her voice was still smooth but her breath was shallower than it had been a moment ago. She took in a silent gasp. The pain from her wounds was getting harder to hide. "A poultice for deep flesh wounds."

I leaned close again to see the page. There were no drawings. Only row after row of symbols. I closed my eyes, fighting off a dizzy headache. "What does it say? I promised Hans I would stitch you up."

She looked up, startled. Her brow wrinkled again. Her lips formed a circle as if she were going to ask a question but when she spoke all she said was "There's a list of herbs. It says to apply them twice a day after the wounds are cleaned."

I nodded. "Read them to me. I'll see if Gran has them."

Comfrey. Burdock. Yarrow. The herbs weren't hard to find in Gran's well stocked cabinet. Snow read the labels to make sure they were right. I washed her wounds with water then powdered the herbs and mixed them with oil. Snow found another recipe to help with the pain. She read the directions to me while I worked. The strength in her voice waned with each word, dwindling into a cold sliver of sound.

I climbed the ladder again, this time more slowly, trying to balance both mixtures in my hands. The ladder's legs wobbled where the wood had cracked and I thought for a moment that I might fall. I gave Snow the pain drought first, a mixture of mullein and valerian tea. I suspected it would help her sleep more than anything else. She drank it slowly as I rolled the edge of her gown off of her shoulder. She flinched at the cold touch of my hand then held still.

Four deep lines were dried over with a deep crimson, almost black, against the smooth ghostly paleness of her skin. The edges of the wound swelled with a milder red I hoped wasn't the beginning of an infection.

Gently, gently, I brushed her hair away from her neck and blew over the wound, hoping the air would prepare her for the poultice. "I don't know if it will sting." I said.

Snow shivered. Her lips curved into a half smile. She swallowed the last of the tea and set the mug down on the loft beside her. "Neither do I."

It didn't take long to apply the herbs. If it hurt, Snow made no indication. I tightened strips of sheet around the wound and tied it tight then tended to her foot in the same way. She lay still, trusting me as I unlaced her boot and peeled the blood-soaked leather and stockings away from her feverish skin and applied the herbs.

"Thank you." Snow said when I had finished.

I glanced down at the herbal and other two books stacked next to her in the straw. "What's in these ones?" I asked, even though I knew she needed to rest. I wasn't ready to be alone in the cottage. Not quite yet. I picked up the smallest book and let it open in my palm. Even I could tell it wasn't as tidy as the herbal. The lines weren't as uniform. Some pages were packed so tight with symbols that I could hardly see them while others held only a single large line.

Snow lifted the third volume, thicker even than the herbal. "This one looks like . . . a recipe book —for food. Not medicine. And this one." She gently took the small one from my hands and fingered through the pages. "Stories. Rhymes. Idioms. The words of a wise woman. Are these . . . The woman from last night. These are her books?"

"My Gran's. Yes." I almost choked over the words. The weight of the last twenty four hours hit me all in one blow. I suddenly wanted to scream or cry or just close my eyes and stop thinking.

Snow brushed her hair out of her face where it had been clinging to her cheek. She looked up at me, her dark eyes distant, almost fearful for a moment. Remembering. Or realizing. Froze in place like a cracked mirror. She blinked. Her lips curled into the ghost of a smile and her pupils were glass again. Solid. Stable. "I'm hungry." She said "Do you think you could find something for us to eat?"

I nodded. The thought of food made my stomach turn but it was something to do. I pushed the books aside and made my way back down the ladder.

The bread and pie in the cupboard was crumbled to a pulp and I'd lost Greta's stew and bread in the wood but there was some dried venison and a basket of apples on the stove. I snatched them up but by the time I climbed back onto the loft Snow was asleep. She lay curled against the straw with her chin tucked into her chest. Her fingertips rested against an open page of the recipe book.

I closed the book and stacked it with the others back into the chest. I poked at the apples and venison but couldn't do much more than nibble.

41

Finally I edged my way back to the other side of the loft and closed my own eyes. My mind and body ached too much to do anything but sleep.

The shrill sound of Snow's screams pierced through my dreams, swimming around me. I dragged myself out of sleep so quickly it almost hurt and forced my eyes open. Snow tossed back and forth in the straw across from me. She rolled from side to side, teetering near the edge.

"Snow." I crawled towards her from the wall side of the loft. Her eyes were closed, her hands clamped over her ears as if she were trying to shut out the sounds of her own screams. Clumps of sweat dripped down her neck and forehead. I placed my hands on either of her shoulders, holding her still. Even through the thick velvet of her gown I could feel the burn of her fever. "Snow." I said "Snow you're going to throw yourself off the loft."

She fought against my touch, wriggling closer and closer to the edge of the loft. I held her tighter, pulling her away from the edge. "It's all right, Snow." I said "The wolf is gone. You're safe. Nothing is going to hurt you."

Her eyes shot open. Quick. Panicked. She looked up at me without recognition. She struggled then lay still. Stunned. Terrified.

"What's the matter?" I asked softly, not even sure she was awake. "What were you dreaming?"

She said nothing. Only stared up at me. Through me as if I weren't there at all. As if nothing were.

I let go of her shoulders and laid down beside her. I draped my arm over her stomach so that she couldn't roll off of the loft and hummed to her the way I had hummed to myself on nights I couldn't sleep in Greta's village house. The way Gran had hummed to me while she spun thread or made stew. Softly, gently, the song wound its way around us. Snow's breathing slowed bit by bit. When I turned to look at her again she was asleep, her eyes closed, her breathing soft. I stayed where I was with my chin tucked over the top of her head and watched the dusk turn to night through the window glass. If I couldn't sleep at least the warm pulse of another heartbeat could dull the aching silence in my head.

We stayed in the cottage for three days. I knew Greta would give me up as lost to the wood but I couldn't leave Snow by herself. Not when she still had trouble climbing down the ladder on her own. She slept most of the time. I tidied the cottage and kept the fire going. When she was awake I saw to her wounds and made sure we were both fed. There was grain porridge and dried peas as well as the venison and apples. Enough for the whole winter if we wanted. Snow offered to help with the washing but the one time I allowed it it was clear that she had never held a scrubbing rag before in her life. Her time was better spent regaining her strength so I could go home.

Not that the village was much of a home to return to. I wasn't sure I could bear the relentless turning of Greta's spinning wheel without the promise of Gran's visits every full moon.

Snow read through the herbal, Gran's journal, and the recipe book to keep herself occupied. In the late afternoon of the second day she fell asleep next to the fire with the journal opened over her lap. I knelt next to her and lifted it out of her hands. I ran my fingers over the crinkled cover for what must have been the hundredth time and gazed at the markings as if I could decode their mystery with sheer curiosity.

"I could teach you to read them yourself."

I looked up, startled by Snow's voice. She hadn't been sleeping as hard as I'd thought. She watched me from the troubled edges of her dreams, waiting for an answer.

I wanted to say yes. A piece of these secrets was a piece of Gran. But what could I expect to learn in another day or two? I was beginning to wonder if I could leave Snow here alone at all. If she didn't know how to wash a dish on her own she wasn't likely to survive the winter --not in these woods --and she hadn't mentioned anywhere else she could go or anyone who might be looking for her.

"Come with me back to Greta's house." I said. "You can teach me there. Greta --well she won't mind for long. She has a good heart underneath it all. And we could use another pair of hands to spin."

Snow laid her head back against the wall and closed her eyes the way she did when she was trying to hide a surge of pain. As her physician I had already learned to see through the attempt. "Who is Greta?"

"My . . ." I stopped, my mouth frozen around nothing. My mother? My sister? My trade mistress? None of the words seemed right. "She's . . . just Greta. I live with her. We spin thread." Why hadn't I ever wondered who she was before? Who I was? I handed the journal back to Snow. "You don't have to come. If you have somewhere else to get back to."

Snow opened her eyes. "I don't" she said. "I'll come."

That evening I went outside to fetch wood. I stood in the dusk, piling fire logs into my arms, humming another one of Gran's songs, trying not to think about the cold nibbling at my nose and fingers. It hadn't snowed since the night the wolf attacked but white ice still lay scattered over the ground as it would for many moons to come. I ran my eyes over the snow-covered vegetable and flower gardens, wondering what they would look like in the warmth of summer.

I stopped.

Impossible.

I blinked, trying to shake the sight out of my eyes, but they were still there when I opened them, sprawling through Gran's flower garden, bright and lively, as if it were early summer instead of winter. I dropped the fire logs, letting them crash into the snow next to my feet, and rushed toward the garden.

The rest of the plants were dormant, gray and thorny for the winter.

I waded through them, expecting the green vines to vanish at any moment--
to melt back into whatever plant was playing tricks on my eyes. But I could
smell them. The soft, tart fragrance filled my lungs. I brushed my fingers
against the petals. They were soft and plentiful and didn't fade away at my
touch. I drew my hand back.

Roses. Roses blooming in the onset of winter. I stared at them.

"Are you the witch?"

I whirred around to face the voice but all I saw were more plants,
dried and gray and dormant.

"Hello?" I said.

Nothing.

If this was another ghost prank I was not amused. "I don't speak to
things who won't show themselves." I said.

"You just did." The voice said, small and scratchy. It sounded like it
had come from somewhere inside the bushes.

I said nothing, waiting.

"Oh, all right. No need to be rude." A small nobbly man no higher
than my knees stepped out from behind a dormant lavender plant. He shook
a collection of dry leaves and snow out of his waist-long beard. He wore shiny
boots tailored for his tiny feet and his clothes were stitched with gold thread
but he looked like he hadn't bathed in centuries. He smelled like it too. "We
just want to know if you will promise to keep your magic away from our
hovel."

"I'm not a witch." I said. "I don't have magic and I don't even know
where your hovel is."

The little man scowled. His pointed grubby fingers, as long as the
side of his face, twitched with irritation. "A simple yes or no is all I'm asking
for. I would expect more respect from Sable's apprentice. Even if you are
only a sapling witch."

I crossed my arms, matching his scowl. "I'm not any kind of witch.
Who's Sable?"

"Ha!" The little man sniffed. "If you're going to play dumb we're not
going to negotiate with you at all. Just remember. If we sniff your magic near
our hovel your gardens might not be as safe as they've been in the past." He
turned and shuffled back into the shrubbery. The brittle plants rustled with
the movement and then every trace of him was gone.

I gathered up the fire logs and went back inside. "There are roses
blooming outside." I told Snow. "And I think I just talked to a hobgoblin."

Snow looked up from the herbal in her lap, her hard dark eyes
thoughtful. She said nothing.

I raised my eyebrows, incredulous. Perhaps she hadn't heard me.
"Don't you ever . . ."

Snow blinked, waiting for me to finish.

" . . . talk?"

"Yes."

But not, apparently, more than one word at a time. I sighed. "You and Greta will get along splendidly."

We left early the next morning. I wasn't about to risk the woods at night again and it was best we started the journey when Snow was the most rested. I gathered the remaining herb mixtures for her drought and poultice along with the books and some apples and venison into a basket and we set out.

The walk wasn't long. The forest was still. Quiet. I was almost able to convince myself it was just an ordinary forest until we passed a large oak and I could hear the cruel tittering of hobgoblins. And once I could have sworn a ghost child winked at me from out of the shadows. Snow kept her knife gripped in her hand in case we ran into anything with teeth but we arrived at the village unscathed. Perhaps the sunlight was enough to keep the dangers at bay.

Or perhaps the forest wanted us out not in.

I shivered at the thought, turning to face Snow. She slid her knife into her belt. I'd given her one of Gran's shifts and bodice to wear since I hadn't been able to clean the blood out of her velvet gown. The dark brown and cream colored fabrics hung loose around her chest and legs and arms, almost as if they were trying to swallow her. I hadn't considered before how small she was. The top of her head only reached my chin.

The village was quiet, even for late morning. Probably because of the snow. Each home was already stocked with all the supplies they would need until spring. There would be little trade in the months to come. Still. I had expected to see at least a handful of women gossiping at the well.

We reached Greta's house across the square. I knocked but there was no answer.

"Greta." I said.

Nothing.

I made my voice louder. "Greta, it's Rose."

Still no answer.

I pushed against the door. It slid open at my touch. My stomach swirled with uneasiness. Greta always kept the latch down. Even when she was only going to the woodshed.

Snow followed me inside. I'd forgotten how small the house was. How gray the walls were.

"Greta." The floorboards creaked underfoot as my eyes adjusted to the shadows. The cupboard door was left open. A shattered plate lay next to the stove, which looked like it hadn't been cleaned out in days. I stared at the piles of ash inside. It wasn't like Greta to be untidy. But there was something else. Something different I had noticed the moment I stepped inside but hadn't been able to place.

"The spinning wheel." I said. "It's gone." Greta would never part with her spinning wheel. Not for anything. It was her livelihood. Her life.

And then I knew. The cupboards were left open because Greta had emptied them in a hurry, not even bothering to pick up her precious china when she'd dropped it, too busy to clean the soot out of the stove or latch the door shut when she'd gone.

Gone. But where? And . . . why?

I couldn't stay in the village without a spinning wheel. There would be no way for me to earn my bread. 'There is nothing there for you.' the huntsman had said 'It isn't safe.' He had been right about the books. Perhaps . . .

I was worried about Greta. I was. But the thought of returning to Gran's cottage --even through the terrible dangers of the wood --sent my blood dancing. As if I belonged there. As if I wondered why I had even left.

A clattering sounded from outside. Faint at first but it grew louder as it came closer. A sharp, grinding sort of tapping. I turned to Snow. "Is that . . . horses?"

Snow already had her hand on her knife. "Soldiers."

No one else in the village had horses. I stepped up to the window and peered out. Half a dozen soldiers pulled their mounts to a stop around the well in the village square. They dismounted, laughing gruffly with each other as they filled their water skins. I turned around to face Snow.

Snow pulled away from the window, melting back into the shadows. She leaned against the wall and clutched the hilt of her knife. "I have to go." She said.

"Where?" I glanced at the door. They would see us the moment we stepped outside.

I looked back at Snow. Her expression was familiar. Dangerously close to the dazed, unseeing way she had stared through me when she'd woken in the night. Pale. Transfixed.

What was she so frightened of? Soldiers in the village was unusual. Especially when the taxes had already been gathered this season --twice. But what interest would they have in . . .

A noble girl with no place to go. A fugitive.

I stepped away from the window, careful not to be seen. "They don't know you're here, Snow. They can't see you."

Snow nodded. A glimmer of understanding returned to her eyes.

We sat down on the floor with our back against the thin wooden wall. The soldiers' voices carried from across the square. I couldn't make out what they were saying but from the tone of their laughter it couldn't have been very polite. Snow closed her eyes. Her breath began to deepen in long slow droughts. Every few minutes her whole body would twitch.

It was late morning by the time the soldiers left. Sunlight pierced through the window, bright and strong over the floor of Greta's abandoned house. I listened as their shouts and laughter died away bit by bit. The square outside was silent but for the low whistle of the wind. I nudged Snow, lying still with her head against the wall. Her eyes fluttered open. Long lashes blinked in the wall's shadow. I held my finger to my lips for silence and together we crawled to the window.

The square was empty. We watched the wind drift across the trampled snow then turned to face each other.

"You're the princess." I said "The one who ---the dead king's daughter. They said you were dead."

"I'm not dead." She said it in a monotone, as if she didn't quite believe it.

"What now?" I asked. I should look for Greta. I should find out why the soldiers had come here, why the villagers seemed to have expected them.

"Back to the cottage." Snow said. "Unless . . . unless you want to stay."

I shook my head. The huntsman had been right. There was nothing for me here. If Greta had taken her spinning wheel she wasn't in the village. If she wasn't in the village . . . I had no idea where she had gone. She had never spoken of any life outside of it. No past. No dreams. She had just lived here with me. And now she didn't.

I followed Snow out of the house and back through the dormant village. Our feet crunched against the snow in the silence. Once I thought I saw a pair of eyes peering at us from inside one of the houses but when I looked again it was only a smudge of dust and frost on the windowpane.

At last we reached the edge of the wood. The long chilling shadows of the trees seemed to welcome us back with a thrill that was almost fear and almost joy. I released a sigh of satisfaction as we walked along the path, listening to the winter birds flutter through the branches above us. Rabbits and foxes —and probably hobgoblins —scurried in the bushes. I listened for ghosts but heard only the wind and the trees themselves. Snow limped a little beside me, already tired from the long pointless walk to the village. I offered her my arm for support but she shrank away from my touch, insisting she could manage on her own.

We had almost reached the bridge. The air was clear but for the warm steam of our own breath. I heard a sound. A whisper though the trees. Only it sounded almost like the gentle moan of a human child. The air began to moisten.

I stopped, turning toward Snow. She stopped too, her deep red lips open in a circle of surprise.

A mist settled around us, thickening from white to silver to a deep unearthly gray. A moment later –hardly more than the drop of an eyelash –I could hardly make out the small dark form of her silhouette beside me. It was darker than night.

"Ghosts." Snow whispered. Almost a gasp.

I opened my mouth to answer but a different voice shivered through me. The quiet hissing whisper of a child.

"Rose."

I shut my eyes. How did a ghost know my name?

"Rose?" That was Snow. Her voice was surprisingly steady. "Are you there, Rose? I can't see the path."

"I'm here." I reached through the fog until I felt the tight grip of her fingers. I closed my hand around hers, feeling the warmth of her skin, no longer scorching with fever. Her pulse beat against mine, both cupped inside our palms. Just the right amount of alive. Just the right amount of steady.

"Did you hear that voice?" She asked.

"Yes." I said. There were two of us this time. We could keep each other from spooking into madness. I fought back a shiver. "Sit down. We'll get lost if we try to find the path. We'll have to wait out the mist the way we did the soldiers."

I sat down, cross legged, onto the ground. Snow lowered herself beside me. She did not let go of my hand. I wouldn't have let her if she had tried. The ghosts could play tricks on our eyes but they couldn't replicate the warm hold of a human hand. Especially not one clammy with sweat like Snow's.

"What if the mist doesn't clear?" She asked.

I didn't answer.

Snow shivered beside me. I could hardly see her through the mist but I could feel the sudden twitch in her wrist as her body tried to fight off the cold. The motion vibrated through me and I shivered to.

"What's that song you hum?"

"Gran's song?" I asked.

"The one you hummed when you mixed the herbs and tidied the cottage. It's always different but also always . . . the same. Warm and rampant. Like fire."

I shrugged, forgetting for a moment that she couldn't see the gesture through the fog. I hadn't realized I'd been humming in the cottage. "Just a song I hum." I said. "It comforts me."

"Me too."

So I began to hum. Softly at first, letting the melody seep into my lungs. Then I closed my eyes. The vibrations took over deep inside my belly. I felt the music shoot up through my throat and scatter into the air, shaking each particle of mist. The droplets collecting on my skin slid off, one by one. A soft, subtle warmth filled the air around me. Snow and I both stopped shivering. Snow leaned her head against my shoulder. Her breath tickled the surface of my neck. Soft. Gentle. I knew she needed rest after our walk to the village so I thought of sleep as I hummed. I thought of soft beds and long, sweet dreams.

Snow's breathing slowed. Her head rolled limp onto my breast. I lowered her onto the ground beside me, never letting go of her hand, and stretched out on the grass next to her. The grass was dry. The air was warm. Snow moaned peacefully in her sleep. My eyes drooped.

I woke with a start. The air was clear, illuminated by a steady stream of moonlight in front of my eyes.

"Rose."

I looked up, propping myself onto my elbow. The ghost child −the first one I had seen that night when I was looking for Gran −stood in front of me. I could see all of her but for one of her shoulders and a leaf shaped piece of her chin where the moonlight didn't shine.

I sat up, my heart pounding. I gripped Snow's hand. Remembering the feeling of warmth. Remembering where I was. Like touching the earth. Like coming home. I took a deep breath and stared straight through the ghost girl.

"What do you want?" I demanded.

"You." The ghost girl said. Then a moment later, as if it took all her strength to pound out each syllable. "Per. . . mis. . . sion."

"Permission? For what?"

"To. . . speak."

"Speak." I said, before I could wonder what it was she might say. What she might know that could drive me mad even with Snow's hand gripped in mine. I could feel the ghost girl's story swirling around her. Fear. Abandonment. A sharp, soul wrenching pain in her chest. Screams no one heard. Soft, delicate hands.

"We are sorry for the mist." Her voice sliced through my mind, pushing it away from the visions of her past with an almost feral force. "Witching hour is the only time we are strong. We needed you to wait. We needed to ask."

"Ask what?"

"You are the witch of the wood. Will you claim us?"

"I'm not −−−what do you mean 'claim' you?"

"If you claim us you will be safe here. If you claim us we will protect you."

"Why?" I asked. I'd never heard of ghosts protecting anyone.

"To hear your song." The breathy monotone of her voice broke for a moment, almost as if she would burst into tears. But ghosts couldn't cry. They could only moan and whisper. "We can't hear it unless you claim us the way Sable did."

I held my breath, almost afraid to speak. "Who is Sable?"

"You know."

And I did. The one who had taught me the song. The one who had lived in these woods year after year, protected by ghosts.

Almost protected.

"I claim you." I said. If Gran had done it there could be no harm in it. "You may hear my song. You may protect my home."

SNOW

Rose said that the wolf creature wouldn't come back. I believed her. She said Hans had told her that it wouldn't. I believed him.

Winter waxed on with Rose and I inside the cottage. Her grandmother had stored enough food to last us until spring. I sometimes wondered why she had stored so much. Almost as if she had known that she would be feeding two rather than one. Two that weren't her.

In the mornings I helped Rose make a fire and boil a wheat porridge. I'd never cooked before. My help slowed her down at first but after a few days I could manage the porridge and even the washing up on my own. Once my foot and shoulder healed I took to chopping wood and resuming my knife practice while Rose rambled through the dormant vines of her grandmother's gardens, but each day there was less and less daylight to work by. Most of our time was spent on the hearth rug as I taught Rose to read by the faint glow of the fire.

She was a quick learner if sometimes impatient. We didn't have any paper or quills to write with so it took some time to show her where one letter stopped and another ended. Especially with her grandmother's thin, inconsistent penmanship.

"I'm tired of repeating sounds." Rose complained one evening. She rolled onto her back, resting her head against the side of her arm. Thick coils of red hair curled around her wrist and the side of her neck like ribbons against silk. A storm raged outside, whirling ice into the windowpanes. "When can I read the words?"

Wind shuddered against the walls outside. A fresh fall of snow gathered in the corners of the window. I held her grandmother's journal out to her. It was her favorite of the three books. I could tell by the gentle way she turned each page as if she expected them to crumble at her touch. I preferred the herbal and the recipe book. The stories in the journal were wild and frightening, changing threads halfway through and usually unfinished. The idioms were cryptic and the rhymes . . . something in their relentless rhythms made me almost afraid to speak them aloud.

"Here." I turned to one of the first pages. A list of spider lore that turned into a story about drowning in dew drops. "Find all the ls on this page."

Rose lifted her head and rested it in the palm of her hand. She took the book from me but didn't look at the pages. "You're different when you're talking about letters." She said. "Almost . . . commanding."

"Find the ls." I pointed to the page again.

Rose smiled. A strange crooked smile that almost made me blush. "Like that. You don't hide."

My fingers tightened around my palms. A habit from gripping my knife hilt. "I don't hide." But it wasn't true. If I didn't hide I wouldn't be here. If I didn't hide . . . .

"Papa used to help me with my letters." I said in almost a whisper. An image entered my mind of Papa lifting me onto his knee to peer at a big book painted with bright ink pictures of birds and angels. It had been so long ago. I must have still been in the nursery.

Rose rolled her eyes toward the loft, almost, but not quite, stopping on the feather bed neither of us slept in. She bent her lip then looked down at the journal. She scanned her finger over the messy scrawl of text, concentrating as she looked for ls.

The wind beat against the four walls of the cottage, howling and screeching as ice caked to the windowpanes all through the night. When morning came the storm had only grown fiercer. We could hardly see through the blurred fog of gray outside and Rose had to fill the cracks in the door with scraps of her grandmother's sheets to keep the icy wind from scattering the embers in the fireplace.

Unable to go outside, we worked on Rose's reading but not even my concentration lasted long. Rose slammed the herbal I'd given her to work with shut after the first hour. A fresh rush of wind pushed against the cracks in the door, forcing its way through the snow drenched pieces of sheet. The soggy strips fell out of the cracks. Bone chilling air swirled through the cottage, filling every corner. I shivered.

"I can't stay in here. "Rose paced back and forth from the door to the fireplace, shaking her head, twitching her nose. "I can't stay trapped inside like this all day. I can't."

I watched her from where I still sat by the fire with the herbal open on my lap. She stopped by the window and pressed her palms against the glass. The wind rattled the door. My palms itched for my knife.

Rose whirled around to face me. "How can you just sit there? Sitting still –it's like . . . it's like hiding, only ---only we have no idea when it will end or if it even will. We're trapped in here. We're trapped, Snow and I can't breathe."

The wind howled. Remnants of nightmares shuddered through me. The sound of the lock I never heard when the pale woman clicked it into place. "The storm will end." I said

Rose glared at me. She bounced her curls against her back and scrunched her nose. "Eventually. That doesn't do us any good now." She turned again to face the blank gray of the window.

The cold hissed outside. It laughed like a snake. Nightmares stirred again inside my head. Vines around my chest. Me unable to move. Pale, soft hands.

I stood and joined Rose by the window. "I don't like it either." I said. "I hate waiting. I hate hiding. When Lucille first came to the manor –before her and Papa were officially wed –I thought I could hide from her. I thought . . ."

I stared out into the gray of the storm. Like empty space inside my head. Empty space that wasn't empty at all. I wished it was.

"Once --preparations were being made for the wedding. The whole manor was turned upside down. There were ribbons and flowers and people practicing marching all over the place. My dancing tutor was helping my flute instructor prepare the music so I had the afternoon free. I went down to the kennels first because I had heard there was a new litter of pups but the mother snarled at me and wouldn't let me near them so I meandered through the halls instead.

"I ended up in the dungeons. I don't remember how. I must have taken a wrong turn or been driven that direction, trying to stay out of everyone's way. It wasn't the first time I had been down there. It smelled of feces and the air was stale and hot. Most of the prisoners were asleep. Flies buzzed up and down over their faces and swarmed their tiny bowls of water.

"There was one prisoner. I have no idea what he had done -- something especially awful because . . . both his wrists had been broken. His hands were twisted, limp and unmoving so that I could see the bone trying to poke up out of his skin. He had fresh burn blisters on his neck and chest and dark purple bruises on his eye and cheek. His eyes were open. He saw me when I passed him but didn't say anything or even move. He just kept staring straight ahead as if nothing around him existed.

"I turned to go. I knew I shouldn't be down there, gawking at prisoners, but as I turned I heard voices. Footsteps. Small, quick steps almost gliding over the stone floor. I slipped behind the nearest corner only seconds before Lucille came sweeping down the hall with a servant at her heels.

"I don't remember what question they asked the prisoner. I just remember that it was the same one over and over and that he said over and over that he didn't know the answer. I don't remember . . .

"Lucille had these strange slippers. They were made of iron. I could tell the first time I saw her in them that they were too big for her feet but the iron was engraved with all sorts of patterns and designs so I had thought that they were some kind of northern fashion I didn't understand. As she questioned the prisoner her servant made a fire in a sort of makeshift stove. I thought that was odd since it was an already hot summer afternoon. Once the fire had come to life Lucille took the shoes off and placed them next to it. I thought that was odd too but I wasn't prepared for . . .

"They turned red first, then orange, then blue, then white. Then Lucille's servant put them on the prisoner. He had gloves and a pair of tongs but even he screamed out in pain as he slipped them over the prisoner's feet. He pulled the man upright so that he had to stand while the queen finished questioning him. Sweat gleamed off the prisoner's skin. His feet jerked up and down and back and forth in a cruel, sickening dance.

"I don't remember how long it took. I don't remember if he ever told Lucille what she wanted to know. I just remember the screaming and the rich scent of his feet cooking inside the shoes. Smoke filled the dungeons, choking out even the smell of feces. I closed my eyes and covered my ears but it did nothing to muffle the sound.

"When it finally stopped I knew that the prisoner was dead. I stayed where I was, huddled against the wall with my hands over my ears, until I heard the servant put the fire out and the soft silken brush of Lucille's gown as she glided back out of the dungeon.

"She wore the slippers to dinner that night. She smiled her warm welcoming smile and laughed at all of Papa's jokes. When the servants brought out the main course —a whole stuffed swan, still sizzling as they placed it on the table —she turned to me. Her laughing emerald eyes locked on mine, intense and malicious for only the flicker of a second. So brief that even I thought I had imagined it. Until she asked me if I wanted to borrow a pair of her shoes for a dance after dinner. It was all I could manage to mumble that I was too young to join her for dancing."

I stopped. Rose stared at me, unmoving. She said nothing. It was frightening to see her speechless. As if I had killed something inside her. Why had I told her this? I had never told anyone before. Not Hans. Not Elise. Not Dana. Not even Papa. If I had told Papa perhaps he wouldn't be ---

I clenched my fist then released my grip. I glanced at the fireplace then back at Rose. "We should start the soup for supper." I said.

Rose nodded. Still watching me. Still speechless. It would take all day for the soup to simmer.

It was two days before the storm finally let up. The ice on the windows was still thick, painting even the gray and black outside white and cracked with veins. I pulled open the door. The pile of snow that had collected against the edge crumbled forward onto the threshold. Thick piles of white shimmered and glittered off the ground as far as I could see, spreading out into the woods in globs beneath the trees, winding like spider webs over the branches. A symphony of bird calls filled the air. We weren't the only ones who had been holed up for the last three days.

I turned around to face Rose, still making her way down the repaired loft ladder. "Does your grandmother have any traps?" I asked. "It might be nice to have some rabbit."

"We can look." Rose dropped herself down. she skipped the last two ladder staves and leapt for the door. She snatched her cloak off the hook and draped it around her shoulders. It rippled around her in a cascade of deep red. Like funeral posies. Like blood. It wasn't the best color for hunting.

"Gran made it." Rose said, noticing my gaze.

Hazel-gold eyes. Red hair. Red cloak. It was as if she were made of flames. I looked down at my own attire. The simple brown dress that had once belonged to Rose's grandmother fit me loosely in the arms and waist. I had hemmed the skirt but it still sank down to the toes of my boots.

It wasn't black, I realized. I had been out of mourning for weeks and hadn't even noticed.

Rose stepped past me into the freedom of the morning. She spun around to face me. Her cloak rippled around her. Her boots pounded through the layers of snow. "Are you coming?"

I grabbed my own black cloak off the hook and rushed after her, crunching my feet hurriedly into the snow to catch up.

The air was still. Almost as if it were frozen in place. Our hot breath sizzled through it in tiny moving clouds. I shivered. Dormant gardens tumbled around us. Thick brittle thorns and long winding bits of gray and brown stiffened with frost from the storm. A single green vine snaked its way through the ice covered mess, smothered in white and red roses. Only a few lone drops of snow clung to the thin delicate petals, somehow unmarred by the storm.

Rose slowed her long impatient strides. She twisted one of her curls, wrinkling her nose as she looked down at the roses. "Out of everything I've seen in these woods those roses scare me the most."

"They weren't there before." I said, catching up to her at last.

"They weren't." Rose agreed. She laughed. "I like them."

The toe of my boots hit a stone hidden in the snow. I tottered forward to keep my balance, almost catching Rose by the arm "You like things that scare you?"

She turned to face me. Her long lashes, already frosted with ice, fluttered over her hazel eyes. Soft. Playful. She looked like she were about to laugh again. She always looked like she were about to laugh. "Don't you?"

I shook my head. The rust sting of blood touched my tongue as I realized I'd been biting my lip.

Rose wrinkled her forehead. She stared at me as if I were one of her grandmother's letters she didn't know the name of. "But the way you jumped at that wolf creature with your knife --like you had nothing to lose. Like--" She stopped. It had been the first either of us had made mention of the wolf creature since the first day.

"I didn't." I said. "Have anything to lose."

We had both stopped walking. I looked down at the sagging brown fabric of my dress then behind my shoulder at the cottage. Smoke shot up out of the chimney in a thin winding stream. The stone walls stood straight and solid, a shield against prying eyes and the press of the wind, almost sacred in the solitude it afforded. If the wolf creature came again maybe I would be more hesitant to risk my life.

Rose and I found half a dozen cage traps and some skinning knives in the shed. One of the cages was water damaged and another had three snapped styles but we could still use the other four. I cut up some apple pieces to bait the rabbits with and we set off into the woods.

It was strange to have Rose chatting beside me as we walked. She seemed to grow more vibrant with each step as if the trees themselves gave her strength. Her nose and cheeks grew rosy as she pointed out the winter birds and evergreens we passed. I couldn't tell if the redness was from excitement or cold. Perhaps both. Or perhaps it was only the shadow of her cloak that made her skin look flushed with fire. She flitted back and forth in the snow as she spoke, kicking up bits of ice and jumping from stone to tree stump along the path. Her steps were so buoyant that I could imagine she was running barefoot in the grass instead of pounding her way through powdered ice in boots too big for her feet.

It took all morning to find places with enough brush to set the traps. I scattered apple scraps inside and around the cages and propped the door so that it would fall if anything stepped inside. When we finished my hands were numb and red with cold so that I could hardly move them. My stomach rumbled for food. Rose and I sat together against a tree trunk and devoured the last of the apples. They went down my throat almost as cold as the ice but they were crisp and sweet and stopped my stomach from cramping.

"Gran used to bring apples to roast in the winter." Rose said "We would stick them over the fire after dinner and wait for them to turn brown and soft, then gobble them down while they were still hot enough to burn our fingers and lips. Even Greta."

The thought of anything warm was enough to make me shiver with longing. I swallowed my last bite of apple and jumped to my feet. The sooner we checked the traps the sooner we could get back to a warm fire.

Something rustled in the bushes behind me. The movement was too heavy for a squirrel or rabbit or even a fox. My heart's rhythm quickened. The only just healed wounds in my shoulder and foot ached as if the flesh were freshly torn. I whirled around to face the sound.

My foot sank into the snow, deeper than I had thought it would be. I lost my balance. A moment later I was on the ground, coated with cold shatterings of ice that melted through my skirts and bodice. My back pressed against Rose's stomach. She coughed, choking on a mouthful of apple. Or maybe she was laughing. The soft rise and fall of her belly tickled against my spine.

I sat up, untangling myself from Rose. I shivered in the cold. "What was that?"

Rose sat up beside me. She swallowed. Her eyes watered as her bite of apple slid down her throat. "Probably a hobgoblin. They're all over the wood." She stood up and brushed snow off her dress. She shook the small white particles out of her cloak, flapping the bright red like a flag in the cold air, then reached her hand down to help me up.

The first two traps we checked were empty. The apple pieces lay untouched beneath the wooden styles. The third had been triggered. The apples were gone but nothing remained but a trail of fox tracks leading to and away from it. We approached the oak I had set the last trap under without much expectation.

The shadows of the tree branches glided over my skin as I approached the trap. The stick had been nudged, the cage door dropped. Staring up at me with wide, round eyes and twitching noses were two young rabbits.

I knelt beside the cage and lifted the hatch. Cold snow bit through my skirt into my knees and shins. I slid my hand into the cage and grabbed the closest rabbit by the back of his neck. His flesh was warm, his fur soft. I pulled him out and dropped the hatch again. He wiggled in my grip. His long ears twitched backward.

I drew my knife. One quick slice across the jugular and he was still. Something crunched in front of me. I looked up to see Rose standing still in the snow. I hadn't noticed her approach.

I laid the dead rabbit down and pulled his brother out of the cage. He fought harder to get away. Because he had seen what I had done to his brother or because he had a wilder nature. When he too had stopped moving I wiped the blood off my fingers and palms in the snow. I looked back up at

Rose.

She stared at me. "You scare me sometimes, Snow."

I almost answered that she scared me too. With her song that scared away ghosts and made roses grow in the dead of winter. With her fearlessly bright scarlet cloak and the way she moved through the trees. But how could I be afraid of someone who had already saved my life so many times?

I reset the trap, sprinkling more apple bits inside, and lifted the rabbit carcasses off the ground.

The journey back to the cottage seemed shorter, almost abrupt, as if we had hardly stepped out of it at all. As much as I longed for the warmth of the fire I was sorry to leave the open stillness of the wood behind us.

I prepared the rabbits in the shed. I stepped into the tiny thin-walled building and pulled the skinning knives off the wall. Alone.

This morning I had thought it strange to have Rose beside me as I worked. Now I found it stranger not to have her. I hadn't realized how long it had been since I had been away from the quiet crackle of her presence for more than a few minutes. The shed felt too silent. Too still. Too much like the manor after Lucille had sterilized it with her soldiers.

It was nearing dusk when I stepped out of the shed with the cleaned cuts of rabbit meat wrapped in linen. I stopped.

Animal tracks. Round, fresh paw markings almost the size of my hand obscured Rose's footprints leading up to the cottage. I could see the deep holes around the edges where claws had pierced through the snow.

My shoulder and foot began to ache. Hans had said that the wolf creature wouldn't come back.

I listened but could hear nothing but the quiet rustle of dusk. Wind through the tree branches. The hoot of an owl. I followed the tracks, pressing my fingers tight around the bits of meat in my hands. They reeked with the mildew scent of death. My stomach felt hollow. Empty with dread.

I turned the corner. The tracks led up to the cottage door then away from it, circling back toward the back of the cottage. Back to the shed where I had stood only moments ago. I resisted the urge to look behind me and darted for the cottage door.

The pattering of footsteps. My own. The deep heavy fall of breathing. My own.

I reached the door and ripped it open. I slammed it closed behind me and bolted it shut. The sound of the iron against wood shattered through the cottage.

The quick pulse of a heart, beating too fast. My own.

Rose turned toward me with a chopping knife in her hand. She set it down next to the bits of onions and root vegetables on the table.

"Animal tracks." I said. "Outside. The size of ---"

"The wolf."

"It could be a bear." I said.

It could. The tracks I had seen up close had been blurred, meshed into Rose's. But I remembered how intently the wolf creature's eyes had followed Rose, how much it had seemed to want her.

Ghost pains burned in my foot and shoulder. "Hans said the creature wouldn't come back."

Rose's eyes flared. "He was wrong."

I turned to look at the bolted door. The wolf creature had seemed so sentient. Would a single lock be enough to keep him out?

I gave the cuts of rabbit meat to Rose. She placed them over the fire with the chopped root vegetables. The scents of garlic and onion filled the air as I slipped behind the drapes in the far corner to bathe. Time moved like the slow burn of a candle, dripping bit by bit into a hardened, shapeless slab at the bottom of the pillar. Any minute the wax would run out.

Rose hummed while she cooked. I tried to focus on the clear, steady purr of her voice instead of the threat lurking outside. Probably circling us. Waiting for the right moment to strike. We couldn't stay inside forever.

At last I managed to scrub the last remains of rabbit blood out from underneath my fingernails. I slipped into my spare shift and got to work on my dress, ringing out every last trace of red and black out of the sleeves and bodice. The scent of searing flesh filled my nostrils, until finally it mingled with the garlic and onions, melting into a rich, pungent gravy. I hung my dress on the wall to dry and stepped out from behind the drapes. My skin felt fresh and light, almost as if it would float away without my body. I sat down at the table a few feet from Rose.

Rose stopped humming. The juice in the apples on the fire dripped down into the ash. A growl sounded from outside. A blur of fur brushed past the window.

Rose glanced at the door.

"Will the lock hold?" I asked.

Rose didn't answer. I reached for my knife but I was only wearing a shift. I'd left my knife with my other clothes.

Another growl scraped against the wind outside. Louder. More persistent. Something scratched against the door. The wood moaned. The iron bolt rattled.

Rose reached for the tongs next to the fireplace. I darted behind the drapes. My dress hung on a hook on the wall, dripping water like saliva onto the floor. I fumbled through the clinging fabric for my knife. The creature's breath heaved outside in clear steady swells. Or was that the wind? Rising and falling, rising and falling, like the great tumbling roar of the sea.

Another growl. Another creaking scrape across wood. The door rattled again beneath the creature's weight. Footsteps pattered across the wood floor.

"Rose?"

No answer. I could see silver at last drowning in the dark brown folds of my bodice. I fumbled through the wet fabric.

"Rose?"

My hand closed over my knife hilt. The lock unbolted with a sudden snap.

"Rose." I flung the drapes back, knife raised to strike.

Rose stood with the fire tongs raised in both of her hands over her head. A mess of fur and claws barreled through the open doorway. The animal's shoulders were almost as high as my chin, his teeth the size of my fingers. But there was something . . . different. He was much too round, his snout too short, his neck too long --too thick --and his fur --the same shiny orange red as Rose's hair.

"Rose. Don't." I lowered my knife. "It's only a bear."

"Only a bear?" Rose's voice was shrill but she didn't strike. It still had claws and teeth. It could still chew us to bits.

The bear turned a pair of round gold eyes toward me. They shifted to Rose, then to me again. He shook his head, releasing a shower of snow out of his red fur. Pieces of ice melted against my skin and hair, dripping down onto the cottage floor.

Thick globs of fur almost as long as his ears stuck up around the bear's neck. He lowered his nose to the ground, crossing his legs almost like a bow, and stepped past me. He placed his jaws over the fire, carefully removing the bits of rabbit meat one bite at a time.

Rose and I watched as he chewed and swallowed the fruits of our day's work. A pair of half cooked rabbits appeared to be easier prey than two live girls. When he had finished he laid down next to the fire, closed his eyes, and went to sleep.

I looked at Rose. She looked at the bear, then me. She lowered the fire tongs.

I strode past her and slammed the door shut. I re-bolted it with a loud clang, not caring if it would wake the bear. I turned back to face Rose, livid. "Why did you open the door? You could have got us both killed."

Rose straightened to her full height, thrusting her chin out. Her eyes locked with determination. "To kill the wolf. It killed Gran."

"Does nothing scare you?" I demanded.

Both our eyes darted toward the bear, sleeping like a baby on our hearth. Even with his heavy jaw and sharp claws he didn't look much like a monster with his eyes closed and his tongue sticking out from between his teeth. He let out a loud, short snore.

Laughter bubbled in my throat and lungs like a stew left on too long. I clasped my hand over my mouth to hold the sound back but it broke through the barrier, gushing past my fingers and into every corner of the cottage.

"You're mad." Rose said but she was laughing too.

I leaned back against the door, clutching my side, unable to stop giggling. My whole body gurgled and hiccuped in rhythm with the noise. I hadn't laughed —I had hardly smiled —since before . . . I couldn't remember when.

Since before the wolf. Since before Lucille.

ROSE

Snow and I climbed the loft. We pulled the ladder up after us so the bear couldn't follow. Snow went right to sleep. If she had nightmares I didn't hear them. Not even a whimper. She hadn't woke screaming since that first night but most nights I could still hear her sobbing in the straw across from me. I lay awake, listening to the bear snore down by the fire. The pangs of Gran's death lay reopened in my chest. Why couldn't I cry? Why did Gran already seem so far away?

I must have slept eventually. I woke a little after dawn to the scuffling of dishes, followed by a grunt and a crash.

"Listen here." It was Snow's voice. "If you want to stay in and keep warm I won't shove you out but you can't have our breakfast."

I sat up, not even bothering to shake the straw out of my hair. Snow stood between the table and the fireplace with a wooden spoon, dripping with porridge, in her hand. The bear looked up from two overturned bowls on the floor. His nose and chin drizzled with white sludge.

"Snow." I jumped for the ladder. "What are you doing? He has claws. And teeth."

Snow looked up at me. She raised an eyebrow. "You believed you could kill him with a poker last night."

"I was angry." I said.

Snow shrugged. "I was hungry. Besides . . ." She bit her lip. The charming traces of a blush spread behind her ears. "I forgot he was here."

I dropped off the ladder onto the ground just a few inches from the bear. He hadn't moved. He looked down at the overturned bowls. The still steaming porridge smeared over the wooden planks. He blinked then licked his nose as if attempting to hide the evidence. He didn't look like he planned on attacking either of us any time soon.

I laughed. Only Snow would wake up with a bear in the cottage and make breakfast, business as usual. It felt good to laugh with all the cracks in my heart reopened.

Snow made more porridge. We left the door open while we ate it. The bear lapped the first two bowls up off the floor then wandered out into the yard. I jumped up to close the door after him. It slammed shut beneath my hand, blocking out the draft. I turned around with my back pressed against the door. "He must have thought our flesh wasn't worth the trouble."

"He must have." Snow agreed. She hesitated. "Pea soup tonight?"

I nodded. I wasn't in the mood to go tromping around in the wood again today and I didn't want to send Snow out alone. Not with a bear roaming through the trees. We stayed inside most of the day. Now that we could leave if we wanted to the cottage didn't seem so small. Night fell with us sitting together by the fire while I tried to make sense out of Gran's journal.

Snow had only just begun to show me how to find the words the letters made. I stared down at Gran's soft, messy letters, mouthing their sounds. Slowly at first. Some were hard to tell apart from the others. A 'B'. An 'O'. That one was probably an 'N' but could have been an 'M'. The dark inky swirls curled over the page, leaking into my eyes. I could hardly tell where one ended and another began. I closed my eyes then opened them again.

Something scratched against the door. The bolt rattled.

Snow looked up from the herbal in her lap. "The bear."

"He can't get in." I reminded her.

"I know." She looked down again but her eyes didn't move across the page. Her forehead didn't wrinkle in concentration the way it did when her mind was floating off to a different world.

I looked back down at the journal. I knew the letters. I knew their sounds if only I could concentrate on them hard enough. I plunged forward, ignoring the grinding pain steeping into the front and back of my head.

The bear moaned. He scratched harder against the wood outside. Snow looked up at the door. "He's probably very cold out there." She said.

"Probably." I agreed.

"And lonely."

I nodded.

"He didn't try to eat us."

"Just our rabbits and porridge."

She looked back down at the herbal, biting her lip.

I laughed. "Oh, just let him in already."

She looked up again, hesitant. "Do you think it's safe?"

"Of course it isn't. He's a bear. Just let him in."

The bear came in covered in ice flakes. He shook them out of his fur, scattering bits of melting snow through the room. He followed Snow to the fire then sat down with her, pressing his damp, warm body against both our backs. He sniffed my fingers then licked them with his big wet tongue.

"He doesn't seem wild." Snow said. "Not the way other animals do."

I shrugged. "He must have already eaten."

"No. Look at his eyes. They don't look like . . ." She stopped. I could see ghosts rising behind her eyes. Fear. The memory of pain.

"The wolf." I finished for her.

She nodded then touched her shoulder, biting her lip again.

I touched her sleeve where I knew her scars were. Long silver slashes like fingers brushing dangerously close to her neck. "Does it still hurt?" I asked.

Snow shook her head. "Only when I remember."

Then I wouldn't make her. I pulled my hand away, brushing my fingertips for a moment against hers, and looked back down at the journal. I knew the letters. If only I could stop looking at them like a riddle and more . . . more wild. Like a song. Like Gran's songs. Something that did not need an answer because it had a rhythm.

B. O. N. E.

"Bone." The word slipped out of my mouth smooth and clear like the sharp edge of a jewel. "Bone of earth and root of flesh. Hidden where the shadows steep. Finger vines and heart strings mesh. Come to me from woodland's deep." I looked back up at Snow. "What do you think that means?"

Snow stared at me with her wide, dark eyes. The flames from the fireplace flickered shadows over the side of her face. "I never taught you that." Her voice came out a whisper.

"You showed me the letters." I said.

She shook her head. "Two nights ago you could hardly make out your name. The writing in that journal is impossible. I can't even make out most of the rhymes." She reached for the book then drew her hand away as if she thought it might bite her.

The bear released a long gentle snore and rolled his snout over behind us.

Snow buried her fingers into the bear's red hair —almost the same color as mine —as if she were looking for a distraction. Something else to touch. "Don't bears sleep in the winter?" She asked.

"He is asleep." I ran my hand along his great spine, feeling the rough locks of his fur between my fingers. They were still wet and looked like they would be so much softer than they were.

Snow wrinkled her forehead. "I mean in a cave. All winter long without stopping. That's what Hans said. He said the best time to hunt a bear is early spring when they're too hungry to be cautious."

I shrugged. "Maybe this one doesn't like caves. I've never even heard of bears in this wood before. Just ghosts and wolves."

The next morning we made extra porridge to share with the bear. After he had eaten it he wandered off again into the wood. He returned after dark and again the night after that. We stopped bothering with the lock until he was already nestled behind us by the fire. He snored and melted snow all over the floor and Snow buried her fingers into his red hair. He ate like the wild animal he was but he was warm to lie against once he was dry and kind as a kitten.

If kittens were kind. I hadn't seen many up close.

At first the bear came only at night but as the days wore on I began to catch glimpses of him watching us from inside the wood, so far back that he looked almost like just another shadow behind the trees. Soon we became used to seeing him in the yard, pulling leaves and sticks out of the snow or sometimes rolling in it like a hog wallowing in the mud. Sometimes he would sit behind Snow while she was practicing her knife throws, just watching her with his big round eyes.

"I think he's sweet on you." I told her.

Snow laughed. "On me? It was your footsteps he followed up to the cottage."

Some nights we didn't climb up into the loft. Instead we slept snuggled next to the fire with the bear, using his big padded paws for pillows. It was nice waking up with his warm fur against our backs but we also woke up in need of a bath which wasn't much fun with the air inside the cottage getting colder every day.

Winter seemed to last forever. Cold night after cold day after cold night. There were more storms than either of us bothered to count, more reading lessons than I needed, more lumpy porridge and pea soup than I had ever eaten in my life. We lit fires and set traps and played with the bear and hummed to one another while we waited for it to end.

At last the trees began to dribble with melting ice and fresh shoots of greenery. The ground thawed so slowly we almost didn't realize how warm it had become until we stepped outside one morning and the earth was green instead of white. The bright tiny blades of grass were coated with frost but the thick blanket of snow was gone.

That night our bear didn't come. We sat by the fire with the door unbolted well into the night, waiting, but there was no scratching against the door. No playful groans, no warm wet mat of fur, not even paw prints in the yard the next morning. Instead I found a ring of crocus stems blooming next to the white and red roses. I stooped and pulled damp bits of dead plants away from them. The hard, frost-coated earth scraped at my fingers.

"We never gave him a name." Snow said.

"He never told us his name." I corrected her.

He didn't come that night either. Or the night after that. Snow burnt the porridge both mornings. She skinned and cut rabbits from our traps and cut firewood we didn't need.

"He's not hurt." I told her "He just went exploring now that the air is warmer. Bears roam in the summer. He's fishing and sampling berries."

"I know." She swung the ax down, splicing a maple log in two. The pieces landed in the dry, brown earth with a dull thud.

The crocuses were only the beginning. As the days passed life cascaded through Gran's flower garden. Deep, saturated red and winter white roses spread out among dark velvety violets, tall fragrant husks of lavender, and bright yellow tufts of chamomile. The single vine of red and white roses that had sprung up through the snow receded into the lush tangles of greenery, just another plant, no more spectacular and no more vibrant than the rest.

The wood tumbled with strawberries and blueberries and blackberries and raspberries. It grew rampant with life. The creek teemed with trout and pike. We found walnuts and hazelnuts buried only a few short inches into the dark rich soil. Squirrels and rabbits and badgers and hedgehogs scurried through the constantly thickening nets of ferns and bushes and there was never a hint of ice. Song birds fluttered through the branches, warbling like drunks at a harvest dance.

No wonder Gran had preferred living here to the stiff, drab village. I abandoned my shoes in the cottage and tended to the gardens, waded in the stream, climbed trees hunting for eggs, and stained my fingers with bright, sticky berry juices. I gathered plants off the forest floor, repeating their names from Gran's books. Meadowsweet for fever. Motherwort for melancholy humors. Sage for —well it smelled better than anything else I had ever held. Was it supposed to chase away ghosts?

If only Gran had been there to teach me the names herself. If only I had come to live with her years and years ago instead of sitting next to Greta with a curding brush, listening to her spin thread all those years.

At midsummer Snow and I lit a fire in the wood to thank the earth for its plenty. I whispered one of Gran's rhymes into the flames and the ghosts gathered in a circle around me. There was no moon but I could see their forms in the glow of the flames. I hummed a hymn of thanks into the night. The song spread through me and into the trees, brimming with promise and new possibilities.

Snow stood beside me, silently staring into the fire. She said she could see the ghosts. She could hear them calling our names but she didn't feel how much they wanted to cry but couldn't, how they melted into the sound of my voice because I had claimed them. She didn't feel each of their lonely, forgotten deaths tangle around her soul like old, dusty cobwebs.

Too soon the leaves faded from green to gold. They fluttered off the trees in thin, crisp flakes, blanketing the great tree roots against the cold. A chill crept into the air a little more each day. My toes grew stiff with cold and I had to remember where I had left my boots.

The morning of the season's first snowfall Snow and I stood together by the window, watching the ice crystals drift like ash in the wind. They landed on the sleeping gardens, clinging to the thorns and gray wood. The red and white rosebush had sprawled through the other plants, winding its way around them and blossoming more brightly than ever. No mere winter could kill it.

"My boots are tight." Snow said. "We should go to the village and see if they will trade a pair for firewood."

"Or fresh game." I said. "The villagers are afraid of the wood. We're bound to have any number of things they would trade for.

I turned to look at Snow. The top of her head only came to my nose but she didn't look like a puppet in a costume anymore. She had stitched pale green vines along the edges of the dress that had been Gran's, pulling the laces tight over the bodice so that I could see the gentle curve between her hips and breasts. She had cut slits in the skirt too, letting the brown drape over the cream white of her shift. Her hair had grown, draping in swirls of black ink around her neck and shoulders. She had filled the top of her bodice with pale, curved breasts but her limbs and middle were still as thin as spinning needles.

I wrinkled my nose, trying to decide if anyone in the village would guess that she was the princess who was supposed to be dead. Her lips were the same deep red they had always been, her eyes filled with the same unblinking gaze.

"I'll go." I said. "They won't ask me as many questions."

I tromped into the village late that morning dragging as much firewood as I could carry in the snow behind me. By midday every piece was gone. Instead I was carrying two pairs of boots only a little worn, a new flint, a sack of flour, a ribbon the same red as my cloak, and a purple ribbon for Snow. I asked if anyone had seen Greta since I'd gone but everyone seemed to have thought she'd gone into the wood with me. No one knew that Gran was dead but they weren't surprised when I told them.

"It's that wood." The miller's wife said, shaking her head as she handed me the ribbons. "Nothing that goes in ever comes out . . ." Her eyes lingered on my cloak then drifted up to my face, never quite meeting my gaze "the same as it went in."

When I arrived back at the cottage there were wide padded tracks leading up to the door. My heart jumped, thinking of the wolf creature, but I had grown used to the shape of a bear's paws. When I opened the door I wasn't surprised to see our very own red bear snoring on the hearth.

Snow turned to me with an excited smile that could have melted iron. I handed her the boots and ribbon I'd brought her from the village and didn't even care that the tea she had made was weak and the porridge lumpy.

When the red bear left again that spring we both knew that he would be back.

The woods sang to me. A wordless song that spiraled with vines and whispered with wind. Some days when I was in the gardens I would close my eyes and just listen.

"Do you hear that?" I asked Snow one day when the trees were thrumming louder than usual. Each oak, each ash, each willow, had its own song. Their tones vibrated through me, reaching their roots into my being.

"I hear birds." Snow said. "I hear the bubbling laughter of the brook and the swooshing whisper of the wind through the trees."

I heard those things too but they weren't as loud as the trees themselves. They weren't as loud as the earth the trees sprang from or the silent cry of the ghost children that rested beneath them. Each child's story grasped at me from the shadows of the forest floor. Their sorrows pattered against the edges of my mind, hungry, exhausted with want, but they didn't envelop me the way they had the first night. When the cutting pain searing a hole through the ghost girl's chest became too much to endure or the soft white hands that seemed to plague all of their memories filled me with unbearable terror, I drew my mind away, returning to Gran's gardens with Snow practicing knife throws across the yard. The rhythmic thump of her blade slicing into wood held me, just for a moment, in the present reality.

That was when I sang. Soft, wild, unpredictable music sprang from my center, through my lips and into the air. The music ignited me, held me like a prisoner in its grasp. I sang of the trees. I sang of the red bear. I sang of fire and ice, melting in dew drops like Snow's tears in the night. I sang of her fear, of the sharp blade of her knife always gripped in her hand. I sang without words of the things words could never quite say.

I sang of the ghost children's sorrow and I felt them settle into the wood, almost as if they could rest the way the dead were meant to. My songs weren't just Gran's anymore. They belonged to the wood. They belonged to me. Some days, when Snow stopped her knife practice to hear my songs, a still half smile dripped from the corners of her lips and they belonged to her. That was when I loved the songs the most.

When I sang the flowers bloomed brighter, the summer berries were more plentiful, and the brook swelled with clearer water. I couldn't help but notice the way the forest spiraled with vines the shape of my song. The forest sang to me and I sang back to it so that sometimes I could hardly tell the difference between our voices.

One evening I went inside at dusk to sear a fish Snow had caught for supper. I knelt next to the fireplace, holding the flint in both hands. Then, without quite knowing why, I set the flint on the floor. I closed my eyes and hummed. Gently, I let the music wiggle its own way out from the deepest part of my being. I opened my eyes. A flame flickered in the fireplace.

"I knew your song was like fire."

I turned to see Snow standing in the doorway behind me. She handed me the cuts of fish, freshly cleaned.

That summer, when we went to light a fire in the wood, we didn't bring the flint.

"Should we bring some wood?" Snow asked, glancing at the fresh pile she had chopped the day before. The bark coated logs and branches lined the outer walls of the cottage. More than we would ever use in the warmth of the summer.

I laughed. "It's the forest, Snow. Wood won't be in short supply. Besides, we want a quick, bright fire, not a slow burn. We need smaller pieces."

We bounded into the wood with a satchel of lavender tea and biscuits, gathering fallen branches as we went. We had only been wandering for an hour when we heard a fierce, persistent rustle scuffling back and forth through a rush of ferns.

"What's that?" I asked "An animal?" But it wasn't scurrying or even hopping, just padding back and forth, back and forth in the same spot.

"Not an animal." Snow stood up. She adjusted the satchel over her shoulder in order to add another branch in the crook of her arm. "It sounds trapped."

"A hobgoblin then." I said.

We kept walking. A moment later I caught sight of his long beard and small wrinkled face darting back and forth through the bushes. He scowled when he saw me and turned his back as if he would run away. He tried but fell, landing on his nut sized knee with a tiny thud.

"Curse it." He rose to his feet. I recognized the long fingers and gold stitched clothing of the hobgoblin I had spoken to in the cottage garden when the red and white roses had first bloomed.

"Are you trapped?" Snow asked.

The hobgoblin stopped. He glared at Snow. "Do you imagine I'm pacing back and forth for a lark? Or did you think this tree is tied to the end of my beard to decorate it?" He tugged on the long gray hairs of his beard. They stuck straight out longways instead of draping down toward the ground. I squinted past the ferns to the roots of a maple tree. The tips of the hobgoblin's beard disappeared into their spindly fingers, pulled tight like thread in a loom.

"What did you do to the maple?" I demanded. "He wouldn't pull your beard if you hadn't done anything to him."

The hobgoblin curled his lips. His tiny black eyes narrowed. "Nothing you two great big things don't do everyday." He glanced at the sticks of firewood tucked in Snow's elbow. "I just needed a branch or two to cook my dinner with. We've all but run out down in the hovel."

I crossed my arms. "There's plenty of wood on the ground."

"No one asked you, witch. Maple gives the meat a better flavor." He crossed his arms underneath the fraying canopy of his beard, mirroring my stance.

We stood for a moment, glaring at each other. A breeze rustled through the branches overhead, shifting the shadows on the forest floor. Something glinted in his hand.

"Well," he tapped his foot in impatience. "Are you going to ask him to let me go?"

"No." I didn't tell him that there was no reason on earth the maple would listen to me. The trees rustled again. I looked down at the round gold disc in his hand. A coin the size of his palm. It was smudged with as much dirt as the hobgoblin was but probably worth an entire village. I had never seen the seal engraved on it before. At least . . . not on any kind of currency.

My hand went to the wooden clasp on my cloak. I rubbed the thin lines carved into it. A single rose. Like my name, Gran had said. And the spindle in Greta's cupboard had been made of gold.

"We can't leave him here." Snow said. "He'll be eaten by foxes." She piled the firewood in her arms onto the ground and drew her knife. She knelt next to the hobgoblin with one knee on the ground and her other lifted over her foot.

"Don't." He swiped his hands at her as if he were big enough to shove her away. "Not my--"

But Snow had already cut off the tip of his beard, freeing him from the hold of the maple roots.

His face went pale. He ran his fingers over the chopped edges. "Look what you've done. My face. My beautiful, distinguished face. I can't go back to the hovel like this. My brothers will laugh like . . . like . . ." He stepped toward Snow, shaking his fists. "You've ruined me, you milk faced child. You brainless harpy."

"Careful what you call her." I took one step toward him. He turned and ran, scurrying through the bushes like a squirrel. "Thankless fiend." I turned to Snow "You probably saved his life."

Snow sheathed her knife. She looked up at me, still kneeling next to the ferns. "Why did he call you a witch? Because you can light fire with your voice?"

I shook my head. "Because I live in Gran's cottage."

Snow rose to her feet. She picked up the wood she had gathered and we continued making our way through the trees. We walked for a moment in silence, neither of us speaking. Bluejays soared overhead with their flat, flamboyant headdresses. A crow squawked somewhere through the trees.

"You live in Gran's cottage too." I said.

"I do." Snow answered.

"Why didn't you say so?" I didn't turn to look at her. The fall of both our bare feet scratched against the leaf covered woodlands. "Do you think I'm a witch?"

Snow stopped. She turned to me with her silent, half smile. "Do you want to be a witch?"

But I didn't know. I was beginning to wonder if I had a choice. Gran had left me her songs. I couldn't just forget them.

We reached the clearing. Snow and I cleaned all the dry brush off the ground, and piled it into the center. We piled the wood we had gathered on top and stepped back.

"We light it at nightfall." I said.

"You light it." Snow reminded me.

We sat on a rock beneath a willow and pulled the tea and biscuits out of the satchel. The satchel had kept the tea from heating in the sun. It trickled down my throat, cool and fresh, tasting of wings and earth. The biscuits were made of oat, crowded with bits of almond and dried blueberry. I looked at the round bit of bread in my hand as I chewed. When was the last time I had done any baking? I preferred staying outdoors as much as possible in the summer so we usually ate fresh nuts and berries with the occasional fish. "Did you make these?" I asked Snow.

Snow nodded. She swallowed a bite, then washed it down with a gulp of tea.

"But . . ." I took another bite, chewing slowly. Sweet. A little tart. A little sticky. "They're magnificent. I never saw them in Gran's books." I thought I had memorized every recipe.

Snow shrugged. A charming cloud of red spread over her cheeks, almost as bright and enchanting as her lips. "I didn't use a recipe. I just . . . threw some things together and baked them."

I stared at her in disbelief. She could hardly manage a decent pot of porridge with clear instructions. How had she invented a magnificent biscuit without even thinking about it? "You are a riddle, Snow." I said.

Snow grinned. It was a smile I hadn't seen before. Playful. Almost teasing. "I'm sorry."

I shook my head, unable to resist returning the smile. "Never apologize for being fascinating."

Dusk crawled around us as we finished the biscuits. The sky's gray darkened and the first splattering of stars glittered overhead. A fox pattered across the clearing. Crickets chirped from the grass. Bright colored beetles drifted through the air around our ears and across the sky. A pair of bats flapped out of the trees looking for their supper.

"The wood is so alive at night." Snow said. "How did I live so long twittering my evenings away at Papa's long suppers inside the manor?"

I tilted my head, peering closely at Snow to see if her eyes held any trace of the haunted look she had when she spoke of the queen, but she wasn't thinking of those times. She was remembering before. "The suppers couldn't have been all bad." I said "They must have had dancing."

"Yes." She smiled distantly "I used to love watching the noble women twirl across the room in silks and ribbons, waiting for the day I would be old enough to join them but . . ." She fingered the edges of her hair. "I think I would rather watch the bats. People are so far away ---everyone at the manor was. Constanze. Dana. Elise. Even Papa. They were always so far out of my reach in some place I couldn't understand. Even when they were right in front of me. Especially then. Things aren't far away here. They just are. The trees. The air. The night. You. I can feel it. I can touch it." She reached her hand out, almost touching mine, then pulled it away.

"You can." I held her gaze, reaching for her hands. "Dance with me." I said. "Show me how. You must be old enough now."

She smiled, biting her lip at the same time. "Almost. But I don't suppose the foxes will care."

My feet were ill tuned for the controlled, delicate steps Snow showed me. I tried to mimic the slow, languid motions of her feet and ankles, but mine fumbled, kicking against her toes and shins. I held onto her hand, resting my other palm firmly against her waist but I still managed to lose my balance. I fell forward as we twisted, landing in her arms. She smelled of ferns and maple sap. I felt her breath, soft and slow, rise against my ear. My heartbeat quickened. I drew back.

The movement was too quick. I had to step my foot back to keep my balance. It tangled between Snow's ankles and we both came tumbling down onto the cool damp grass. My knee pressed into her thigh. My elbow pushed down against her shoulder.

"I'm sorry." I muttered, barely able to get the words out.

Snow laughed. It sounded like rain. Like thunder. "That was much better than my first lesson. I was so stiff my feet hardly moved at all."

I pulled my elbow away from her shoulder. "I doubt that. You were probably born with complete control of every movement you ever made."

Except when she was asleep. And making porridge.

"It's dark." Snow said.

"Yes."

She looked at me, waiting. I didn't move.

"Time to light the fire."

"Yes. Yes, of course." We untangled ourselves and I followed her to the kindling piled in the center of the clearing. We stood in silence for a moment, listening to the calls, and scurries of the night. At least that's what Snow heard. I heard the deep thrum of the trees, the enveloping roar of the earth, and the wordless cries of children who had died years before I was born. I closed my eyes.

I felt the fire, already burning deep inside my chest, brighter than ever before. It spread through my limbs and belly and up into my throat. It rollicked there a moment, dancing to the tune of the earth, then I opened my mouth and let the music out into the night.

The song I sang was unlike any I had ever tasted before. It gurgled and soared and screamed and laughed all at once, swirling in the air as if I had more voices than one. It warmed me like liquid light then doused me with the chills of a summer rainfall. I felt lightning in its melody and thunder in its rhythm. My mind screamed for it to end while my body wanted it to go on forever.

Music poured into the night, drowning out every bird chirp, every deer's rustle, every owl's hoot or insect hum. Even the ghosts had fallen silent. All I could hear were the trees and the earth itself, thrumming louder and louder from inside me. I was their voice, their soul, their song. Or were they mine? I wasn't sure if there was a difference anymore. I was the maple the hobgoblin had tried to take branches from. I was the old oak Snow had once killed rabbits under. I was the willow we had sat beneath to drink our tea.

Snow. I was the grass beneath her feet. The breeze pouring through her inky black hair.

No. I was Rose. I lived with Snow in Gran's cottage. I might be a witch.

I opened my eyes. The fire burned high in front of me, lighting the night brighter than a full moon. The heat scorched the surface of my skin. I slipped my hand into Snow's beside me. Her fingers twitched, tightening their grip around mine. The life inside them pulled me little by little back to myself.

I was Rose, standing next to Snow in the wood. We had come to thank the earth.

Ghosts flickered in the light of the fire. Children grinned at me with hopelessness as their faces turned from gold to red to blue. "Lost." They whispered, over and over "Lost."

Shadows fluttered in a circle overhead. I looked up, staring for a moment before I realized they were bats and owls, gathering in a ring around the fire. Other woodland creatures stepped out from behind the trees. Badgers and fox and mice and rabbits and deer and squirrels. They stood silently in a perfect circle, watching the flames. Watching me. Watching

Snow.

I was Rose. Singing a song I had learned from my Gran.

I stopped singing. Silence never touched my ears. The owls and bats beat their wings, diving into the clearing with a fluttering roar. Insects I hadn't seen resting in the trees took flight, buzzing across the sky, past our ears and mouths and eyes. Rabbits and mice and deer and fox and squirrels darted into the clearing, squeaking and chattering as they pattered through the grass with a brittle hiss.

The ground crawled with shadows. A bat flew into the side of my head. Snow ducked as an owl flew past her ear. We held on to each other for balance. Small woodland animals scurried over our bare feet and brushed their tails against our ankles. Tiny claws scratched between my toes. Whiskers tickled the arches of my feet. Insect legs landed on my hands and neck and ears. Snow held on tight to both my hands. Our foreheads tapped against each other as we tried to shelter one another's faces.

The river of forest life seemed to go on forever until all at once it stopped. A final pair of mice remained, chasing each other through the grass. A moth landed on my nose then flew away. Whatever had brought them had also sent them away.

Snow and I straightened. Snow coughed, sputtering an insect into her palm. His wet, shriveled wings clung to the creases of her skin. We looked at each other, then at the fire, still burning amidst the swirl of ghosts.

I let go of Snow's hands and stepped toward the flames. My heart thumped louder than the thrum of the trees inside my chest. My breath heaved, rough and shallow, through my lungs. I had memorized all of Gran's rhymes but none of them seemed right for tonight. Not quite.

"Thorn and briar." I whispered "Wing and claw. Spare us from your clenching jaw. Wild wonders, rich and sweet. We lay our treasures at your feet."

"You wrote that one." Snow said. "I've never heard it before."

I nodded. I didn't tell her it had come to me in almost that very second. Instead I turned toward her, watching her pale face change colors like the ghost childrens' in the firelight. "Do I scare you?"

Snow shook her head. "You could never scare me."

I wished I had her faith. Tonight I was scaring myself. "I think I'm a witch." I said.

She smiled. A sweet smile. An understanding smile. "I think so too."

I looked back at the fire. Its warmth rippled against my skin. "I never had a friend like you before, Snow. Greta always kept me away from the other villagers."

Snow stepped closer. I could hear the gentle rise and fall of her breath only an inch or two from my shoulder. "You had your Gran."

I sniffed, wiping a tear off my nose with the back of my hand. When had I started crying? I never cried. "I only saw her once a moon and . . . she wasn't like you."

"No one's going to keep you away from me." Snow promised.

In the warmth of the summer night, under the canopy of more stars than any being could hope to count, I believed her.

SNOW

We saw the hobgoblin again toward the end of summer. A hint of cold had already begun to seep into the nights and mornings. Rose and I followed the brook downstream, looking for one last string of fish before the chill of autumn set in and it was too cold to wade up to our shins in the cool liquid ripples. I walked ahead of Rose with my skirts pinned to my bodice so that they didn't drape past my knees. I had a pole and fishing line in one hand and a satchel of strawberries and truffles slung over my shoulder, rubbing against my hip as we walked. A slur of wet gravel beneath the water squashed between my bare toes. The leaves whispered in the branches overhead, caressed by the still, soft breeze. I turned back to look at Rose, feeling the wind twirl through the loose strands of my hair. Rose's head was tilted, her eyes distant, her berry-stained lips bent in a distracted smile.

"Listening to the ghosts again?" I asked.

She shook her head. "The trees."

"That ghost child who speaks to you." I said. "The girl."

Rose pulled a stray curl away from her neck. It dangled from her fingers like a dancing thread of fire. "They all speak to me."

"But the one who speaks the most—I've seen her before. When she was alive."

"Where?" Rose asked but I knew she had already guessed.

"The manor. Just after Lucille came. One of the soldiers brought her in, cold and hungry, out of the rain. No one knew what happened to her after that."

A dragonfly landed on Rose's bare shoulder. She stared straight at me, not bothering to brush it off. "You know."

I nodded. "Lucille ate her heart."

I had heard Lucille and the Hunter —Hans --discussing a fine delicacy to be brought up to her room late in the night after Papa had gone to bed. I had pretended I thought it was an animal's heart but why drug an animal first so that no one would hear it scream? Later I had seen the girl led down a corridor up toward the tower rooms that no one used. I'd never told anyone.

Rose touched my shoulder, pressing her palm warm and comfortably into my skin. She held my gaze. Her wild amber eyes didn't quite smile and didn't quite cry and then we moved forward with the water's current.

The brook widened into a stream. The bank grew smoother and wider, covered with rocks and moss instead of gravelly earth. We stopped at a place where the the rocks were wide enough for us to climb up onto and sit cross legged while we waited for fish to bite.

I leaned next to the water and cupped my hands, lowering them into the gurgling ripples. I waited until the wings and legs of a water bug tickled my palms, then closed my fingers around him. I pulled him up out of the water. His legs squirmed as I held him by his wing and tied him to the end of the fishing line.

Rose sat beside me, watching. She could have easily called the water bug —or even the fish—to us but she refused to use her powers against the forest. She would take what the earth offered her, she'd said, but nothing more.

She laid back with her long bare arms stretched over her head. She had taken to wearing only her outer gown when the weather was warm, and leaving her shift buried in the cupboard with her boots. The pale gray fabric draped loosely over the sleek curves of her body. "I hope we catch something soon." She said. "It's going to rain."

I didn't ask her how she knew that when the sky looked as clear as glass. She knew. That was enough.

The water bug wiggled his legs over the water's surface. The current drifted past us. I let my feet drape over the rock's edge, dipping my toes back into the cold, dark water. Something stirred in the rushes. Rose looked up. Her eyes narrowed. I followed the line of her gaze. The hobgoblin poked his long smudged face and now shortened beard out of the long green stalks.

He scrunched his face up into a knot. "You two. Can't I go anywhere without seeing your big gawking faces?"

Rose flicked a gnat away from her eye with her finger. "We were here first."

"Ha. Think you'll make me leave do you? This is the only place I can catch a decent mouth of fish." The hobgoblin planted himself cross legged onto the bank and set to work stringing his fishing pole.

"Do you have a name?" I asked.

Rose shot me a look.

The hobgoblin glowered. "You think I would tell you my name with the witch just laying there next to you? I'm in no hurry to die."

I narrowed my gaze. "Rose would never--"

"Leave him, Snow." Rose said "He's just a nasty little man with no manners."

I turned toward her, strewn over the rocks with a reed between her teeth, her ankle crossed over her knee, her toes wiggling. My tutors would have been horrified. "You don't have any manners either." I pointed out.

Rose snorted. "No. But I have that other thing. What's it called?" She twisted her face, wrinkling her nose as she continued to chew the reed. "Charm."

I shook my head, unable to resist a giggle. "You mean audacity."

The hobgoblin cast his bait into the water and sat back with both hands on his pole, waiting for a bite. We left him alone and concentrated on catching our own dinner.

The wind and the water rippled. Sunlight streamed out of the sky, soft and warm like a farewell kiss. Rose and I caught three fish. Rose braided herself a crown and bracelet out of rushes. I told her that they looked ridiculous on her but I was lying. The green made the bright red of her hair and the gold of her eyes sing. She looked like a dryad or a siren. Like Rose.

We were deciding whether or not to cast the fishing strand one last time when we heard a cry and a splash from across the stream.

We turned toward the sound. The hobgoblin hopped up and down on the bank, gripping his fishing pole. He moved closer and closer to the water with each leap. The current was already pouring over the arches of his feet.

Rose arched her eyebrows in amusement. "You will scare away the fish if you go for a swim now."

The hobgoblin continued hopping, edging closer and closer to the water. He gripped his fishing pole tight in his hands. "Idiot. Can't you see my beard is caught in the thread? The fish is pulling me in."

I turned my head, meeting Rose's gaze. Without a word we both slid off the rock, down into the water. We waded across the stream. It only reached a little past our knees but the hobgoblin was small enough to drown in it. My foot slipped on the soft carpeted slime of the moss and Rose had to catch me to keep me from falling into the slow dribbling current.

We reached the hobgoblin. Rose grabbed hold of his fishing line with both hands and pulled a grayling the size of a hare out of the water. The fish thrashed his long silver tail wildly, his scales glinting like tiny mirrors in the sun.

I climbed out onto the bank next to the hobgoblin and knelt next to him in the gravel. The water lapped around my knees and thighs, stirring the edges of my skirt. The hobgoblin stopped hopping as I fumbled to untangle his beard from the fishing strand but the knots were too tight. The wind stirred the rough strings of his hair even as I worked, tightening their hold around the strand. The hobgoblin kicked and snarled like a trapped badger. Finally I gave up and cut him loose with my knife.

The hobgoblin stopped struggling. He stepped back, stunned as if I had slapped him. He looked down at his beard, now reaching the center of his chest rather than his waist.

"Are you alright?" I asked.

"Oaf." He said "Temptress. Fiend. You're worse than the witch. Distorting my face once wasn't enough for you, eh? You had to come back and finish the job?"

"I--"

Rose came up beside me with the grayling in her hand. The fish had stopped flailing. His gills moved slowly now as he struggled to breathe. The hobgoblin jumped up and snatched it out of her hand. Clouds were closing in overhead, draping us in sudden shadows, but I still saw something glint around his waist. I squinted, peering at it more closely.

It looked like a gold ring hanging from around his belt. In its center was a large pink amethyst but around that, engraved into the gold, was a marking I had seen before. Perhaps the insignia of some noble I'd seen at the manor.

"What's that?" I asked him, but he had already darted off into the rushes, disappearing into the forest floor.

"Next time," Rose said "we will leave him to die."

We waded back across the stream. I had the three fish on a string in my hand and Rose had the fishing pole and empty satchel hung over her shoulder when the first streak of lightning cracked across the sky.

"The rain." Rose said. "Let's race it to the cottage." She grabbed my hand and darted into the trees, pulling me after her.

The first roll of thunder sounded. Our feet beat against the earth like a drum. Cool, hard soil beneath my soles. Crisp, dry leaves. Rough, brittle twigs. We sprinted forward, side stepping through the trees like a dance, first one way then the other. At first Rose raced ahead, pulling me by the arm to keep up with her, but as we ran her breath began to shorten and then I was in front, pulling her after me.

Lightning cracked. Thunder roared. Cool dusk air crawled past my face and into my hair, fondling my feet and ankles. My heart hammered in my chest, matching the pulse of my feet. Water rushed beside us, trickling through the earth as we ran upstream.

At last we reached the bridge. I stopped, jerking Rose to a stop beside me. Her arm pulled taunt then slackened between us. Her fingers tightened around mine, pulling our palms close. Her cheeks were flushed from running, her eyes and mouth filled with laughter. A thread of lightning flashed, the same fire as her hair. The air was thick and damp, preparing for the coming storm.

Thunder shattered against the silence. The sky broke apart, pouring heavy streaks of rain down over our heads. I screamed, then laughed. Within seconds we were drenched through, every inch of our clothes soaked and clinging to our skin.

Rose dropped the fishing pole. I dropped the fish. She took my hand, already smothered in rainwater. Water drizzled out from between our palms and down our wrists. We flung our heads back, letting it pour into our mouths. Drops danced over my face, collecting on my lips and eyelashes, then dripping down my cheeks and neck. We spun around, whiling in circles until we were dizzy.

When both our heads were spinning too much to stand upright we pressed our foreheads together, holding onto each other for balance. Our bodies swayed together, rocking back and forth in the cool of the evening. I could smell the crisp flora of the forest, heightened by the rain, and the warm honey scent of Rose's breath, brushing against my nose and cheek. Slowly the dizziness began to fade.

I shivered. "Winter is on its way." I was unable to keep the wistfulness out of my voice.

Rose tightened her fingers around mine. We ignored another flare of lightning. Another crash of thunder. "So is our red bear."

But he wasn't.

Winter came. The rain hardened into ice, coating the cottage roof and covering the brittle windings of Rose's gardens. Only the red and white rose vine continued to bloom in the persistent howl of harsh winds. We filled our cupboards with turnips and dried peas and beat the dust out of our stockings so we could repair the holes.

"We need more thread." Rose said, fingering our last spool. Her red cloak lay spread over her lap, the last of the hem's tears newly stitched together in tiny neat little 'x's.

"We can get some at the village." I said "We need more flour too."

Rose shook her head. "Greta and I spun the thread in the village. When I was there last winter the villagers said they had to go to Copshire to buy thread."

"Can't we go to Copshire?" I asked.

"It's a day's walk and there are bound to be soldiers."

I bit my lip. Would Lucille's soldiers even recognize me now? It had been so long. Surely they had stopped looking for me. It wasn't a risk I wanted to take. "We can wait until the red bear comes. He'll keep me company while you're gone."

We waited. The frost grew thicker. The wind grew stronger. I helped Rose build a sled with the wood from her grandmother's old bed so she could carry more wood with her into Copshire. The bear didn't come.

"We can't wait any longer." Rose said "Another moon and the roads will be iced over."

I sighed, looking down at a new hole in the heel of my stocking. Black threads frayed around the edges, threatening to snap if they were pulled. The wind moaned outside. Or were those the ghosts?

I shivered. I didn't remember my nightmares. Not anymore. But some nights .... It was good to wake up and see Rose, alive and warm, a few feet from me in the loft. Her presence chased away the lingering traces of darkness before my mind could form names for them. And I always dried the tears away before she woke.

"Take me with you." I said.

Rose shook her head. "It's dangerous."

But I couldn't spend two whole nights without Rose's song or the warm thick fur of the red bear's coat. Being awake and alone for so long would be nightmare enough. "It's been two years." I said. "Most of the soldiers didn't remember what I looked like when I lived in the manor."

Rose pounded her palm against the pastry dough laid out on the table. She drummed her fingers over the wood surface.

"We can carry more wood with the two of us." I said.

Rose tossed her curls and tapped her foot and wrinkled her nose but eventually she agreed that I could come. We baked what was left of our flour into bread for the journey and set out the next morning.

The first part of the journey was familiar. We followed the same road through the wood to Rose's village as we'd followed before. I felt a shudder as we stepped out of the trees. My pulse quickened. I closed my fists around my palms. Open space with only a few buildings cluttered together to shadow the ground. The air was colder out here. The sun was brighter.

Rose felt it too. She turned to me as if to ask if I was all right. I nodded and we kept walking.

The children in the village waved to us as we passed through but the adults hung back, watching us with wary eyes. We stopped at the well for a drink but didn't linger long. It was hard to rest with cold, unwelcoming stares hounding us from the yards and windows. Rose stopped for only a moment to gaze at the house she had lived in with Greta. Another family lived there now. Two children chased a dog through the yard while their father sharpened a set of carpenter's tools.

After the village was the heath. Bits of purple heather prickled up out of the thick blanket of snow. A pair of hawks circled over our heads. The creaking pull of the sled of firewood dragged behind us as we trotted up the road. Large black stones lay scattered over the fields, coated with ice. So much stillness felt lonely after the stagnant bustle of the village. A chill swept through my cloak and skirts. They flapped back and forth with a hard snapping sound but the snow kept the grass and heather still. The stones stood solid and unmoving, smothered in cold, hard ice.

Past midday, after we had eaten our first portion of bread, a hawk soared over the heath, clutching something in her talons. I thought it was a snake at first but it was too thick and had too many limbs. It thrashed back and forth in its struggle to get away. The hawk landed on one of the tall stone ledges. The sun glinted off a streak of torn gold threads. Then we saw the matted gray beard and long grubby fingers.

Our ill-mannered hobgoblin friend.

Rose cursed. "Can't he go anywhere without almost getting himself killed?"

We rushed forward, lifting our feet up and down in quick, snow-covered crunches until we reached the bottom of the stone. It was at least twice as high as Rose. Maybe even three times my height.

"I think I can climb it." I said "If you can distract the bird."

Rose nodded. She edged over to the other side of the giant rock.

The climb was harder than I expected. The stone wasn't high but it was covered in ice. My feet and knees slipped. My hands turned red and numb from grasping at the cold, slippery surface. I bruised my shin and cut the inside of my palm. At last I pulled myself up onto the ledge.

The hobgoblin turned his face toward me from inside the hawk's nest. His little black eyes were frightened and dazed. Rose's song carried up from below. The hawk tilted her head, hopping a little on her sharp talons as she fluttered toward the sound, closer and closer to the edge of the stone. Her wide, all-seeing eyes blinked, fixed on the heath below.

I crept toward the nest and helped the hobgoblin untangle his beard out of the dried brush and heath. It had already begun to grow back, reaching almost to his waist. I wrapped both my hands over his middle and pulled him out of the nest. He struggled for a moment then held still as I set him down beside me.

Rose's song stopped. The hawk turned her head. Her eyes lighted on the hobgoblin. He made a dash for the edge of the rock but she was faster. Her talons closed around the gold threads of his coat, pulling him up off the ground. He kicked his tiny legs back and forth, trying to set his feet back onto the stone.

"Rose."

I stood and reached for the hawk and hobgoblin. They rose higher and higher into the air. My hands closed over the hobgoblin's shoulders. I pulled. His coat ripped. The hawk pecked at the back of my hand, piercing the skin with her sharp beak. I lost my balance and teetered toward the edge.

"Rose."

Her song started again. Slow. Simple. Twirling and tumbling like the wind itself. The hawk let go of the hobgoblin and took off into the sky.

I fell forward, landing on my knee with the hobgoblin in my hands. I let go of him and swung my legs over the edge of the stone. The climb down was quicker but I was still out of breath when I reached the ground. The hobgoblin dropped beside me with a tiny crunch in the snow.

"You're far from the wood." I said.

He pulled a feather out of his beard. "Not by choice, you clumsy oaf. Look what you've done to my coat. It's in tatters."

The back had been ripped so that I could see the white of his shirt in six long stripes where the hawk's talons had been but a day or two with a needle and thread would mend it easily enough.

Rose stepped around from the other side of the stone. "Are you alright?"

I nodded. "What happened?"

"I thought saying hello would be enough to distract her but she was very hungry. I had to tempt her with the sky." Rose scanned the cold, empty heath, barren of all signs of life save for a sliver of black in the sky. The hawk soaring off into the early winter sky. "It will be some time before she finds another meal."

The hobgoblin crossed his arms, scowling. "I don't care if it takes her the rest of the winter so long as it's not me or one of my brothers she finds."

"You ought to take better care of yourself." Rose said.

The hobgoblin shook his head. I noticed for the first time a string of pearls around his neck tucked beneath his shirt so that I could only see a few of the pearls. Between those pearls hung a small gold disc with the same insignia his amethyst ring had had. He snorted. "That's rich, coming from you."

I raised an eyebrow, catching Rose's eye.

"What?" she asked.

I grinned. "He's right. You open doors for wolves, talk to ghosts, light fires in the wood. You court danger every day."

"I don't think that's what he meant." Rose fingered the wooden clasp on her cloak, feeling the rose engraving. The engraving of a single rose. The same as the string of pearls. The same as the amethyst ring.

"I meant that she's a greater danger than anything else."

"Because she's a witch?" I turned toward him, anger taking precedent over my curiosity about the necklace and the clasp. "Rose would never --"

But he had already scurried off through the heather. The snow spread apart, falling from the tall purple plants in a long winding line as he scurried past them, already too far away to hear me.

It was past nightfall when we reached Copshire. The shops and markets were all closed. I wanted to sleep out on the moor but Rose said we would freeze to death. I reminded her that she could light us a fire bright enough to make it seem like summer but she said it would draw too much attention to me so we knocked on tavern doors until we found one willing to give us a room in exchange for firewood. It was a small tavern near the edges of town, a long walk from most of the markets, but there were few rats and the landladies gave us a room to ourselves.

I lay awake most of the night, listening to the rise and fall of the conversations in the hall below us. Murmurs turned to anger or excitement then softened again, almost masked by the scuffling of tables and chairs. Rats scurried. The stairs creaked as new guests were shown to their rooms. Dishes clinked in the kitchen. Rose slept in the bed beside me with her head rested against my shoulder. I wished we had our loft. The mattress was hard and we had to huddle close together to keep from falling off the sides.

"Don't look so nervous." Rose whispered to me the next morning as we pushed our way through the hall, looking for a table to eat our porridge at. But it was hard not to look nervous when I was. I had been to town before. I had even been inside taverns while Papa discussed prison penalties and guild taxes with the local authorities, but I had never been pushed or shoved or stepped on or whistled at so many times in a single morning. I bit my lip and tucked a piece of hair back into my scarf. Rose had insisted I wear it in case anyone knew that the old king's daughter was short and thin with big eyes and ink-black hair. But I was supposed to be dead. No one was likely to recognize me even if I hadn't had my cloak on to cover the strands of black that poured out over my back where the scarf couldn't reach.

We eventually found a table nearer the center of the room than I would have liked. I brushed crumbs off the warped wooden surface and sat down.

Rose sat down across from me. "We should sell the wood first." She had to shout in order to be heard over the noise of the cooks and patrons, packed like strings of salted venison around us. "It will be easier to find everything we need if we have coins instead of wood to trade with."

I nodded. A baby started to cry. One of the landladies shouted at someone not to spill beer on the floor, already soaked with melted snow. Someone whistled. I poked at my porridge but it was already cold and crusted around the sides, lumpier than any concoction I had ever tried to make. I waited while Rose gobbled down hers faster than she could taste it then we stepped out into the streets, tugging our load of firewood behind us.

The streets weren't much quieter than the tavern but at least there was room to walk and the crisp chill in the air masked some of the rank scent of human sweat.

It took us an hour to find the market, then the rest of the morning to find buyers for the wood. Rose and I both held our breath when we saw a soldier follow us from around the corner. He made straight for us but all he wanted was a fee for using the market. We hadn't sold enough wood yet to pay it. He offered to let us stay for a kiss each. Rose offered to light his hair on fire. He stopped talking, tried to look her in the eye but couldn't quite manage it, then said that since we didn't have much to sell the three pennies we had offered would be enough. Just for this once. He took the money and left, moving through the crowd as fast as he could without running.

By the time we had sold all the wood our fingers and noses were red with cold, our stomachs gurgling for food, and our feet sore from standing still. Rose wanted to head for a tavern for some hot cider but I said we had better buy what we had come for first.

We started in the dyers district where we bought a whole basket of thread and seven yards of pale blue fabric. Next we went to the granary for three sacks of flour --the only food we couldn't grow or hunt or collect for ourselves in the wood. We went to the smithy next but we didn't have enough left for a kettle or a new ax.

I passed the bookshops and silver smiths with a wistful eye. Papa had given me all of Mama's silver long before Lucille had come to the manor. She had hated seeing me in it. I wondered if she had melted it all down after I had gone or if she kept it and wore it herself. I wrapped my fingers around my knife hilt as Rose and I ducked past a pair of soldiers out on patrol. They didn't even turn their heads.

It was dusk by the time we arrived back at the tavern. Rose and I were both dazed and dreary eyed, our feet dragging like the sled behind us. I considered going straight upstairs and throwing myself onto the small, hard bed but my stomach had long since stopped gurgling and started screeching for food. Rose headed for the kitchens to see what she could find us while I pushed through the crowd for a place to sit.

The tavern was almost louder than it had been at breakfast. There was twice as much beer and three times as many whistles. Two separate songs had broken out on opposite sides of the hall, tangling together so that I couldn't tell what they were even if they hadn't been toneless sounds almost screamed from large bellies and red beard-covered faces. I spotted a table towards the edge of the hall. It only had one bench but Rose and I could squeeze onto it together. I stepped around a pool of melted snow and spilled stew and headed toward it.

"He had red fur and eyes that looked almost human."

The words jumped at me from out of the noise, smooth and clear. I stopped, dead still. A fist tightened itself in my belly. My hunger vanished all at once. The few bites of porridge I had swallowed this morning swished and swelled inside my stomach.

"I've never seen red bears this far north, Boris." Another voice said.

Boris laughed. The same rich, charming laughter that had filtered over so many dinners in the manor after he and Lucille had come to live there. If I hadn't heard it before I might have thought it was pleasant. Friendly even. "Do you think I would make up an animal that got away from me? He was out on the heath almost a moon ago --too close to the town for safety-- so Beor here and I went out to catch him. Clever bugger he was. Gave us the slip right out in the open. I swear his eyes were almost human."

"Beor's?"

"The bear's."

"You only say that because he gave you the slip."

I sighted the three men circled around a large table by the fire. Then I realized what they were talking about. The red bear. Our red bear with fur the color of Rose's curls. I had seen the hint of humanity in his eyes too, hidden in the corners as if his animal instincts had pushed it aside. But even his animal eyes had been gentle. There was no reason to fear him being close to the Copshire. I stepped closer to listen. The rush of my heartbeat was almost enough to drown out the noise of the tavern.

"A red bear." The larger of Boris's companions mused. "Could he have been the red witch's familiar? Perhaps she can change her form."

Beor shook his head. "She never leaves the wood, right Boris?"

But Boris wasn't listening. He was staring straight ahead with a crooked half smile on his lips. He set his beer tankard down and ran his fingers through his brown curls. His amber eyes danced.

His companions chuckled on either side of him. "Boris never could talk hunting when a girl was near."

I followed the direction of Boris's gaze to see Rose, pushing her way toward me in her blood red cloak with two bowls of stew in her hands.

My blood turned to ice in my veins, too cold to even let me shiver.

Rose smiled at me, raising the bowls with a questioning look.

I shook my head, forcing myself to move. I turned and headed toward the staircase. The crowd seemed to fight my every move, someone always standing where I needed to put my foot next. If they would only hold still the way the trees did. I kept my head down, swiveling and dodging my way toward the stairs.

Rose caught up to me. "What's the matter?" Her nose scrunched into confusion. She turned her face toward the crowd, then back to me. "Did someone recognize you?"

I shook my head. "I recognized someone." If anyone would tell Lucille that I was still alive it would be Boris. I hated to think what would happen to Hans if she knew. What would happen to me.

And I didn't like the way he had been staring at Rose.

We ate our stew --thin and salty with more turnips than beef and more broth that turnips-- in our room, hunched on the floor next to the bed, and left at the first sign of light. I had slept worse that night than the night before, getting up every hour to make sure the door was still latched, but Rose tripped twice trying to keep up with me as we dragged our sled through the pale gray streets. We passed beggars and drunkards, half frozen, on the side of the road. There were a few smithies and bakeries with furnaces lit but the rest of the buildings were quiet except for the scurrying of rats and stray cats.

We reached the heath but I still felt a shadow behind me, always watching me, always just out of sight. "No one will find you." Rose promised over and over but I still kept looking back, jumping at the sounds of animals scurrying through the heather.

Lucille would find me. How could I have ever believed she wouldn't? One day she would find me and she would eat my heart the way she had eaten the lost girl her soldiers had brought in from out of the rain.

It was dusk when we reached the edge of the forest. I still felt eyes on me but perhaps that was only the villagers, watching us step into the shelter of the trees.

It was warmer in the wood without the wind biting and clawing at our faces as it had out on the heath. I trudged alongside Rose, listening to the welcoming rustle of the leaves overhead, the constant scurry of the animals in the bushes. It was good to be home again but the haven seemed different now. Tainted. Breached. I resisted the urge to swivel my head around and try to peer into the trees behind me.

Rose stopped suddenly beside me. She grabbed my hand. "Did you see that?"

We crept toward the rustling. Careful. Soundless. There, sitting on a fallen branch, was our hobgoblin friend. He had the pearl necklace pulled out of his shirt, the gold insignia held up to the last of the woodland light.

Rose fingered her clasp.

The hobgoblin looked up. "You." He stuffed the necklace back into his shirt. "What are you two clumsy clogs gawking at? Go away and leave a fellow in peace."

"What is that?" Rose asked. "Where did you get it?"

The hobgoblin didn't answer. He jumped to his feet then turned and darted off into the snow.

"Come back." Rose called after him but he didn't stop. She cursed. "If he had told us his name I could make him stop. Curse his cleverness."

We left the sled and darted after him, following the long slither of footprints in the snow. We were faster than him but he was defter at moving through the trees. We split up, trying to trap him between us but he weaved back and forth, crawling under tree roots and hiding beneath the thin, brittle windings of the shrubbery. I craned my neck, looking for the limp shifting of the snow, the tiny trail of footprints, the movement of thorns and dead leaves. The hobgoblin made it halfway up an oak before I spotted him clinging to the wide bark covered cylinder with his little smudged hands.

I darted after him, one foot pounding after the other. My heart pumped heat to the surface of my skin. The cold death kiss of the wind sliced across my face. Nothing would ever catch me so long as I kept moving. Nothing could touch me. Not even Lucille.

I stopped. Rose stepped out of the trees a few paces away. The hobgoblin stood between us, backing toward a tree trunk. His big round eyes wobbled from Rose to me to Rose again. He clutched the pearls tight in both hands.

"Tell me where you got the necklace." Rose said.

The hobgoblin snarled. His face wrinkled with an almost animal ferocity. "It's mine."

"Where did you get it?" Rose asked again. "Where did you get the amethyst ring and the gold coin? What does the insignia mean? Why did Gran carve it on my cloak?"

I felt something move behind us. A shadow blocked the streams of sunlight pouring in through the canopy. Phantom shivers of pain swept through me. I reached for my knife hilt. "Rose."

The hobgoblin took another step back. His eyes bulged. His thin little limbs shivered with fear.

"Tell me." Rose demanded.

A growl sounded behind us, soft and quiet but deep like the roots of the trees. Like the morning call of a soldier's drum. I gripped my knife, trying to ignore the phantom pains in my foot and shoulder. I bit my lip to keep from crying out and tasted the warm, familiar salt trickle of blood.

The hobgoblin backed further and further away. He had almost reached the tree now. He pulled the pearls up over his neck and threw them into the air with as much force as his grubby little fist could give. "Here. Take them."

Rose and I both turned as the necklace soared past us. A mass of red fur stood in the snow, towering over us on two legs. The red bear raised his front claws. He shook his thick, massive neck and sharp jagged teeth at the hobgoblin.

As if the little man could have done anything to hurt us.

The pearls struck the bear across his snout. Suddenly he was shorter. Suddenly he had less fur. Suddenly his neck was smaller and his limbs were thin. The necklace landed in the snow, inches from the pale, round, naked toes of a human foot. A young man with hair the same amber red as Rose's blinked at me.

"Hello." He said. "I'm Otto. Could I please get some clothes? It is very cold.

ROSE

I snatched the pearls up out of the snow. I could hear the hobgoblin behind me, scampering off into the wood. Otto –the bear who wasn't a bear anymore –stared at me, shivering. I peeled my cloak off of my shoulders and handed it to him. He clutched it around his shoulders, still staring at me, still shivering.

"You were a bear." I said.

"Yes." He nodded slowly. Uncertainly. "I remember . . . steel. Iron. Heat. A rich, sultry smoke. The queen from the north did this. The witch queen. Lucille."

I looked at Snow then back at the man who had been a bear. His teeth started to chatter in the cold. His nose was red.

"Come with us." Snow said.

We made our way back to the path to fetch the sled we'd abandoned in the chase then went home. It was dusk when we reached the cottage. The stool and chair and china cabinet blended into the dark shadows of the room. Otto swiveled around, taking in every corner as if he were trying to memorize it.

"I know this place." He said "It's . . . home."

I hummed, lighting the logs already set in the fireplace and sat our guest down on the stool next to it. He looked up at me, staring. Snow filled a kettle and set it over the fire.

"It must have been a long time ago." Otto said. "You had only just been born. How old are you?"

He was babbling, mad from the cold or the transformation or both. "Seventeen." I answered.

"Seventeen. I was –a bear you said? --for seventeen years." He twitched his nose and scratched behind his ear. "Was I a savage bear?"

"Don't you remember?" Snow sat on the chair across from him and folded her hands in her lap.

Otto shook his head. "No." He stopped, then looked around the room, his eyes quizzical, confused. "Yes . . . I don't know. Some of it . . . I think. Mostly I just remember . . . before."

"What was before?" I asked so he could grasp something that made sense to him. "How did the queen turn you into a bear?"

Otto closed his eyes. "A castle. Stone cliffs. Fierce, howling wind. I remember . . . there were two witches in the north. One was beautiful. The other was wise."

I glanced at Snow. Was she ready to hear how Lucille had left another life in ruins? She sat where she was. Still. Unblinking.

"The beautiful witch came to my christening feasts." Otto continued. "She danced before the king and queen. She opened up the skies and created lightening with her voice, then blew the clouds away so that the night was clear again. Her laughter was warm and her hands were soft and all the court was enamored of her powers.

"The wise witch came to the feasts too, but she didn't dine and dance with the guests. She drifted through the kitchens, sprinkling blessings into the dishes. She wandered the gardens, singing to the plants. She sat in the attic, spinning while she told tales to anyone who would listen.

"I was the king and queen's first born and a son. The feasts lasted months. I learned to crawl with the celebrations still tumbling around me. One afternoon I climbed out of my crib and padded my way past the silken slippers of dancing lords and the rushing scamper of the servants' feet out into the garden. The wise witch found me trying to grab tadpoles out of the pond. She brought me back to my mother. The king and queen were so grateful that they made her my nurse.

"I loved her instantly. I sat on her knee while she spun, listening to her sing and tell stories. So many songs. About so many things. Spiders. Ghosts. Rivers. Some of them would frighten me but then Nurse would laugh. The corners of her eyes would crinkle and I knew that no matter what monsters lay in wait for me I would have the strength to fight them. Only . . . I didn't. Not in the end."

Otto told us how he had grown up in the castle, learning to hunt and fence and fish. He told us that he would creep out of bed at night to watch his mother and father dance in the feasting halls. He told us that he was a good horseman but a poor falconer, that he used to steal lemons from his father's groves, and that he was betrothed to a princess with freckles and soft lips from the east who visited every Christmas. He told us that when he was sixteen, against everyone's expectation, his mother gave birth to a young princess and the feasts began again.

"But they were tainted with sorrow" Otto said "because Mother was weak and died three days after the birth and when the beautiful witch came to the feasts the second time it was with an army behind her. She called lightening and hail out of the sky, smashing the castle to bits while the soldiers flung fire into the gardens. The trees charred black, the violets and roses turned to ash, and the frogs and tadpoles choked to death on the smoke, their damp bodies shriveling in the heat.

"I fought with father's soldiers on the outer walls, pouring hot oil down on the attackers, but even if none of the men had been drunk from the feasts' wine they could never have withstood Lucille's men. The castle was ravaged, Father killed, the servants beaten until they agreed to serve Lucille, but when she came to me she ordered her soldiers to stay their hands.

"And she sang.

"She sang of bones and ashes. Of flesh and fear. Of running and of chasing. Of cold winter nights and long lonely marches in the wilderness. I felt my breath deepen. Smoke filled my lungs, scratching at my throat and turning to a growl. The tips of my fingers itched, bleeding and swelling around the nails. Just before I turned I heard her speak. A whisper that seeped into my lungs and memory.

"'So that you will be a wild beast. So that you will never love again as you loved your foul, common nurse.'"

"So that you will never love again." Snow repeated. She rose and pulled the kettle off the fire.

"I remember the battle." Otto turned to look at me. "I saw an iron stake drive through father's back and everything else I had ever known crumble into nothing. But it's . . . distant. Like a dream or another world. I never saw what happened when they reached your nursery. How did you escape?"

I stared at him. I'd thought he'd finally found some shreds of sanity in the details of his story but perhaps it was still too soon. "My nursery? You mean your sister's."

"You are his sister." Snow said. "You have the same hair, the same nose and your eyes are only a few shades lighter."

How could she possibly know what shade his eyes were in this dim light? I shook my head. "He's the same age as me ---perhaps younger. My mother and father were never royalty. They died in the village when I was a baby."

Had Greta told me that or had Gran? I had never thought to ask who exactly they had been. Perhaps they hadn't died. Perhaps they simply hadn't wanted me. Or couldn't want me.

"Your clasp." Otto took the wooden clasp Gran had made off my cloak and handed it to me. "It bears our family's insignia. So does that necklace." He pointed to the string of pearls still clutched in my other hand. "It was Mother's. I think that's what changed me back. Touching something from my life before. It made me remember who I was." His nose twitched. Parts of him were still having trouble remembering.

"I've touched your fur these last two winters." I said. "If I were from your past wouldn't that have turned you back?"

"You were a baby." Otto said. "I never held you. It's not something princes do, hold babies."

"That's mad." I said.

He shrugged. "Just a custom."

"I mean you're mad." The idea that a prince could be my brother was mad. The idea that I could have any brother.

"Our family is quite sane." His round dark eyes misted over, tainted with memory the way Snow's were when she talked about Lucille. "What's left of it. You and I."

I shook my head. "That's a lot to believe based on a clasp."

Otto twitched his nose again. "I remember flashes from the last seventeen years. Ideas. Smells. Feelings. Things I know I didn't know before but now I do, only I can't remember how I learned them. Like this cottage. I knew it was home the moment I saw it. I felt safe. I felt welcome."

"You are welcome." Snow assured him. She was calmly steeping dried chamomile in three mugs as if the entire world hadn't just been turned on its head.

Otto nodded. "I know. And I know Rose is my sister. Animals know their own blood. They don't have to be told and it doesn't have to make sense. I think that's why I came here at all. When I was a bear I knew who she was and now I know because . . . I knew then."

Then I remembered. I remembered the gold spindle locked up in Greta's cupboard. I remembered the way she had pressed her lips and gritted her teeth when Gran had brought me the cloak, hiding it from sight as if it were deadly. "Like your name." Gran had said, throwing it over my shoulders.

Greta had always kept me from the other villagers. Always alone. Always apart. Could she have known who I was? Could she have been hiding me?

I turned from Otto and stepped toward the cupboard on the other side of the room. Next to the door where Gran's bed had once been. My feet clopped against the floor in the dead silence. The cottage was small. I reached it much too soon. I pulled it open and dug under the folds of our extra clothes, our basket of needles, Gran's books.

There. My hand closed over the hard, cold object. I pulled it out so that Snow and Otto could see it in the dim burn of the fire. Light danced off the surface. I ran my fingers over the engraving. The wide, curved petals of a single rose.

"That was nurse's." Otto said. "She used it to spin while she told stories."

I looked up at Snow. "You're the princess." There was panic in my voice. "You're the one with the mysterious past. I'm ... just Rose." I dropped the spindle. It landed on the floor in front of me with a loud, heavy thud, then rolled to the side. "We're the same age." I said. "How can we be the same age?"

Otto smiled weakly. "The curse must have held me frozen in time."

I felt cold, smothered in evidence. I couldn't breathe. I turned toward the door. "I'm going for a walk."

"Take my cloak." Snow said.

I didn't. It was a cold night. I stopped when I reached the fence and considered going back for it. Traces of firelight twinkled from the cottage's windowpanes, dark but full of life like the pupil of an eye.

I didn't dare go back in. Not with my mind spiraling out of kilter the way it was. The cottage was too constricting. Too warm. I climbed over the fence and stepped into the wood where there was no one to ask me questions, no one to tell me I was wrong about who I thought I was. There wasn't even a road. Just me and the night.

The moon was bright but I didn't need it to see by. I knew where the trees were. I knew where the bramble and ditches and rabbit burrows were the same way I knew where my hands and feet were. They were a part of the wood. They were a part of me. Ghosts drifted past me. I pulled my mind away from the gentle lapping of their grief. I ignored the whistle of wind in the leaves, the soft trickle of the stream, even the deep thrum of the trees themselves.

Greta had vanished like a ghost in the night. Had that been because of me? Because of who I was. Had she been ... found?

But she had taken her spinning wheel. No soldier would have allowed her to take her spinning wheel.

A fox drifted past me a few feet away. I stepped around a rotting log, grinding my feet into the twigs and leaves beneath the snow.

I wished I'd never asked the hobgoblin about the necklace. I wished we'd never disenchanted Otto. I'd been much fonder of him when he was just our red bear.

I closed my eyes, listening to the pulse of the earth. Another night it might have soothed me. Another night its calm might have enveloped me. I might have absorbed its stillness like a draught of fresh rainwater. Tonight it only fueled my anger. Tonight its strength intertwined with my being like a vine. Fire gushed through my veins, filling my eyes and my lungs with a song I was too furious to release.

The ghost girl who Snow had seen alive, whose heart Lucille had eaten, flitted across my consciousness. This time I let her come, pouring her pain and anger into me like hot smelt. Fear turned to hate as a knife cut into my chest. I felt the cold edge of the blade, the firm sweaty grip of hands around my wrists, and elbows pushing down against my shoulders. A scream boiled in my throat but I couldn't move. My arms, my limbs, my whole body was stiff and unable to move.

Only it wasn't because I was stampeding through the wood like a soldier off to battle. I opened my eyes so I could see the twigs and snow as I stomped down on them. So I could see the branches as they brushed against my face, damp and cold. I breathed deep, letting the ghost's pain seep out of my chest. I placed my hand over my breast as if to remind myself that my heart was still there, beating as quick and strong as it always had. I had never let any of the ghosts in that far before.

"You feel that." I said to the ghost girl. "Every day."

"Gone." A child I couldn't see hissed into my ear. And then, in soft wispy syllables hardly distinguishable from the wind. "For . . . got . . . ten."

I shook my head. "Not forgotten."

But they were. No one had even known the girl's name. A nameless morsel brought in out of the rain.

Something stirred behind me. The familiar crunch of human footsteps.

"Snow." I said but the steps were too heavy to be hers. Too quick and hurried. Perhaps they were Otto's.

The steps moved closer. I could hear breathing now.

"Lost." The ghosts lapped at my mind and soul but the girl's story had already taken too much from me. I couldn't bear to feel even the smallest trickle of their pain anymore. I pushed them away, shaking them off like droplets of water, and turned around.

A familiar set of sharp cheekbones and amber eyes hovered over a ridiculously charming grin. "I almost didn't recognize you without your cloak."

I stared, searching my memory for his name. "Boris."

Boris laughed. "You don't sound pleased to see me." His smile grew wistful, almost sad. "I suppose you wouldn't be, the way I disappeared on you."

I lifted my chin. The last time I had seen him I had found Gran's mangled body. I had screamed for help but he hadn't come. Snow had. I moved to step around him.

"Wait. Rose. Please." He placed his hand on my shoulder, then pulled it away as if I had burnt him.

I was considering it.

"I've never been as brave as I should be, Rose." His voice was pleading, almost as if he were in physical pain. I winced, remembering the ghost girl's heart. "My nightmares are plagued with the memory of leaving you that night. I relive the horrors you must have gone through over and over. Not a day goes by that I don't wish I'd stayed. Then . . . when I saw you in Copshire I . . . I just wanted to come to make sure you were well and . . . and to apologize. I'm sorry, Rose. I should never have left you in danger."

I sighed. "I wasn't hurt. There probably wasn't much you could have done." Not everyone was as mad and brave as Snow.

Boris smiled again. A soft, crooked smile that almost glittered beneath the gibbous moon. "I'm glad you weren't hurt. Here." He unclasped his cloak and flung it over my shoulders. "You must be cold."

I wasn't. Not anymore, but I let him hook the clasp anyways. His cloak was thick and heavy. I couldn't see the color in the dark but the fabric was soft like drying moss. "What were you doing that night?" I asked. "Why were you even in the wood?"

He let out a long sigh, almost a whistle between his cheeks. "I was looking for excitement. I didn't know that when I found it I would run." He touched the back of his neck, brushing his fingers through his curls. "I work at the manor. It's only a few hours walk from here. Do you live in the cottage we saw that night? The one your Gran lived in?"

He wasn't telling the truth. Not all of it anyways. "I'm a witch." I said to discourage anymore lies.

"I know." He grinned. "The red witch. You're a legend. The villagers near the wood say that they can hear you singing at night, laying a curse on anyone who would defy you. They say that last summer you nearly burnt down the wood in anger."

I didn't tell him that the rumors were false.

"Rose." His rich, smooth voice purred my name in a way I almost liked and almost hated. "The red witch. I'm not surprised she turned out to be you. I saw sparks of magic in you even then. And you told me you'd been talking to ghosts. Most people just scream when they hear them. Or run. They don't bother to talk back."

"Then most people are foolish."

He nodded. "Most are. And they're not nearly as --do you know the cliffs just after the creek turns into a river?"

I nodded.

"Meet me there next new moon. I want to show you something."

I raised an eyebrow. "The moon's darkest night?"

He winked. "When else?"

I laughed in spite of myself. The danger of being on a cliff with only the stars to light my way was enticing. "I have to go." I handed him back his cloak and moved to step around him. This time he didn't try to stop me.

"Rose."

I turned back.

Boris clasped his cloak, letting the long heavy folds of the fabric drape around him in the shadows. He tilted his head to the side, smiling his ridiculous smile. His eyes danced with mischief. "When you come to meet me, don't trust me."

"I won't." I promised, and left him there, staring after me as I disappeared into the wood.

It wasn't until then that I wondered how he had found me when I hadn't even been on the path. Or how he had learned my name.

I awoke the next morning to the sound of Snow's tender giggle. Straw scratched at my chin as I crept to the edge of the loft and peered down.

Snow sat next to Otto by the fire, stitching a pair of trousers out of the pale blue fabric we'd bought in town. She pulled the thread through and cut it with her knife. "I told Rose you had followed her here." She said. "I knew you couldn't be an ordinary bear."

Otto smiled. Slowly. Shyly. I wanted to throw something at him. "When I'm near Rose I feel happy --glad that she's safe and glad that we found each other—but when I'm near you . . ." His neck and face turned suddenly very red "You must have been very kind to me when I was a bear."

Snow looked back down at the would be trousers in her lap. I shook the straw out of my hair and headed down the ladder.

After breakfast I took a walk through Gran's gardens while Snow finished stitching together the trousers. I had grown used to the dormant plants in the winter. Most of them were all but buried in the snow with only the brittle edges of their thorns poking out. But something seemed different today. Sadder. Drearier. As if the tumbling, abundant life of summer would never return. As if the roses and lavender and ivy and chamomile weren't merely asleep this winter, but forever and irrevocably dead.

When I slipped back into the cottage I found Otto sitting on the stool with Gran's journal in his lap. His head was bent over the pages, red curls smothering his neck and ears. Snow had finished the trousers. They looked especially soft and pale next to the bright sting of my cloak. Otto looked up when he heard the door close. He smiled. I wondered if his smile were anything like mine. I doubted it.

"This is Nurse's writing." He rested his hand on the pages of the journal, almost stroking them. "I recognize some of the stories but others . . . I had no idea she had such darkness in her. The way she tells of a simple fox out hunting. How the rabbit can't even shriek when he dies. Where did you get this?"

"It was Gran's." I said. How could his nurse be my Gran? But then, it made about as much sense as anything else.

Otto's eyes softened with sadness. For a moment he looked almost like our red bear. "Was?"

I nodded. "A wolf killed her. The night I came to live here."

Otto buried his forehead in his palms. He ran his fingers through his curls. "It's all gone then. Everything. I had hoped . . . I know it was seventeen years ago but it feels like it was yesterday. Like . . ." He looked up, gazing into the fire. His eyes reflected the bright orange and gold as it danced and rollicked like a witch in the night. "Like it never happened at all."

He wanted proof. Something to show him that he hadn't dreamed it all. I picked up the gold spindle from where I had dropped it the night before. I walked over to him knelt next to the stool. I placed the spindle in his hand, pressing it against his palm. He tightened his fingers around the cold, smooth gold.

"Where's Snow?" I asked. She wasn't in the cottage and I hadn't seen her in the yard with her knives.

"She went to the village." Otto's voice was monotone, his mind still somewhere seventeen years into the past. "She said she was going to trade for a pair of boots so I could help her hunt."

I straightened, drawing my hand away from the spindle. "By herself?"

Otto nodded.

"It's dangerous." My voice grew shrill with worry. "Did she tell you who she is? Who she's hiding from?"

But it was more than that. It had been so long since either of us had gone anywhere without the other. She hadn't even told me that she was leaving.

I stood and walked to the window. At least the sky was clear. It didn't look like there would be another snowfall today. "When did she leave? I should go after her."

"It must have been Nurse who saved you." Otto said. "How else would you end up in the wood together miles and miles away?"

I turned around to face him. I didn't want Gran to be his nurse. I didn't want to share her. "But why would she leave me to live in the village with Greta instead of keeping me here?"

Otto shrugged. "Maybe she thought you would be safer there. Or happier."

I sighed and turned back toward the window. Ice glittered in the branches. A bird swooped down out of a tree and pecked at the ground, trying to unbury something to eat. "I wasn't. I should go after Snow."

But I didn't. Because I knew she would be safe. Because I knew that the villagers had already seen her and anyone who would report what they saw to the queen had already done it. Because I knew she had her knife with her and her aim had become swift and precise in the last two years.

Because I knew she didn't need me the way she thought she did.

Maybe she knew that now too.

"Lucille was wrong." Otto said "I will love again."

Then I remembered what had been wrong with the gardens, why they had seemed so dead. The roses, red and white, tangled together in a long vine. The roses I had sung into being by wishing before I even knew I had the power in me. The roses that bloomed every day of the year, wide and soft and fresh as if it were the beginning of summer.

They hadn't been blooming

SNOW

"It's unmarked." Otto said.

"Yes." I stared down at the soft rounding edges of the grave where the snow rose over the earth. It was a soft bed, a quiet place to sleep despite the cold, and close to the cottage as if even in death she couldn't stray far from it.

"Does Rose ever come here?"

I looked up at the man standing next to me near the edge of the forest. He looked nothing like the red bear. Nothing like the friend who nuzzled me in the cold of winter and watched me practice throws. I gazed past him into the trees. There were so many shadows even in the daylight, each covered with tiny pieces of ice. "I've never seen her here but . . . sometimes she goes on walks by herself. Maybe she comes here then."

"Maybe." Otto said. "Why is the grave unmarked?"

The wind whirred around us, tangling the loose threads of my hair. I pulled them out of my face. They stuck in my fingers. "I don't know."

Otto knelt. He pressed his hand into the snow. It looked small on top of the cold, icy mound, almost like a child's hand-print. "Her Gran. My nurse." He stood and dusted snow crystals off his hand. They sprinkled onto the ground, disappearing into the thick layers of white. His face was so much like Rose's. He even set his jaw tight with determination the way she did when she had made a decision. He turned toward me. "Rose said you are hiding from Lucille too."

I nodded.

He looked back down at the grave, then turned around and headed back toward the cottage. I followed him.

Rose wasn't inside. She had started the laundry but then abandoned it, leaving a pile of our stockings on the floor and my extra shift soaking in a bucket of ice-cold suds. Our bedding drip dried from the washing line she'd strung across the room.

I turned to look at Otto. "I think you've been a bit of a shock to her."

Otto stared at the dripping cottage, tense, distracted. "I've been a shock to myself."

I finished the laundry and Otto and I left to find something alive to put in our stew. We brought the rabbit traps, but I hoped that with the two of us we could bring home a deer.

"How?" Otto asked. "We don't have a bow."

"I have a knife." I said.

Otto looked unconvinced. He held on to the traps as we moved through the trees in silence, listening for the sounds of our prey. We couldn't see the ghosts in the daylight but we could hear them from time to time, whispering with the trees. "Lost." They said over and over, a softly hissed warning caught and tangled into the wind, sticking to our ears like dusty cobwebs.

"How do you get used to it?" Otto asked.

"They won't hurt us," I assured him. "Rose says that they are our protectors."

Otto shook his head. "Rose scares me."

I turned to face him. "Why? She's your sister."

Otto ran his fingers through his curls, raising both eyebrows. "She talks to ghosts and lights fires with her voice. Doesn't that scare you?"

I shook my head. "Never. She talks to the trees too. And the animals. If she were here with us she could call a deer so that we wouldn't even have to look for him."

"Really?" Otto stared at me with interest. "Would she?"

I shook my head again. "She doesn't like to see things killed."

Otto and I had already set up three of the cage traps, hidden neatly in the right kinds of shrubbery, when I first saw the deer tracks. They were minted into the snow like a scattering of summer leaves. I turned to Otto, placing my finger to my lips. Otto abandoned the last of the traps and we followed the thin, whisking trail of prints through the trees.

The tracks led us through a thick mess of blackberry bushes with thorns iced over like tiny knives and leafless branches weighed down with heavy globs of snow. The bushes tore and scratched at my cloak and skirts as Otto and I made our way through them, trying not to crunch the snow with our heavy boots. Oaks canopied the sky overhead, obscuring the tracks with their shadows, but we moved forward. Slowly. Carefully. Following the light brushes of prints until we reached a clearing.

I stopped. I knew this place. It was where Rose and I had lit the bonfire at midsummer. I stepped back, not wanting to be there. It made me wish . . .

"Lost," a ghost whispered over my shoulder. I tried to ignore the cold shiver that ran through me. A whisper of fear, tiny enough to melt against my skin.

I turned to look at Otto. He stopped at the edge of the bushes beside me. His human bear eyes were intent, scanning the clearing for any other signs of life. His nose scrunched exactly the same way Rose's had when she had first begun to make sense of the writing in her Gran's books.

Otto caught my glance. He smiled. "What is it? Did you see the deer?"

I shook my head, pointing to the untouched white of the clearing stretched out in front of us. It glittered in the thick piles of sun like hallowed ground. "The snow iced over. There are no more tracks."

Otto twitched his nose. I wondered if he were resisting an urge to sniff the ground as he would have as a bear. "Then we'll have to search the edges of the clearing for them. If he isn't here he went back into the wood somewhere."

I nodded and stepped out into the clearing. The ground was hard, frozen solid beneath my feet. I almost slipped. Otto put his arm around my waist to help hold me upright.

Something stirred inside the trees.

Otto let go of my waist. He straightened, turning his head from one side to the other. He looked at me. "The deer?"

I shook my head. "The tracks weren't fresh enough for that."

The bushes moved again.

"Rabbits then." Otto said but the sound was more like footsteps than scampering. The hurried footsteps of two tiny feet.

"Hobgoblins." I said.

The word had hardly slipped out of my mouth when our ill mannered friend stepped out from behind a willow tree. The ice crystals clinging to the dormant vines dangled over the top of his head. He crossed his arms over his chest, glaring at us. His matted gray beard draped over his wrists, smothered in bits of snow. The tiny wrinkles on his forehead bunched together like bark knots. "Where are my pearls?"

"Your pearls?" I asked. "They belong to --"

"You can have them." Otto stepped in front of me, his voice eager.

"If you tell me where you found them."

The hobgoblin's expression did not change. He tapped his foot. He looked from Otto to me and then back to Otto. "Will you tell the witch?"

"No." Otto promised. "I won't breathe a word to her."

The hobgoblin sighed. I would never have imagined so much air could be kept in his little lungs. "Meet me here tomorrow. Bring the pearls. I will tell you then." He turned. The bushes rustled. An icicle fell off the willow vines, crashing into pieces against the ground, then he was gone.

We found the deer tracks again on the other side of the clearing. They were fresher here without any collapsed bits of snow around the edges. The droppings were fresher too.

"It's a young deer." I said "The prints are pressed lightly and the hooves are pointed in the front."

"Who taught you to hunt?" Otto asked.

"An old friend." I said, remembering Hans's quiet, meticulous lessons in the still hours of the morning. It seemed a lifetime ago. How much had he really risked by letting me go? I didn't know what freedom was until he had sent me out into the wood alone.

We followed the tracks deep into the wood, stopping only now and again to examine rubbings against the younger trees. Otto had brought turnip and mushroom pies but we were gaining on our quarry too quickly to want to stop and settle the rumbling in our bellies. When it started to snow and we could still see the hoof marks, minted crisply into the mask of white, I pulled my knife out of my belt. We moved forward more carefully than ever, peering into the trees for signs of life.

"There." Otto touched my elbow. He pointed ahead, just a little to the left.

The deer was barely visible through the trees. He had his nose to the ground, looking for bits of green beneath the layers of snow.

I lifted my knife and edged toward him, one silent step at a time. When I was close enough to take aim I planted my feet into the ground and pulled the knife back behind my ear. I held the blade steady, tilted upward, just a little to the right.

The deer looked up.

No hesitation. I flung the knife into the air. It whizzed through the cold, landing hilt deep into the animal's throat. His eyes widened in surprise. His legs wobbled, then he toppled onto the ground. Flakes of snow scattered into the air as he hit the earth. I waited a moment, letting the bulk of the blood drain into the ice before we approached. There was no point in watching him struggle the last short breaths of his life away.

"I've never seen anything like that." Otto said.

It was late afternoon when we returned to the cottage. Rose was still nowhere to be seen. Otto followed me to the shed and set to work, helping me skin and carve the deer carcass.

"This is what I was doing the night I met you." I told him. "Only it was a pair of rabbits."

Otto laughed. "Did I try to take them from you?"

"No." I pulled a carving knife off the wall and handed it to him. "Not until after Rose had cooked them into a stew. You scared us nearly to death. We thought you were a wolf."

It was dark by the time we finished. Rose hadn't returned. Otto seared three long cuts of venison in the fireplace while I bathed. They were still hot when I devoured mine, hungrier than usual from the day's work. I glanced at the remaining two cuts cooling on the table next to a bowl of apples. One for Rose when she decided to come back and one for Otto when he finished his bath.

"Is it too cold?" I asked him through the curtains. I had tried to hurry but there had been so much blood and the warmth of the water had been so delicious.

"It's perfect." He promised.

I picked up an apple, balancing it for a moment in my hand, but I was too tired to eat anymore. I set it down again and let my eyes droop for a moment.

I woke with Otto standing over me. I lifted my head. My neck was sore. A glittering stream of white light leaked in from the window, spilling over the floor. I rubbed the sleep out of my eyes and twisted my neck to see Otto more clearly.

"You were crying."

"What?" I turned my neck the other way.

"In your sleep." Otto said. "You cried." He reached for my face as if he would wipe what remained of the tears away then pulled his hand back.

"Nightmares." I said. "I can't remember them now."

Otto knelt next to the chair. He placed his hands on my shoulders. His grip was gentle but firm. Almost authoritative. "It's because of Lucille isn't it?"

I said nothing.

"We have to fight her, Snow." His voice was urgent, as if all the world depended on what I would say next. "We have to take back the things she took from us."

I shook my head. "We will die." Like Papa. Like Dana and Elise and Constanze. Traces of the nightmares fluttered back through my head. Traces that took no shape but made me want to close my eyes again and shake my head until they went away.

Otto sighed. He let go of my shoulders and shook his head. "Better death than fear. I will fight her, whether you want to help or not. She's taken too much from us. All of us. When spring comes --as soon as the snow melts-

- I will go back to the north. I will gather whatever remains of the castle garrison and together we will defeat Lucille."

"Your soldiers will all be loyal to her now." I said.

"Not all of them." Otto insisted. "We had a very loyal garrison."

"Then they will be dead." I said.

"Please, Snow. Believe that I can do this. Help me do it."

I stared at him, confused. "What help would I be?"

"You know the manor. And you are an expert with a knife. "

I shook my head. "I'm a hunter not a soldier."

"Then teach me." Otto said "I can teach my soldiers when I find them. We will need stealth. A way to attack that the queen won't see coming."

I shook my head again. He was mad if he really thought he had any kind of chance against Lucille.

That day I made Otto a waistcoat and overcoat out of the pale blue fabric we had bought in Copshire. Rose, who had come home at last during the night, had hoped to make us both new dresses but there was only enough fabric left for a single sash. Rose trimmed and hemmed the edges then sat across from me, embroidering violets and vines on it with purple and green thread while I stitched the finishing touches into Otto's waistcoat. Every few seconds the sound of a mason hitting the roof cut into the silence. Otto, patching up the leak in the roof. I told him that I could manage it myself but he had insisted.

"Do princes even know how to fix roofs?" Rose asked. "I thought they had their own thatchers and carpenters for that."

"Princes are soldiers." I said "They learn what they need to to lead men into battle."

She looked back down at the sash in her lap. I watched her pull the thread through in silence. The wind whistled outside, sending a shiver of cold through the hole Otto hadn't finished repairing. I'd never seen her concentrate so hard on anything before. Almost as if she had forgotten her own existence in the precision of each stitch.

"Rose." I said.

She didn't look up.

"Rose, are you all right?"

She kept stitching.

"You're so quiet." I said.

Her head snapped up. Her eyes flared, almost the way they did before she lit the fireplace with her hums. "Can't I be quiet if I want?"

I blinked, startled by her sudden irritation. "Yes. Of course. It's just . . . not like you."

Rose looked back down at the sash. Soot sifted in the fireplace. Otto's mason hammered against the roof. The wind howled. The windows rattled. She pressed her lips together. Finally she looked up. "Otto tells me he wants to fight Lucille."

I nodded. His proposal had been nagging at me all day. I had been hiding from Lucille for so long. I had never even wondered if I could defeat her. I couldn't --of course I couldn't -- but I had never even wondered.

Rose snorted. "If he believes that I will help him simply because he says that I am his sister, he is mistaken."

"Aren't you tired of being afraid?" I asked.

Her eyes burned, staring straight through me, scorching a hole into my mind. "Who's afraid?"

Not her. Never her. It had been a silly question.

"I am." I looked down at the unfinished waistcoat in my lap, fingering with the thread but not pulling a stitch. "I let Lucille do things – terrible, terrible things --because I was afraid she would eat my heart. I was afraid she would poison me. I was afraid she would make me dance in her iron shoes. I did nothing. I said nothing when I should have spoken. And then I ran."

Rose shook her head. "You didn't run. You survived."

"I didn't even want to do that." I remembered the tempting sweetness of the fruit Lucile had sent up to my room that last day. How I had longed for oblivion, for sleep without nightmares.

"But you did." Rose said. "You are strong, Snow. I can see that, even if Otto can't."

I looked back up at Rose. "I ran. I'm still running. We both are."

Rose set the unfinished sash down onto the table between us. "Snow, don't let Otto use your suffering for his revenge."

I clenched my left hand as if the familiar handle of my knife rested there. "It's my revenge too. I have every reason to hate Lucille."

"You've decided to fight with him then?"

I bit my lip. "I don't know. I only know that Lucille took Papa and everything else I ever knew away from me and then sent me into the wilderness to die. She took your birthright too, Rose."

The door burst open. Otto stepped in, trailing dribbles of melting snow onto the floor. He shook the delicate flakes out of his hair and hung Rose's cloak up on the hook. I almost laughed. He looked for the first time since he had changed almost like the cold, wild animal who had first wandered into the cottage.

The three of us ate supper in complete silence, listening to the structureless howls of the wind outside. Rose went to bed before we started on the roasted apples and I was left to show Otto how to roast them myself. They turned blacker than they should have and I burnt my fingers pulling them off the fire. Otto knelt next to me, blowing on my fingertips to cool them.

It was dark out, the lightless night of the new moon, and for a moment I thought I heard the chilling call of a wolf. My neck and foot and shoulder ached with the memory of their wounds. I touched the thin, silken scars that ran across my shoulder to remind myself that that was all that remained of the gash that had once been there, and bit into the warm, tender apple flesh.

I slept hard that night and dreamed long.

I dreamed that the vines of a dead rose bush wound their way around me, holding me still, grinding their thorns into my flesh. Drips of blood tickled their way over my skin, scattering onto the ground beneath me like a gentle pattering of rain. I hovered over the ground, suspended, unable to move, unable to speak. I tried to cry out for help but sounds withered inside my throat, choking me until I could no longer breathe. The vines pulled tighter and tighter around me. The thorns cut deeper, scraping the surface of my bones.

And then I was free. I was running through the wood. My feet landed, one after the other against the ground but I couldn't feel the impact. I seemed to be floating through the trees, whisking over the fallen leaves like a piece of the wind.

And then I had a dagger in my heart and I was dead. The pain hardened inside my chest so that my ribs almost shattered. Cracks wove their way across my skin, each with its own unique stab of pain. I looked down and saw my feet —no my hooves —leaving soft, dark footprints in the snow as I kept moving, trying to pretend that I was still alive. Trying to pretend that I could still move. My legs gave out. I collapsed onto the earth.

Pale, soft hands rolled my eyes shut.

The creatures from the carvings in my room in the manor danced in a circle around me. I couldn't see them but I knew that they were there. I knew what they were doing. They shook their dark wings and reached for me with long hissing tongues. They whirred around and around, brushing against me with their claws, opening their mouths to reveal sharpened teeth poking out of black, rotting gums.

The largest creature winked at me. He lifted a double clawed finger up to his lips, motioning for my silence. He grinned. His lips spread wide apart, cracking, and dripping brown blood down his chin.

Or were those my tears? Seeping into the ice. Crystallizing onto the ground.

A woman laughed. Soft, gentle laughter brushing against the air like a painter's stroke. Kind laughter. Playful laughter.

And then there were the screams, rolling on and on in the distance, growing louder each second. I tightened my eyes, wanting it to stop. Why wouldn't it stop?

"Lost." A child said.

I opened my eyes. The girl blinked at me. The girl I'd seen in Papa's manor. The girl I'd seen led through the corridors in the dead of night when Lucille had thought I was asleep. The girl I hadn't heard scream.

I woke, wet with tears and sweat. Bits of straw clung to my neck and cheek as I lifted myself up in the loft. The glow of the fire shifted off the walls. Rose stirred across from me. Her wrist almost touched her forehead in her sleep. I crept to the edge of the loft and peered down into the shadows of the cottage.

Otto sat on his knees next to the fire. He stared into the flames. At the future. At the past. Bits of soot clung to his nose and chin, dusting the red curls around his face.

"Otto."

He turned, looking straight up at me, almost into me.

"Was I screaming?"

Otto shook his head.

The sting of salt water grazed my lips and tongue. I wiped it away with my palm but the tears kept pouring down my face like unstoppable screams. "I will teach you to throw knives." I said "And when you come back in the summer with your soldiers I will teach them.

ROSE

I didn't go to meet Boris on the new moon but when I went to that place in the cliff the next day there were two words imprinted into the snow.

NEXT TIME

I didn't go the next new moon either. Or the one after that. Or even the one after that. But when spring came and Otto showed no sign of leaving I began to consider it. I grew tired of watching Snow and Otto practice knife throwing together in the yard. I grew tired of listening to them talk about Lucille and how she would pay for all that she had done. They didn't understand why I wouldn't join their plans. They didn't understand why I didn't hate her as much as they did. I felt myself drifting further and further away from them until I could hardly stand being at the cottage at all.

The trees offered some solace. I wandered through them, singing as I listened to them thrum from deep inside the earth. I asked them if they had been getting enough water, enough sunlight, if anyone had bothered them, how the squirrels nesting in their roots or the birds sleeping in their branches were. Few had many complaints. They had lived too many years to mind an inconvenience that would be gone by the end of the season. Still, they liked to be asked. They began to move their roots and branches out of the way as I passed them, as glad for the company as I was. There was a willow who would sometimes lift her roots, bending them into a perfect seat for me to rest on. It was a comfortable place to sit. I would sing to her, forgetting for a moment how alone I was.

Some days the animals would join me. They didn't have names the way Snow and I did. They didn't speak with words or ask me what I had had for breakfast. But if I closed my eyes I knew where they were. They would hear me calling and they would find me. The birds perched in the tangles of my hair. The squirrels ran in circles around my feet. The rabbits sniffed curiously at my fingers and the foxes stopped a few short paces from me and stared with wide knowing eyes.

It was the ghosts whose company I enjoyed the most. They understood why my song had grown so mournful. Still, I couldn't tell them how beautiful the sky was or that I couldn't wait for the summer berries to be ripe again. I couldn't tell them that I couldn't be a princess because I belonged here. All they understood were tears. Tears and the long, mournful melodies that sometimes soothed them.

It was still the afternoon of the new moon four months after Otto had joined us in the cottage. I returned from a romp in the wood. I placed my hand on the door, then stopped. Laughter came from inside. Otto's, soft and deep. There was humming.

Snow trying to hum anyway. Whatever melody it was supposed to be was obscured by the course, uneven way she jumped from note to note. Still, my ears lingered on the sound. The corners of my mouth lifted in an unwilling smile. I had tried to teach her to sing --so had her tutors --but her music was as useless as her cooking.

Most of her cooking.

I crept over to the window and peered inside. Snow and Otto were dancing. He had one hand on her waist and the other bound inside her fingers, leading her around the tiny little cottage as if it were a ballroom made for nothing but the gentle rhythm of their steps.

Snow's voice may not have made music but her feet did. She glided alongside Otto in perfect unison, dipping and twirling. Both layers of her skirts spun outward then rested against her bare ankles. Against her bent knees. I'd been concentrating so hard on my own feet when she'd tried to teach me to dance that I hadn't realized how beautiful her movements were, how precisely and gracefully she melted from one position to the next. Like a goddess. Like a swan.

Otto didn't kick her shins. He didn't trip and pull her to the ground.

They should have been dancing in a ballroom, not a tiny little cottage that didn't even have a bed anymore. They should have been dressed in silk and dazed from too many courses of wine. Lucille had taken more from them than she had ever taken from me.

I stepped away from the window. They wouldn't thank me for

interrupting. And what would I do if I joined them inside? Stand on the stool and watch? Spin around in my clumsy country feet?

I turned around and headed for the cliffs where Boris had said he would be waiting for me. The walk wasn't long and the ghost kept me company.

It was dark when I reached the cliffs. Like soot. Like the black center of an eye. Even the stars were blotted out by the thick foliage over my head. I stood at the edge of the cliff, imaging that I could see down. Imagining that there was no bottom.

I didn't see Boris when he appeared behind me. I didn't hear him. I just knew he was there. The same way I knew where the woodland creatures were. I felt him moving across the forest floor the same way I felt the night sky brush against my skin.

"Hello." He said.

"Hello." I turned around to face him, though neither of us could see the other in the darkness. I had expected a more enthusiastic greeting.

"I thought you would come." I could hear his smile. His mad, ridiculous smile. "If I waited long enough. You don't trust me, do you?"

"Of course not."

"Good." He lifted his hand. His fingers touched the curls running alongside of my face. "I am, without a doubt, the most dangerous thing in these woods."

I laughed. "Hardly."

He drew his hand away from my hair. "You don't believe me?"

I rested my hands on my hips. "I'm a witch, remember? The trees speak to me. The forest creatures come when I call them. I can light fire with my voice and I don't need light to see. If one of us should be afraid it should be you."

Boris laughed. "You may be right. There's not much a mere man can do against that kind of charm. Come." He dropped his voice to a whisper "You shouldn't stand so close to the edge."

I took his hand and let him lead me away from the cliff. A stone rattled off the edge and dropped over the side. I listened, counting how many seconds before it hit the bottom. Twenty six. Twenty seven. It must have been a heavy stone.

"Do you hear water?" Boris asked.

"Of course." I said. The brook widened to a river just before it met the cliffs. The crash of it pouring over the edge could be heard for miles like the purr of a giant cat.

"Let's find it." Boris tightened his hand around mine and we followed the edge of the cliff, moving toward the sound of water. The steady pour rose to a roar as we got closer. We had to shout to hear each other speak.

We stopped when we reached the water. Drops of it sprayed up at me out of the darkness. I closed my eyes, memorizing where the sharp rocks were, where the deepest bits of water were.

Boris let go of my hand. He took off his cloak, then his shirt and dropped them in a heap on the ground.

I opened my eyes. "What are you doing?"

"Going for a swim." There was that smile again. I could hear it in his voice. "Come with me?"

"You're mad." I said, but the cold liquid rush of the water sounded more enticing every second. Even though it was only just past the last frost. Even though we were standing on top of a cliff in the dead of night. Or maybe because.

"You said it yourself." Boris reminded me. "You don't need light to see by."

That was me. How he planned not to fall onto a sharp rock when he hit the bottom was another matter. But I had already flung my cloak off and dropped it next to his.

"Do you want to go first or should I?" He asked.

"Together." I said. We clasped hands again and approached the edge. The distance down was a little lower here but not much. I closed my eyes, trying to calculate the depth of the water. It was only just deep enough. If we landed feet first. If we didn't hit a pile of rocks. I took a step to the side, pulling Boris with me.

"Ready?" He asked.

"Ready."

We jumped. The fall lasted only a second. It lasted forever. The cold chill of night ran its fingers through my hair, whispering over my arms and legs and neck. My heart lifted, bubbling up inside my throat. And then we splashed through the water's surface.

Cold. Colder than cold. It rushed over my head. It pushed against my arms and legs and skirt. It tried to leak into my lungs. I twisted, pulling my breastbone away from a sharp rock. I pulled my elbow in just before it grazed across another dagger edged stone.

Down. I was still tumbling down. Further and further as if the stream had no bottom. The water wasn't cold anymore. It was almost warm, lulling me to sleep with the force of its motion. I struggled not to draw breath.

My feet touched the soft and grainy ground. Boris let go of my hand, freeing it to pull myself up through the water. I kicked my toes into the gravel and then I was moving up. Slower now, zipping through the pull of the river, savoring the promise of breath in only a few short seconds.

I stopped. My skirts pulled at my hips, caught on the edge of a rock. Why hadn't I tied them around my waist before I jumped?

My lungs swelled with pain. They beat at my chest in anger at not

111

being fed. I pulled back at my skirts then reached down to find the snag amidst the folds of floating fabric. My head swam with dizziness. My chest demanded air.

There. My fingers closed around the rough wool fabric caught between the rocks. I pulled. The fabric ripped and I was moving upward again.

Boris's hand found mine just as I burst through the surface. Cold air struck my face. I gulped it into my lungs then hiccuped out a procession of laughter, almost choking on the sound.

"What happened?" Boris asked. "I thought for a moment you'd turned fish."

I grinned at him, shivering. My wet hair clung to my neck and face. "My dress caught in the rocks."

"Come on." He moved toward the shore, pulling me with him. "Let's get warm. I know a cave near here."

My teeth chattered as I pulled myself out of the water. My head and limbs felt heavy. Drops of river rolled off my skin and out of my skirts. Boris and I left a trail of wet footprints leading up to a small cave hidden behind a collection of hawthorn bushes. The berries weren't ripe yet but I could smell the blossoms beginning to sprout as we crouched and crawled through the leaves and thorns. They scratched and prickled at my skin.

It was warm inside with plenty of room for both of us to stretch our legs or even stand if we had wanted to. Boris piled some kindling together in the center. "Can you really light fires with your voice?" He asked.

I answered with a quick hum. Deep. Sad. Dark, but full of energy. I felt the flames catch in the kindling, then spread with their own force. The cave glowed a soft shade of orange, darkened by our shadows against the earthen walls. A steady stream of smoke rose up over our heads like a silken thread, disappearing into the cracks in the earth above us.

Boris smiled, his lips crooked, his eyes mischievous. The smile was even more ridiculous than I remembered.

I moved closer to the flames, letting the heat scorch the surface of my skin. Shadows and stones littered the uneven ground. I touched a dark piece where the earth bent inward in a deep round curve.

"You shouldn't trust me, Rose." Boris whispered.

I looked up at him. "You keep saying that. Why? Do you plan on running away again as soon as there's danger?"

Boris looked away. "You don't know what I am, Rose. You don't know . . . I told you I work at the manor. That's not true. At least . . . that's not everything."

I leaned back against the wall, not taking my gaze from him. "Tell me the rest."

He sighed. "I can't. You wouldn't . . . I don't know where to start."

"Try."

He closed his eyes. "I don't work at the manor. I live there. My mother is the queen."

I stared at him. He was Lucille's son. Another blasted prince.

Boris opened his eyes. He looked straight at me, his smile gone. "My mother seduced my father to conceive me then killed him. She wanted a son and she always gets what she wants. I never had a choice. She made me what I am. A ---you shouldn't trust me."

"I don't." I said. The fire flickered. I looked down at the dark imprint in the ground then back at him. "You have a choice now. You don't have to go back to her. Not if you don't want to." I didn't hate Lucille the way Otto and Snow did but it still made my skin crawl to be alone in a cave with her son.

He shook his head. "She finds people, Rose. No one can hide from her. Not forever."

Snow did. Why had she never mentioned Boris before? Were there things about her life in the manor that she was still afraid to tell me? I looked back down at the dark imprint, fingering the shape's round edges.

"That's not all." Boris said.

He had left me. All alone in the wood with a monster on the prowl. He had left me to find Gran's mangled body myself. I stared down at the dark imprint. Suddenly the shape seemed less arbitrary, less round and more blotted. There were smaller imprints scattered around the edge. Tiny, sharp little circles. Claw marks.

"I'm a wolf." Boris said. "A were."

Sick swirled inside my stomach. I looked up at him. Slowly. Afraid of the surges of fire coursing through me. "You killed Gran." The words dropped out of my mouth one after the other like smooth, heavy river stones.

He nodded. All traces of his smile were gone. His head remained bent. As if he were tucking his nose in shame. As if shame would do him any good.

"Why did you bring me here?" I demanded. "To kill me?"

He shook his head. "Never. Why do you think it had to be tonight, on the new moon, when there was no chance of me turning? I told you not to trust me."

I stared at him. A wolf. I could see a hint of wild hunger in his eyes. "You can't control it?" I asked, skeptical.

He shook his head. Drops of water rolled off his hair and splattered against my face. His wet hair stuck up around his ears like the hair on a dog's hunches. "Sometimes. It's unpredictable, but when there's no moon . . . that's the only night I'm fully human. The only night I can choose who I am. It's the night I choose to be here. My mother doesn't know."

"You killed Gran." I said again. "What did you choose that night?"

I remembered her corpse laying in her bed with hollow eyes, smothered in blood and quilts. I remembered her throat, gashed open. Her ear falling away from her face.

"My mother wanted a monster, Rose. She chose my father because he was a wolf. I never had a choice."

No choice. Like Greta had never asked me if I wanted to spin thread. Like the wood had never asked me if I wanted to be a witch. Like Otto had never asked me if I wanted to be his sister.

I stood up. I stared down at Boris in the hungry glow of the firelight. It flickered against the pale surface of his skin.

His lips lifted into a crooked hint of his smile. "When I look at you I know what I want to choose. I want to be human. I want away from my mother and the monster she's trained me to be but it's not so simple. She finds people. And the things I've done . . . if you knew, Rose. If you knew even half of it."

He'd killed Gran. That was enough. Enough to make my stomach churn over and over as if it were trying to make butter. And yet . . . I couldn't hate him. Not the way I had when he was only an animal. Not with him gazing up at me with those wide, pleading eyes. I didn't want to hate him.

"I'm going home." I turned around, crouching so I could fit through the mouth of the cave.

"Next new moon." Boris said. "I'll be waiting."

I didn't tell him that I would come. I didn't have to.

It was dawn when I got back to the cottage. For once the wood and glen were still, quiet but for a lone skylark warbling a greeting to the morning. The edges of the cottage glowed green then yellow then white as I approached. Otto stood by the door, leaning against Snow's tidy, well stocked woodpile.

"Didn't you sleep?" I asked him.

He raised an eyebrow. "Didn't you?"

"I will." I placed my hand on the door.

"Where do you go, Rose?"

I turned toward Otto. He had straightened away from the woodpile. Bits of dust glittered in the air between us, lit by the first streams of dawn. I wasn't about to tell him about Boris. He would only wake Snow and run after him with his knives and hatred.

"Who's the heir?" I asked. "The daughter who is older or the son who was born first?"

I knew the answer of course. The son. Not that it really mattered. I didn't want to live in his kingdom, much less rule it.

Otto sighed. He ran his fingers through his messy red curls. "Snow is worried about you, Rose."

"Snow should worry about herself. Her nightmares have been

getting worse, or haven't you noticed?"

"I've noticed." He pressed his hand against the side of his face. Tired. Weary. "Do you think I like hearing her cry at night?"

At least he slept below the loft. He didn't hear every moan and sniffle -- each a tiny wound inside his heart-- just a few feet across the hay. "Then why do you make her remember?" I asked. "Why do you ask her so many questions about Lucille and her life with her in the manor when you know it hurts her?"

Otto looked at me with his hand still pressed against his face. He looked like a knobby tree trunk choked in vines. "Because we need to know all we can if we are going to defeat her. You think you're safe here, Rose. You're not. Lucille will find you one day and she will kill you unless she is stopped."

I shook my head. One day could be years away and yet . . . would she send Boris after us? Would he obey her the way he had been trained to? My mind traveled again to Gran's corpse, mangled and bloody on her bed.

"Lucille took everything from us, Rose." Otto said. "Our father. Our home. It was because of her that we grew up strangers, me scouring the woods as a wild animal, and you spinning thread inside a dreary little village."

"Maybe I liked spinning thread." I didn't like the way he spoke of my village as if it were stupid and insignificant. Even if I had grown up hating it for those very reasons.

Otto sighed. The light drained out of his eyes. He looked away. "Don't you wish . . . I wish I had known you as a child, Rose. I wish I had been able to teach you how to ride a horse and take you exploring in the mountain cliffs. There was a cave about half a day's ride from our castle. It was on the very top of the mountains and you could see for miles and miles. So many villages. So many woods and streams. A stream ran next to the cave and all the animals came there to drink. I used to go there to hunt or sometimes just to watch the world live. I think you would have liked it. I wish . . . is it really too late, Rose, for me to be your brother?"

"We had the same parents." I said and went inside.

I climbed up the ladder and onto the loft, too exhausted to care that I would have to eat cold, lumpy porridge if I didn't make some myself before I went to sleep. I covered my mouth, yawning, as I crawled toward my half of the loft.

Snow lay on the other side of the hay, her eyes closed, her arms stretched above her head as if she were reaching for something in her sleep. Her bright lips curved in a peaceful almost smile but her cheeks were still damp with tears, resting on her cheeks like drops of dew. Which of her dreams would she remember when she woke? Only the peaceful ones I hoped. Of her and Otto dancing together in his castle in the north. Of rescuing hobgoblins in the soft summer rain.

I laid down and closed my eyes, letting the heaviness of sleep overtake me bit by bit. Visions of the night floated, lawless, through my head. The dark cold of the river water. The dangerous charm of Boris's smile. Otto's worried warnings.

Snow stirred across from me in the hay. The wood of the loft creaked as she sat up.

"Rose." The sound of her voice, soft and wild, brought me away from the edge of dreams. "Rose." She said again. Less of a whisper this time. More of a promise. I could feel her leaning toward me. Her knees hovered near my half of the loft.

I wanted to open my eyes. I wanted to smile at her and tell her how it had felt to dive off a cliff in the dark. I wanted to laugh with her about the willow who liked to make her roots into a seat for me and the hobgoblin who still ran whenever he saw me coming. But I didn't. Because if I opened my eyes she might leave. Because if I spoke I might tell her about Boris and because she was bound to ask me again if I would help her fight Lucille.

The door opened below, then closed again. Otto's heavy footsteps plodded across the cottage. "Let her sleep," he told Snow. "She only just came home."

Snow drew away. She stayed in the loft a moment, straightening her bodice and pulling pieces of straw out of her hair, then climbed down the ladder. It creaked and wobbled as she made her way down, then I fell asleep, listening to her scrape and rattle the dishes near the fire as she made breakfast.

SNOW

Otto was a patient student. He wasn't used to the stillness before a knife throw but he was diligent in his practice and consistent in his progress. Within a month he could strike my straw man in the throat from yards away. Within four he could hit it swaying back and forth on a pair of ropes.

Most days, after practicing, we sat inside by the warmth of the fire while I told him everything I could remember about the manor. We each constructed a map of it in our heads and tested each other on our memories. Then we would discuss which points were likely to be weaker, where it would be best to begin the attack. It was strange to be planning to destroy a place that had once been my home but after we destroyed it ---once Lucille was dead –we would rebuild it.

"Every stone. Every passage." Otto promised.

Some days he ventured off into the wood to speak to the hobgoblins. He said that they hated Lucille as much as we did and would do anything to see her dead. Except tell the Red Witch where their hovel was. Or tell me.

"Nurse gave them the jewelry." Otto told me one afternoon after practicing knife throws. He had managed a throw from halfway across the clearing and landed it only a few inches short of the heart. "She gave it to them as a gift when they helped her find Rose."

"Find Rose?" I closed the door behind us. "But I thought ---"

"So did I." Otto said. "They said the Old Witch –that's what they

117

call Nurse –came to the wood sixteen years ago from far away, asking every tree and woodland creature if they had seen a child princess born on the sixth moon of the year. She didn't believe the hobgoblins when they first came to her but she went to the village anyway and found Rose living with a spinner. She gave the hobgoblins the jewels and built herself this cottage here in the wood to be near her as she grew up."

I glanced at Rose's sash, lying on the floor unfinished. She had spent all winter stitching and restitching the patterns but had never been satisfied with them. How had she come to live here instead of in the north if her Gran hadn't brought her here? Who had rescued her from the massacre in her family's castle?

"Why are they so afraid of her?" I asked Otto. "Your nurse was a witch too. They weren't afraid of her."

Otto sat down beneath the loft. He took my hand and pulled me down beside him. "There used to be eleven hobgoblins in this wood when the old king –your father--was still alive. All brothers. Lucille learned of certain powers they had and her soldiers combed the wood for them. She caught four. The other seven almost didn't recognize the bodies they found washed up on the river bank two days later."

I shuddered, remembering the body Rose had found the night we came to the cottage. "What does that have to do with Rose?"

"Lucille is a witch. Glen says the bodies were shriveled dry with magic. They didn't even trust Nurse anymore after that."

I pulled my knees into my chest. "I was there --in the manor-- when she did . . . so many things. I should have stopped her. I should have--" I remembered the dreams now. Every night I remembered every scream and atrocity.

"You were hardly more than a child, Snow. What could you have done?"

"Spoken." I said. "I could have told Papa the things that I had seen --the things that I knew."

Otto shook his head. "What could he have done? He had already let her in."

"Because he was powerless against her." Because he wanted to save me from Boris.

"I'll get your manor back." Otto promised. "I won't let Lucille keep it from you. Not forever."

ROSE

I thanked the wood alone that summer. Snow didn't come with me. I didn't see any hobgoblins as I gathered fallen wood to burn. I considered asking Boris to come but midsummer didn't fall on a new moon and he was very insistent about only seeing me when there was no chance of him turning. Our visits were few and far between.

I sang as I piled the wood in the center of the clearing. Animals gathered around the edge of the wood to watch. The ghosts drifted just out of sight in the dusk, not quite whispering in my ears, not quite telling me their stories. I had begun to suspect that they all had the same story for as many years as Lucille had been eating human hearts.

I stood still, waiting for the darkness to fall, listening to the deep, deep, thrum of the wood. Crickets chirped. The air stirred. A woodpecker pounded his beak furiously into a pine. The bushes rustled.

And then it was dark and I was dark. I didn't need to sing to light the fire. The heat was already burning in my breast. The piles of wood burst into flame the moment I wished them to. The earth swelled inside me, claiming me as I claimed it. The trees thrummed on and on and on, my own voice, quiet and long, stretching over centuries upon centuries of time.

I saw the trees as saplings, reaching their tiny sprouting roots into the soil. I saw them age through season after season. Their leaves turned green then gold then fell and grew again until finally, one by one, they fell and others emerged in their place. I felt their bark thicken as they grew and grew, each size more painful than the last, each change using more of their strength. The force of each moment was so strong that I could hardly stand and yet I stood straighter and stiller than ever before, drinking in the power of the wood as everything happened at once inside me.

"Lost." The ghosts whispered over and over as they flickered in and out of sight. "Lost."

But I wasn't lost. I was found. I was the wood and nothing would ever stand in my way. Nothing would take me from myself

SNOW

Spring came. Otto did not leave. Every day I thought would be his last day at the cottage but he lingered, hunting, practicing his knife throws, and drifting off to speak to the hobgoblins. He went to see them more and more each week. Some days I thought he had gone at last without bidding me farewell only to come inside with a string of fish or bag full of walnuts and find him stretched out beneath the loft. It was strange to have him at the cottage when the weather was warm. It reminded me how much had changed since he had transformed into a man.

"I'll go soon." He kept saying but spring warmed into summer, and still he stayed.

One evening, at last, he didn't return. It was dusk when I realized I hadn't seen him since breakfast. Rose had gone off to roam the woods, he had gone —I'd assumed —to the hobgoblins' hovel, and I had stayed at the cottage, washing laundry, airing out the windows, fingering through the herbal in the garden, practicing my own knife throws. My knife's blade had gone dull from all of Otto's practice. I pulled a pair of sharpening stones out of the shed and sat on the woodpile, rubbing until the blade could cut silk.

The air was warm, grey and soft, as it settled around me. I could hear a woodpecker, hammering his beak into his home some ways into the wood. I squinted at my knife, hardly able to make out the vines engraved on it in the fading light. I hadn't realized how late it had grown.

"We'll need a fire soon, Rose." I said, forgetting that she wasn't in the garden, trimming and pruning the way she used to in the summer. I looked up and stared out at the flowers and vegetables running rampant through the yard. It had been so long since I'd seen her crouched among the plants. They had grown tangled and crowded. Wild. Some flourished in spite of her inattention. Others looked as if they were on the verge of choking to death. I missed the sound of her humming. I missed the sound of her laugh.

I slid my knife back into its sheath and rose to return the sharpening stones to the shed. I filled the pot with water to start a soup but I wasn't very hungry and we didn't have a flint to light the fire. Rose always did that. I stood in the doorway for a moment, staring out into the wood, feeling as if I had forgotten something. Something important. A light breeze fluttered through the rampant flower garden, rolling the plants like a ripple in a pond. I closed the door, climbed up into the loft, and went to sleep.

Neither Otto nor Rose had returned when I woke. Rose came back mid-morning, grumbling that I only had raw nuts and berries for her to eat. I reminded her that she was the only one who could light a fire and went to collect more nuts.

She was gone again when I returned. It was past dark but there was a fire frolicking beneath a boiling pot of pea soup. I opened my mouth to curse her for almost burning the cottage down when I saw a flint lying on the hearth. I looked up at the table. A large book I had never seen before lay on the surface, thick and smooth and rectangular. I stepped toward it and ran my fingers up and down the thick leather binding, fresh and glossy and neatly cut. I touched the cover, then pulled it open, slowly.

Memories splashed through my head, drifting through me with the clean, dusty scent of the pages. My tutor standing over me as I practiced my writing. Papa, in the library, looking over maps and ledgers while I fingered through books of stories, admiring their bright colored paintings and wondering why there seemed to be so many kings in the world, and why everyone always seemed to want to kill them and take their land. Sometimes, if I waited long enough and quietly enough, if I had practiced my music and dancing and stitching and penmanship, if I didn't fall asleep before he finished his work, Papa would sit me on his knee and tell me a story of his own.

His stories weren't about kings or land or battles. Sometimes they were about princesses like me who were brave and kind and cunning, but mostly they were about birds that talked or water that sang, trees that danced, or boxes that could lock a person's heart away so that it could never be found and they could never be killed. I would fall asleep, listening to the deep, rich sound of his voice and wake in my bed with Dana and Elise waiting in the anteroom to dress me and a hot plate of sausage and biscuits on the table.

My world had been so small, so clean and neat. I had even believed it was safe.

I touched the strong inky swirls on the page in front of me, reading the first line

Behold, the tale of King Agar, seventh son of the mountain god, ruler of the eleven forests.

There had been so many books in Papa's library, dozens --more than dozens-- and I had read them all, then I had read them again. It had been so long since I had touched a book apart from the three little ones tucked away in our cupboard.

"It's for you." Otto said.

I turned, startled by the sound of his voice. I hadn't heard the door open. He stood just inside the cottage with a pile of chopped wood in his arms. His hair was combed back, his curls tucked neatly behind his ears and he wore a new waistcoat and trousers.

"How did you know?" I asked.

He smiled. "You always linger when you tell me about the libraries."

"Thank you." I closed the book. "I thought you'd left. To the north."

"Not yet." He knelt next to the fireplace and unloaded the wood onto the hearth next to the flint. He rose and pressed his hand against the back of his neck. He looked toward the window but didn't seem to observe the stars beginning to scatter across the sky. He pulled in a deep draught of breath and pulled the stool up to the table, motioning for me to sit in the chair. I did as he instructed.

"I'm leaving soon." He said.

"I know."

"Tomorrow, I think. Or the day after."

I nodded, waiting. There was more. His voice was pregnant with it, fluttering around inside him, not sure how it wanted to come out.

"Can I take you to see the hobgoblins?" Otto asked, not quite looking at me. He kept on glancing out the window. "I would rather leave knowing that you and Rose have someone to look after you."

"They don't want me at their hovel." I said.

"They don't want Rose. Please, Snow. Let me leave with my mind at rest. There is something--" he touched the back of his neck again. "Something I want to show you before I go."

I folded my hands in my lap, unsure what to say.

"Please." Otto said.

I bit my lip. I stared down at the book on the table. Finally I nodded. "I'll go." I said. "We can leave in the morning."

Rose was in the herb garden when we left. She had let the flowers run wild but the sage and tarragon were still lined in neat, pungent green rows. I could hear the fiery lull of her humming as we stepped out into the wood.

"If you stayed a few days more" I told Otto "you could come with us to light our midsummer bonfire."

"Midsummer was two nights ago."

I stopped, turning to look over my shoulder at the cottage. The space between me and the building was draped by the greenery of the forest. If I listened hard enough I could still catch whiffs of Rose's song. So that's where she had been the night Otto hadn't come back.

"This way." Otto said. "It's a long walk."

I expected Otto to lead me toward Rose's village or perhaps downstream a ways where the best hunting spots were but we trekked north, moving closer to the manor. The trees seemed taller than they had ever been, silent, watchful, reaching for me with their brittle fingers. I had never considered before how close to Lucille I had hidden from her. I glanced over my shoulder, almost expecting to see her lurking behind the trees, but there was nothing but oaks and pines and firs, crowded together in clusters.

"Run." A ghost whispered somewhere next to my ear but I wouldn't. Not this time.

It was still daylight when we stopped in front of an old oak. The familiar form of a hobgoblin stepped out of the hawthorns with sticky leaves stuck to his beard and his usual smear of dirt on his face and hands. Only the face was new, narrower, sharper, and his beard was scattered with splotches of brown.

Otto cleared his throat. "We've come to see Dale."

The hobgoblin gave a single curt nod.

Otto dropped to his hands and knees. His belly brushed against the earth as he moved forward. I followed, mimicking his movements, slithering like a snake. Prickly leaves caught in my hair and skirts and I kept my lips closed and face down to keep the plants out of my mouth.

The opening to the hovel was small but big enough for Otto's long legs and broad shoulders. I felt the ground in front of me, unable to see in the darkness that enclosed me as I crawled in after him.

A scattering of harp notes echoed from below. Light, jolly notes, full of moss and dragonflies followed by another sprinkle of sound, much darker and deeper than the first. We crawled downward. Blood trickled slowly to my head, rolling along the tilting slope of the earth. I could see a warm hint of orange up ahead.

Music soared and trickled and wove around me. A light, cheerful melody strung together with heavy, angry notes that made me want to scream and cry and laugh. My tutors would have been pleased if I could hit a single note so lovely. Mesmerized as I was by the music, I almost didn't notice when the tunnel ended. Otto took my hand and helped me down into a large, cavern, flickering with shadows.

The air was stale but at least there was enough of it. I blinked, letting my eyes focus. The walls were a rich earthen brown. Stalagmite dripped from the ceiling too high above our heads. I was reminded for a moment of the domed ballroom in Papa's manor. A fire burned near the center of the cavern crowded by a tiny cluster of hobgoblins. Their small, doll-like forms made the cavern look even bigger.

A hobgoblin with a harp sat cross legged next to the flames. His melody reached a crescendo, strong and rich and cluttered with uncertainty then he set his harp down. He was the smallest of all his brothers and obviously the youngest. His hair and beard had only just started to go gray. Most of it was still blond.

The stink of fish and sting of nettles wafted through the air. Another hobgoblin stood next to the fire. His beard was better kept and a paler shade of gray. He stood over the fire, stirring something in an iron pot the size of a helmet. He lifted a ladle to his nose and sniffed in concentration. He gave his stew an experimental taste, twisted his nose in dissatisfaction, then looked up at Otto and I. "This the witch then?"

Another hobgoblin clamored to his feet. This one I had seen before. He was the troublemaker who'd nearly been swallowed by a tree, drowned by a pike, and clawed to death by a hawk. He crossed his arms and looked up at me, scowling his usual scowl. "That's the other one. Snow."

I blinked, startled. He had never called me by my name before.

"Sludge." The hobgoblin cook set his ladle back in the pot and held out his hand. I rested the tips of my fingers in it. He kissed my knuckles.

"She doesn't need to know what you're called ye daft willie." A fourth hobgoblin looked up from a scroll in his hand ---an old scroll made with parchment instead of paper—from where he sat next to the harpist. He held a torch in one hand lifted over the scroll so that I could see the thick inky writing, wrinkled and knobby like his face. I hadn't noticed the rug he and his brother sat on before, woven entirely out of gold thread that glinted and shimmered in the flicker of the fire.

"It won't do any harm, Quill." Sludge said.

Quill looked back down at his parchment. "Ha! A witch in our hovel."

"Not all witches are cruel." I glanced at the hobgoblin troublemaker, standing with his arms crossed, still scowling. He'd be dead by now if it weren't for me and Rose.

"These aren't our real names." He said "We never use those. Not even among ourselves. Names hold power. When you name something you get to decide what it is."

"What do they call you?" I asked "They must call you something."

The hobgoblin's scowl deepened. Only it almost didn't look so much like a scowl anymore. It almost looked like a smile trying very hard not to be seen. Almost. "Trouble." He said.

I laughed.

The harpist picked up his harp and strummed. Notes dusted the air like particles in the sunlight. He strummed again, clawing out a hard, heavy chord.

Quill shook his head. "Those gloomy dirges will draw the misfortunes here if anything will."

Sludge sniffed at his soup again. "Lad! Fetch me some pine nuts and mushrooms and be quick about it. I want this stew ready for our guests."

A thin scruffy figure stepped out of the shadows. His beard was black without a trace of gray, reaching down past his waist. His shoulders were hunched, his hair frayed and tangled, and his fingers purple with blackberry juice. He looked at me, his eyes wide and curious, then popped a blackberry from his pocket into his mouth and scrambled back into the shadows.

"Where's Glen?" Otto asked.

Sludge gave his stew a long, slow stir. "In the treasury."

Otto pulled a candle out of his pocket. He lowered the wick into the flames then pulled it away, flickering with a tiny ring of light. "We'll go see him."

I followed Otto across the cavern. The sound of our feet echoed in the dark space as we drifted further and further from the hobgoblins, a rhythm beneath the fierce, continuous pluckings of the harp. Even the slow, ragged huffs of our breathing bounced off the walls, filling the emptiness around us. The candle flickered in Otto's hand. I held onto his arm to keep from tripping in deepening shadows.

Another candle flickered up ahead at knee level. It moved closer. A moment later it was hovering just beneath us in the closed fist of a white haired hobgoblin with stern eyes and a sterner mouth. He stopped. His big round eyes wandered up to my face then back down to my toes. He turned toward Otto. "This the girl?"

"This is Snow." Otto said. "Snow, Glen is the eldest of the brothers. If anything happens while I'm gone he will protect you."

I bowed my head in a half curtsy. "That is very kind of you, sir."

"Don't get lost." He said and stepped around us, moving toward the fire near the cavern opening where his brothers were gathered.

"They're a tight lipped clan." Otto said "But reliable. This way. I want to show you something."

The opening to the treasury was only a few steps further. Otto and I had to lower our heads to fit through. This cavern was smaller. Otto lifted his candle so I could see the walls, cluttered with shadows.

Dark objects of every shape and size filled the space. Axes, candlesticks, dishes. There was even a spinning wheel, threaded and ready to spin, resting in the corner.

"They're magpies." I stopped next to a small open chest full of coins and jewelry. The pearl necklace that had changed Otto back into a man rested on the top next to an amethyst ring encrusted with the emblem of a single rose.

"This is how I am going to pay my soldiers." Otto said.

I picked the ring up and turned it over in my hand. It was heavy, smooth, more intricate than anything I had held in a long time. The box of treasures were worth a village at least but I was certain Lucille had much more locked away in Papa's manor and in her castle in the north --Otto's castle. She could more than double whatever Otto offered his soldiers.

Then I remembered the silver Mama had brought with her from her home. The comb, the long chained cross, the short chained diamonds, the earrings, the three matching rings. If Papa hadn't given them to me when I was still small I might have forgotten she had ever existed most days. Otto's family was dead too. This was all he had left of them. "Are you willing to part with the heirlooms?" I asked.

His lips twisted in the shadows. "The hobgoblins aren't. The chest is staying here." He stepped to the side of the cavern and lifted his candle. The light fluttered against the spinning wheel and spool after spool of spun thread, sprawled and piled on the ground around it in no particular order. Otto stooped to pick up a spool and held it out to me. "This is what will pay for the army."

I set the ring down and reached into the shadows to take the spool, confused. "Thread?" But it was heavier in my hand than it should have been. Realization struck me in an instant. The rug the hobgoblins had been sitting on. The thread all of the hobgoblin's clothes were stitched together with. "Gold." I said. "Gold thread."

Otto nodded. "They've been spinning it for me these last months. It's their skill —the one Lucille tried to take from them. I can bring a handful to show my recruits and pay them when they arrive. I wanted to show you in case . . . in case something happens to me on the journey. So you can pay the soldiers. So you can lead them if you must."

With this kind of payment I wondered why he had to go to the north at all. Surely there were plenty of men here who would want thread spun of gold. There was no reason they had to be loyal to Otto's family.

"Why did they spin it for you?" I asked "What did you offer them?"

"Protection from Lucille." Otto said "And a place in my castle if they want it but I think they would have done it without the promises."

"Because of what Lucille did to their brothers."

Otto nodded.

I handed the spool back to him.

Otto balanced it in his palm, running his thumb over the threads. "The caverns will be a good place to hide once the battles start. We could fit armies in here."

We could. The caverns were wide and the passages tall, but was it a good place to hide or a perfect place to be trapped? I had only seen the one entrance.

"How long will you be gone?" I asked Otto.

"Until spring."

Almost a year. That gave Rose and I one more winter in the cottage. The next would be spent either in a coffin or a castle. Probably without Rose.

"Snow," Otto lowered his voice. He knelt and placed the spool back on the ground with the others. "Snow," he said again. He rose and reached for my hand. His fingers were warm and tight around mine. Light from the candle flickered across his eyes. Earnest. Eager. "When I come back, after we defeat Lucille, when my home is mine again to offer you, I want you to marry me." He paused to take in a breath. I could feel the pumping of his blood quickening even just from inside his hands. "Would you do that?"

I nodded, remembering, as if I had never forgotten, how such things were done. "That would bind my land to yours. It would be a good alliance."

My land. The words felt strange. It had never been my land before. It had been Papa's. It had been going to be my husband's, whichever prince he turned out to be.

Otto wrinkled his forehead. He looked confused, disappointed, hurt. "Snow, I don't want to marry you to join our lands. I want to marry you because I love you."

I stared at him.

Love me? Papa had loved me. So had Hans, and Rose, and probably my attendants, Elise and Dana --at least they had been fonder of me than my tutors had been-- but Papa hadn't loved Lucille and he hadn't loved my mother.

I didn't remember her. She had died four days after I was born from too much bleeding. Papa had told me that she had been good and kind and that she had stitched the best embroidery in all the plains. He had been sorry when she had died because she had been a good wife in the year that they had lived together. He had even mourned her an extra month but he had never loved her. Not the way the stories spoke of love. Nobles married because their lands were too close together and they did not trust each other not to attack and because they needed heirs to look after their land when they were gone.

Perhaps things were done differently in the north.

"Please say something." Otto said.

"Did you love your other betrothed?" I asked, curious.

He let go of my hand. Hurt and disappointment gave way to pure bemusement. "What?"

"The princess from the east you were betrothed to before. The one with the freckles and the soft lips. Did you love her too?"

Otto shook his head. "No. Of course not. We had fun together as children but she was . . . we were fond of each other. That was all." He stared at me, waiting for me to say something else but I had no idea what it was he was waiting for me to say.

"I will marry you." I said at last. The words were final. Sticky and wax-like as they sealed my fate. Otto's plans to fight Lucille had never seemed real until that moment.

Otto sighed. He ran his fingers through his hair then looked down at me with a sad, wistful smile. He shook his head. "No. Not yet. You aren't as cold and sullen as you appear, Snow. I know you aren't. Maybe one day you will be ready to marry me." He paused. "Or maybe you will discover that your heart lies somewhere else."

I had no idea what he meant. We stood for a moment in the darkness, neither of us speaking.

"Should we head back to the opening?" He asked at last.

I shook my head. "I want to stay here for a moment. Alone."

Otto nodded. He fished another candle out of his pocket, lit the wick, and handed it to me. Then he turned and left. I listened to the heavy, solid sound of his footsteps fade, dripping like wax off the candle in my hand.

Love. Otto had spoken of it as if it were real, as if it were something we could touch, something we could own. I turned and wandered through the cluttered space of the cavern, the glittering odds and ends the hobgoblins had earned and stolen over the years. There was a goblet just like the ones Papa and I had drunk from at the manor. There was the chest full of jewels that had once belonged to Rose's mother.

I knelt and lifted the amethyst ring again. The gold stone looked like fire. Like a midsummer bonfire. Would Rose want it, a piece of her mother? I never knew what she wanted anymore. I seldom even saw her. Sometimes it almost felt like we were strangers.

I looked at the candle in my hand. The wax was dripping steadily now, crusting over the tips of my fingers. Something glinted next to the chest. Not a gold glint. Lighter, paler, more like moonlight than sunlight. I lifted my candle, bringing it closer. An oval disk leaned against the stone wall, draped in a rich purple fabric. All but one corner was covered. The corner shimmered.

A mirror. Silver, carved with vines and violets, almost exactly like the one I had had in my bedroom in Papa's manor. A seeing mirror, Papa had called it before Lucille had taken it and moved it to her own room. He had never said what I was meant to see in it besides myself. Without wondering why, I pulled the cover off.

Green eyes gazed at me, untouched by the warm smile beneath them and smothered in long nut brown locks, not quite straight, and not quite curled. I touched the side of my face with the back of my hand just as she touched hers but this woman was not me. She was too certain of herself, too boisterous and alive. And she wasn't trapped in a cluttered hobgoblin's treasury. I recognized the domed ceiling, ornate carvings, and cluttered shelves of Papa's study behind her.

Lucille rose one perfect eyebrow over her perfect forest colored eye. "Snow." I saw her laughing mouth say but couldn't hear her voice. "Alive."

They were her eyes, her real, magic filled eyes. She had found me at last.

My candle went out, burning my skin as the flame reached my finger, and the cavern turned dark

ROSE

I was in the garden, plucking tarragon and basil leaves when I felt the footsteps pressing down into the grass. I felt them pushing over the the tall thin blades as distinctly as if they had been pressing into my own skin. They were close, not far into the wood at all, moving steadily toward the cottage with slow, prickling movements.

I stood up. Listening. Feeling. A whisper of wind brushed across my face. It sighed through the tree tops and tangled itself into a thick, coarse coat of fur, only a few feet now from the forest's edge. I looked up at the sky. It was gray, filled with the smoky haze of dusk. Suspended above my head, just a little to the west, was a bright silver tinted orb. Not full, but almost. An apple with a bite gauged out of it.

I could hear the footsteps now. Not with the murmuring senses of the woodland, but with my own tiny human ears. I started at the sound. It tickled my flesh like the hum of an insect. Soft, consistent pattering over the creaking wood of the bridge at the edge of the wood. Nearer and nearer until I could see the wolf creature stepping out of the shadows and into the clearing.

Wide amber eyes. Pale, yellow fangs. Dark fur that looked almost charcoal in the blackening dusk air. He was bigger even than I remembered with shoulders that would have reached past my knees had I been standing.

131

He didn't look anything like Boris but I knew it was him. The monster who had killed my Gran. The monster who had almost killed Snow.

He stopped for only a moment at the edge of the clearing, sniffing the air with his snout as if to be sure he had come to the right place. He fixed his eyes on me and moved forward again. Quickly. Effortlessly. Snow and I had never repaired the gate. He leapt over its shambles, gaining speed as he neared me.

I stood where I was, holding my hand out in front of me for him to sniff. Basil leaves and strips of tarragon scattered over the earth next to my feet. Perhaps he would recognize me. Perhaps he would be strong enough to resist his mother's commands.

I focused inward, into the part of my soul where my songs came from. Where Gran had told me stories and where I had stood with Snow next to the midsummer bonfire. If he wasn't strong enough I would be ready for him.

Boris stopped when he reached me, close enough that I could feel hot air coming from his snout. The hair on the back of his haunches settled flat across his back. His pointed ears stood straight. His gums lowered over his teeth, covering the growl that had stopped before it started. I looked into the deep, unsaturated gold of his eyes and saw exactly what I had hoped to see.

Recognition.

The coals of the fire inside me turned to ash. My whole body went cold.

Boris brushed past me. He rubbed his shoulders against my legs. The fur on the back of his tail tapped against my fingers. I watched him plod toward the cottage then disappear through the door I had left open.

Fire bubbled anew in every piece of me, cracking against all compassion, singeing the corners of my rationality. I breathed deep, collecting the last remnants of my restraint and followed him into the cottage.

Boris stood next to the wash basin with the bath curtain wrapped around his naked human body.

"You recognized me." I said.

He smiled incredulously. "Of course I did. How could I possibly not recognize you?"

I glared at him, letting my anger seep into every corner of the cottage. For a moment I almost thought I heard the tar in the walls sizzle. "You killed Gran."

Boris furrowed his forehead in confusion. Sweat painted a shiny glint over his face, gleaming down his neck and bare chest and shoulders. "I told you I did. It was the full moon. My mother--"

I shook my head, lifting my finger to point at him like a dagger. "You killed Gran. Not your mother. Not some monster that possessed you. I saw your eyes a moment ago. Your eyes without that smile and face to hide behind."

"The moon--"

"I know wild beasts." I continued, ignoring his interruption. "I speak to them. They're hungry and feral and vicious but they don't know when they hurt you. They only know that if they don't eat you you might eat them. If I hum softly enough and deeply enough they will trust me, let me pass by them closer than any human has, touch them even. Your eyes -- just now-- they were wild and hungry but they weren't the eyes of a dumb beast. Whatever the moon does to you, you are still in control."

Boris sighed. He ran a hand through his hair. He clutched the curtain in his fist with the other hand. "Sometimes. Mostly. But it's more complicated than that. It's . . . unpredictable. An animal in me does take over. Maybe it's not the wolf. Maybe it is myself but . . ." He looked up, meeting my gaze. "Rose, I do remember that night. I remember the way your Gran screamed and begged me to let her go. I remember . . . so much more. Snow's dagger piercing into my gut, my mother's joy when she heard that the deed was done, how pleased I was that I had been able to please her. I live with those memories everyday but Rose –Rose all that was before I knew you. Before you made me want to be different."

"You should leave." I told him but he kept talking.

"I love you, Rose." He took a slow lingering step toward me. "I wish I had never taken your Gran from you. I wish I had never hurt anyone but I could never hurt you, Rose. Never."

I stared at him. His voice was fervent, his eyes sincere. He believed he was telling the truth.

He took another step towards me, encouraged by my silence. Then another. A few seconds and he was standing close enough for me to hear his breathing, heavy and shallow like mine. He lifted my hand in his, running his thumb over my palm.

"What are you doing here?" I asked. My heart was beating faster than I would have liked.

"I came to see you." His voice was soft, lilting, hardly more than a whisper. He was close enough now for me to feel his breath, warm and close, so, so close to my face. The curtain he was still holding around his waist brushed against my shins. "I want you to come with me."

"Where?" I asked. "Why?"

"Anywhere." He pulled back just a little, smiling his ridiculous smile. "My mother knows that Snow is alive. When she comes looking for her you won't be safe here anymore."

I pulled my hand back. There was only one part of that speech that meant anything to me. "Snow's in danger." I said "We have to warn her."

Boris raised his eyebrows. His lips twisted into a pout. He tilted his head in a way he might have thought was charming. "Now? Can't it wait a few minutes or . . ." He leaned his head down, close to mine again "seconds."

A hot rush of blood spread over my cheeks. The rest of my body went cold. "No." I placed both my palms on his naked chest and shoved him away. "It can't." I turned around, stepping toward the door.

"Rose." His hand clamped around my wrist. He pulled me back around to face him. "Say you will come with me. Say you will let me take care of you."

The anger coursing through me wasn't hot anymore. It didn't consume me or cloud me with passion. It was cold and empty and clearer than anything I had ever felt before. My heart beat faster and faster with each second. "Take care of yourself." I said, clipping my way through each syllable to be sure that he understood. "Leave before I burn you to cinders."

"Please." Boris begged. His hand clamped tighter around my wrist. "Don't send me away."

"You would have killed Snow." I said. "If Hans hadn't come in time. You would have killed her."

He scoffed. His human eyes glinted with contempt. "Hans the Hunter. Mother's favorite pet. We thought he had finished the two of you off. I don't imagine he'll live long now that his secret is discovered."

My lip curled. His loyalty to his mother might have been reduced to tatters but he was still jealous of her affection. She had trained him well.

Boris saw my expression. The disdain drained from his eyes. "I didn't mean it that way."

"You did." I said.

"Old ways are hard to change, Rose, but I will. For you, I will. It's hard tonight with the moon out."

"You are in perfect control of who you are." I glanced at his big sweaty hand still clamped around my wrist. "I won't tell you again."

Boris let go of me. He stepped back with his eyes still locked on mine. His shoulders hunched. He yelped then snarled. His limbs jolted first in one direction then the other. His skin thickened and grew fur. His flesh shriveled then expanded and I was staring once again into the harsh, gold eyes of the wolf who had killed my grandmother. He shook his head, snarled, and darted out the door. The bath curtain lay spread over the cottage floor like an old rag.

I followed him outside. He had already disappeared into the trees.

I closed my eyes. I planted my feet against the ground and let the remaining shards of sunlight leak into my skin. I listened. I listened deep into the heart of the wood. I listened for Snow's careful, low-lifted steps against the earth. I listened for the wind through her long, straight braid, over her soft lips and long eyelashes.

Nothing.

Fox paws pattered against the ground. Birds' wings fluttered in the wind. The delicate hoof beats of woodland deer sounded over and over like a drum. I felt the rushed push of Boris's wolf feet as he made his way back to his mother's manor but not a human step touched the earth. Not where I could feel it. Not in my wood.

Where is she? I demanded but the trees did not answer. My pulse rushed like a waterfall so that I could hardly manage to stand still. I struggled to hold my concentration. Where is Snow?

Oak leaves rustled in a circle around the cottage glen. Willow vines swayed deep in the forest. The trees did not answer.

I inhaled, trying to dig deeper, trying to feel into the roots of the trees, into every ring of their trunks. My mind burned with fire. Where? I asked again, frantic for the answer. Where is Snow? She had to have gone through the wood to leave the cottage. The trees had to have seen.

They did not answer. Perhaps I had asked them too forcefully. Perhaps they didn't know or perhaps . . . perhaps another magic had bound them into silence.

Please. I begged, one last time. Tell me where she is. Tell me she is safe.

Silence.

There wasn't time to tramp through the wood looking for her. Lucille's powers were a hundred times stronger than mine. She knew Snow was alive. It was a matter of hours —minutes even —before she discovered where. Where would Snow go? The village? Perhaps but . . . I needed to know where she wasn't first. As long as I knew that I knew she had a chance.

I ran back to the cottage, moving faster than I could ever remember moving before. I pushed the door open. It slammed against the wall and bounced on its hinges. I looked around the room for something to . . . there. On the table was a book. Not Gran's. One I had never seen before. I opened it to the first page.

Ink. I needed ink but I knew there wasn't any. There wasn't time to boil walnuts or squeeze berries either. I grabbed one of Gran's china cups and broke the rim against the table. I pressed my finger into to the broken edge, pushing down until my skin split open. A red ribbon of blood bled through. I smeared it onto the book page, writing as quickly and neatly as I could manage with my heart thundering inside my chest. My heart felt sick. I couldn't let anything happen to Snow. I couldn't.

SHE KNOWS. GET OUT.

The words were hardly legible but it was the best I could manage. I left the cottage and darted through the gardens, across the glen, and out into the wood. I wove and ducked through the trees, dodging birches and oaks. Leaves and thorns stuck in my hair, pulling at my roots, trying to make me stop.

I listened as I ran. I listened as I had never listened before. To my feet bouncing off the woodland floor over and over. To the blood pumping through my limbs and chest like the roar of a storm. To the crunch of the leaves and the flapping of bat's wings, the chirping of insects, the hiss of the wind. If I listened hard enough perhaps I would hear her. Perhaps I would hear Otto. Perhaps I could get to her and warn her in time.

But I didn't hear her. Not anywhere on the woodland floor. Not out on the plains of the village. My thighs burned. I struggled to keep control of my breath. Then, suddenly, almost as if I had appeared there by magic, I was standing in front of the manor, staring at the black iron gate.

I had never imagined that a single building could be so large. It poked up from behind the thick, stone walls that surrounded it like a giant tree stump in the growing darkness. I could hear voices and the trampling plod of feet coming from inside, only ---something was missing. The sounds were harsh and regulated with none of the laughter and grumblings I had grown up with in the village.

I stood just inside the trees, catching my breath, gathering my thoughts. I would gain nothing if I marched up to the gate and demanded information. Nothing but a night in the dungeons. Or worse. I needed a plan. No one but Boris would have any idea who I was. I could ask for shelter or work or . . .

Boris was already inside the manor. Wolves run faster than girls, even witches. I'd felt him slip out of the wood long before I'd reached the edge.

It didn't matter. If he claimed to know me I would deny it. If he tried to stop me I would burst him into flames.

I pulled as many of the leaves as I could out of my curls and ran my fingers through them so I would look more like a village girl and less like a wild thing from the wood. I approached the gate. It was some time before anyone came but the warden assured me that he could find work for me if I had any skills worth noting. I told him I could spin thread. He grinned at me, telling me that the queen had said only a day ago that she wished she had someone who could spin some decent thread. He let me in, rattling on about his wife's broken wrist and how it had grown back crooked, leaving her to learn to cook all over again as if they were newly wed —only she wasn't as handsome as she had been then and not as willing in more ways than one.

I asked him if he had ever been in the dungeons or seen any of the prisoners. He waved his hand. "The prisoners never last long enough to recognize, girl. Most don't make it through the night. You needn't bother worrying though. Little of the noise carries into the servant's quarters. The queen is very tidy with that kind of work."

He led me through a courtyard of soldiers marching back and forth in formations. I had never seen so many men dressed alike. I had never seen so many weapons, sharp and clean and glinting in the golden glow of the sunset.

"This way, girl." The warden led me past the stable and the kitchen into the manor's ground level. The inside was lined with doors and staircases. The warden led me to a plainly decorated room near the kitchen. It was lined with benches and cluttered with basket upon basket of silk threads and luxurious fabrics. They glittered and shone and swagged in all colors, bright and gauzy and delicate. The velvet gown I had first seen Snow in looked like rags in comparison. I touched the sash around my waist --the blue one embroidered with vines and birds that I had made for Snow but had never given to her. It was nothing compared to the gifts she must have been used to.

The warden left me without a word and I was left alone in the empty room. I could hear the sizzling of meats and the cook's muted orders coming from the kitchen outside but I doubted if anyone would notice if I slipped out the door and went to look for the dungeons. I wished to anything that I could speak to the stone and wood of the manor house the way I could the woodlands.

"You are beautiful."

I whirred around, surprised by the clear, rounded voice. I hadn't heard the woman approach. I hadn't expected her to arrive so soon.

She smiled at me. A warm, glittering smile. As if she had been waiting for me to arrive all day and here I was at last. As if she wanted nothing better than to sit down with me and a cup of mead and chat about nothing all day long. She was beautiful too. Hair the color of the earth after a storm. Eyes like the forest. She had a thin, delicate chin and cheeks flushed just enough to lighten her expression. "He said you would be beautiful." Her voice was like mist.

"Who said?"

She laughed. Like ripples in a thick, rich cream. Like a trumpet on harvest day. It was hypnotic, riveting.

Was this the queen? Lucille herself? But of course she couldn't be. She wasn't old enough to have given birth to a child of ten and certainly not to a man of Boris's age. At the most she could be his little sister.

"The warden, silly goose. He said it was a wonder you were looking for work and not a husband." The woman lifted the side of her lips into a half smile. "He sounded disappointed that he no longer qualifies for the job."

I stared at her. I needed to find Snow, not a husband. "I just want to spin." I said. "I'm also quite good in the garden."

"What an interesting combination of skills." She glided across the room, the movement quick but balanced and unhurried. She brushed her gown back —plain blue wool; I had hardly noticed it before —and sat down on one of the benches next to the spinning wheel. "Let's see your spinning first since the garden will take days to prove."

I suppressed a sigh and sat next to her. If I couldn't explore the manor perhaps I could draw some gossip out of this woman. She seemed friendly enough if I could manage to phrase the questions right. "How long have you worked here?"

"Not long." There was a hint of laughter still lingering in her voice as she watched me examine a pelt of wool from a basket.

I lifted the pelt in my hands. White, pure and unstained. I could only imagine the trouble the sheep shearers must have gone through to wash it. It felt strange scratching against my palms, familiar but from a life so far away I wasn't even sure it had been mine.

"But you must have met the queen." I wrapped the end of the wool onto the spinning needle.

"Only the soldiers and the serving staff meet the queen." The woman said. "Unless you anger her of course but no one in the manor has."

Somehow I did not think that that was because the queen was not easily angered.

The woman reached into her pocket and pulled out a small thin piece of linen. She held it out to me. "For your finger." She nodded toward the cut from Gran's mug, clotted now but still dark with blood. I'd forgotten how much it hurt. "So you don't stain the thread."

I took the linen and wrapped it around my finger, tying it tight next to my knuckle. "What angers her? The queen."

The woman's lips quirked. "Too many questions."

I held the wool between my fingers, pressing it back onto the spinning needle. I placed my feet on the wooden pedals and began to pump. The sound was like going back in time to the constant, relentless hum of Greta's house in the village where we had sat, day after day, spinning. The wool pulled through my fingers, gently, steadily, scratching, whispering at my calluses. I concentrated on holding still. I had never been very patient with a spinning wheel. Greta had never been quite satisfied with my work.

"The queen had a sister once." The woman said. "Not many

people know that. I suppose she was the first woman to truly anger her. The first to question her ways."

Gossip of the past. Nothing about where Lucille was now or what prisoners she had.

"What are her ways?" I asked. "What did her sister question?"

"Her livelihood." The woman answered. "Her right to survive. But it doesn't matter anymore. Her sister is dead."

The wheel thrummed. I kept pedaling, guiding the wool onto the needle, searching my brain for another question. One that would lead the direction I wanted it to. I forced myself to spin slowly, fighting against the rhythm of my heartbeat.

"You are fortunate to be so beautiful." The woman said. "If you chose you would never have to work again. There are men who enjoy indulging a beautiful wife —or mistress —if she is accommodating enough at the right times."

"I like to work." I said "It helps me think."

The woman laughed. "It doesn't really matter what you like. Or think. Have you ever seen an ugly woman? Not a plain woman. A plain woman can get by. She works hard and stays out of everyone's way and when all the pretty girls have been claimed there are men willing enough to take her if she is a good cook and promises to keep the floor well scrubbed. I mean a hag; old and shriveled with teeth falling out of her mouth and hardly any hair left. She might have been beautiful once but it doesn't matter anymore. The men who had always thought she was silly and dim no longer wish to indulge her whims. They no longer wish to look at her. They spit on her as she walks by. They laugh at her. They steal from her whatever small possessions she's managed to hoard into her old age because she is too weak to fight them. And the women? They are worse. They draw back from her, refuse to look at her, terrified because they know that she is their future. Beauty, my dear, is the only power a woman can claim. Use it while it is still yours."

The silky monotone of her voice stopped. The wheel kept spinning, dragging her thoughts on into the almost silence, turning them over and over inside my mind. I shivered then shook my head. The wool moved in my fingers, leaving a glitch in the thread. "That's not true." I said. "My Gran was old and she was beautiful. She laughed. She danced."

Her joy had made her beautiful. Her love.

"Then she was fortunate to have had you, blinded by your love for her." Her voice grew terse, hints of anger or mockery pushing against the careful, syllabic lilt. She stood, brushing her skirt down, freeing it of wrinkles. "Enough spinning. You've done well. Only one hitch and you chose the most well carded wool. If the queen is pleased with the thread you will have work to keep you awake and thinking for weeks. Let me clean that cut for you."

I lifted my feet off the pedals and let go of the wool then stood and followed her to a pitcher of water set out on a high table near the corner of the room. She sprinkled salt into a bowl and poured the water in after it, swirling and swishing them together inside the pewter. "Pricks and cuts are very common down here, as you might imagine. We are kept prepared."

I gave her my hand. She peeled off the wool strip and dipped my hand down in the water. The cut stung. Like nettles. Like bee knives. I bit my lip, holding back a gasp. Bits of red floated off into the water in an inky cloud, dark at first, then paler and paler until I could no longer tell it apart from the murky liquid.

"You didn't get this from spinning." The woman ran her thumb over my finger, just next to the wound. "How did you get it?"

"A broken cup." I didn't say that I had broken it on purpose or that I had used my blood to write Snow a warning. I was wasting so much time with this woman. "Do you really believe that no one will love you when you are old?" I asked because it seemed to be the only subject that interested her and I didn't want to sound overly inquisitive about the queen.

"I know that no one will, child. Men rule the world, child. They will always believe that they are stronger than us. They will always believe that they are wiser. What do we have left to offer them when we are no longer beautiful? It is the only power we are allowed." The stroke of her thumb against my finger grew softer, slower.

I pulled my hand out of the water and shook it dry. Bits of water brushed against my nose and cheeks. "Shall we show the queen the thread?" I asked.

The woman smiled. Her eyes glittered like the forest at sunset. "Of course. Hand me the needle. I will take it to her at once."

Lucille was in the manor. That at least was something. She might have sent men after Snow but she hadn't gone herself. And there had been no men in the wood. If they were searching they were searching in the wrong place.

I walked back to the spinning wheel, reaching for the needle covered in fine white thread. Like spider silk. I pulled it off the neck of the spinning wheel. The cool, silver-colored steel touched the open wound on my finger.

It tingled. It stung.

Involuntarily, I dropped the needle. I turned to look at the woman with an apologetic smile. She watched me, still smiling.

My finger went numb. My hand was tingling now, then my wrist, then my arm.

I looked down at the needle, lying on the ground with pure white thread wound around it. Poison. How had I not guessed? This woman, smiling at me, urging me to hold on to every ounce of power I had, was Lucille —somehow, despite her age —and she had poisoned me. How would I ever warn Snow now?

I turned and stepped toward the door. I pressed my weight down into my knee. It gave way. I wobbled and fell to the ground, barely able to catch myself with the palm of my hand --the one that hadn't touched the needle. That one dangled at my side, slack and unmoving. My skin was hot, my insides cold. I could hardly move.

Suddenly I remembered the ghost girl. The one whose heart Lucille had eaten. The burning pain in her chest. How she had struggled and struggled, unable to move as a knife blade sliced into her. This poison wouldn't kill me. I wouldn't be released that painlessly.

Down on my knees, my stomach swirling with sickness, my vision blurred, forcing myself to stay conscious, I looked up at the queen. At Lucille. "Power isn't everything." I said.

She stepped toward me. Her smile didn't change. Her dark brown curls swished and swayed around her perfect neck and chin. "It is. You have much of it. I can feel it in the air around you. Raw, unbridled power, there for me to take."

And then I couldn't move at all. The floor pressed hard into my face. My head ached and ached and ached. I felt drool drizzling out of my mouth onto my chin but I couldn't move to wipe it away.

I was conscious and then I wasn't and then I was again. There was blackness, everywhere inside me. Blackness instead of a fire. Blackness instead of a song. Blackness instead of a heart. Blackness instead of a mind. I wasn't sure who I was. I wasn't sure what I was doing. My arm twisted under my chest. My elbow stuck into my gut. It hurt.

People were shouting. There was an argument. Someone didn't want me on the floor. I tried to get up. I couldn't move. How long had I been here? How long had I not been here?

More shouting. The room swam, teetering back and forth, up and down. Feet clattered around me. Two pairs. Three pairs. Six. And then only one. Hands gripped firmly around my waist, dragging me away.

I don't remember how I got to the room. I don't remember being stretched out on the sofa or hearing the lock to the door click shut.

I just remember his lips, pressing down onto mine, hard, desperate, greedy. His tongue, wiggling inside my mouth. His whole body, stretched out on top of mine. His hot, sickening touch, pouring into my lungs, choking out my breath, rubbing against my stomach and back.

I tried to scream. I tried to kick and writhe and pull his eyes out with my fingers but Lucille's poison held me still, unable to move, unable to summon the song, dying inside me. I tried to melt his flesh off of his bones.

I felt his hands run down the nape of my neck, his fingers dig into the back of my shoulders, his tongue flicker between my breasts. I felt him pull up my skirt and push open my thighs.

He didn't try to be gentle. Why would he? There was nothing I could do to stop him.

SNOW

I sat in the dark, waiting. Otto had said that he would be back as soon as he told Rose why I wouldn't be home. He wouldn't let me go with him. He wouldn't let me leave the hovel. "This is the safest place you could be." He had insisted, over and over. "She knows you're alive now. She doesn't know where you are."

But I hadn't been willing to let Rose think that I had left her without saying goodbye.

Sludge, the hobgoblin cook, handed me a cup sized bowl of hot pike and pine nettle soup. Bits of mushroom bobbed in the broth. I could hardly see it in the dim light of the fire. "Eat up, girl." He said "You're going to have to get used to my cooking if you're going to stay here until your prince gets back."

I set the bowl down, untouched. I hated the dark. I hated being kept in one place against my will, even for my own safety. Especially for my own safety. Why shouldn't Lucille find me here as easily as anywhere else? I couldn't stay here, waiting, all the way until spring.

The hobgoblin Trouble came up to fetch his soup from Sludge. "I suppose the witch will be here next." He glanced at the empty bowl beside me. "Wasting our food alongside of you."

I lifted the bowl off the ground and handed it to him. After we had saved him so many times it was galling to hear him still speak of Rose as if she were a thing. "She would never hurt you."

The little man shrugged. "Them that have power don't often know how much." He swallowed three spoonfuls of soup almost without chewing. "I don't suppose she would mean to though."

"There." I said "I knew you weren't solid hard all through."

Trouble gulped down the rest of the soup without using the spoon and wiped his beard with the the back of his hand. "No more than you're solid cold." He handed his empty bowl to Sludge and joined the rest of his brothers on the other side of the fire.

The harpist hobgoblin struck up a string of melodies, one after the other. His fingers never stopped. They flung out soft tunes and lively tunes and fast tunes and slow tunes in quick succession so that I could hardly tell when one had ended and another had began. When the other hobgoblins finished their soup, one by one they began to dance. Their shadows flickered and fluttered against the earthen walls, swirling and kicking to the pull of the music.

I leaned against the wall, holding my knees next to my chest, watching, waiting.

Hiding.

The hobgoblins spun and pivoted and leapt to song after song but none of the melodies were anything compared to Rose's song. I wished I could hear her now, humming in my ear, keeping the nightmares and memories away.

At last the harp stopped. The hobgoblins ended their dance and slunk away to the edges of the cavern. They wrapped themselves in blankets spun from gold thread and went to sleep. I remained where I was, watching the smoldering remains of the fire and listening to the rough uneven symphony of their snores.

Lucille had found me at last. I wasn't as afraid as I had always thought I would be. I wasn't as afraid as I ought to have been.

Shuffling echoed through the passageway. I stood up, listening. Closer and closer, the shuffling came. Hands pattering. Knees dragging against the earth.

One of Lucille's soldiers? No. I was certain it was Otto. Why then was there only one pair of hands and knees instead of two? Where was Rose?

He appeared at last, a shadow at first, rising up off the ground. As he came nearer I could see the rust red of his curls and the long form of his nose glowing in the remaining smolder of the firelight.

"Where's Rose?" I asked.

Otto's face was drawn, his eyes worried. "She wasn't there."

"She'll come back." I said. She always did. After hours and hours of wandering the forest, all night or all day or some of both, she always came back.

Otto shook his head. For the first time I noticed the book he had brought back from Copshire folded under his arm. He handed it to me.

I opened the book. The words were hard to read in the faint, flickering light, but I recognized the messy scrawl of Rose's handwriting. It was a warning for me written in pale rusty brown ink like dried--

I looked up at Otto. "Is that blood?"

Otto nodded. "I waited to see if she would come back but . . ." He hesitated. I had never seen him so pale.

"What?" I demanded.

"Snow, there were wolf tracks. Leading into the cottage and leading out of it."

I rolled my hand into a fist by my side, aching for my knife hilt.

"The wolf must be a servant of Lucille's." Otto said. "That's how Rose knew she had found you."

I shook my head, closed my eyes. "It's my fault. It's my fault again."

"No." Otto stepped toward me. He took my hands in his. "It's not your fault, Snow. It was never your fault."

I stared at him, cold, unable to move.

He brushed his fingers against my cheek, hardly touching it at all. "I will find her, Snow. Lucille has poisoned your life, your inheritance, your sleep, but I'm here now and you don't have to be afraid anymore."

"You're right." I pulled back away from his touch. "I don't have to be afraid." I pulled my hands out of his and stepped past him toward the cavern opening.

"Snow." I could hear his footsteps pattering after me. "Where are you going?"

"I'm not going to hide anymore." I said without turning. I didn't even slow my pace. "Find your army, Otto. Bring down Lucille. I'm going to find Rose."

"Alone? Snow, you won't get past the guards."

But I didn't care. I was already in the tunnel, already crawling as quickly as I could manage toward freedom. The earth scraped my hands and face and knees and shins. I bumped my head in the darkness and cut my ankle on a sharp stone.

"Snow." Otto's voice grew fainter and fainter. "Snow, we don't even know if she's alive."

I moved forward, feeling my way through the tunnel, crawling upward, frustrated that I couldn't move faster. More than once I pulled myself up only to slide down again, scraping my knees and chest and face against the hard earth. At last I could feel the night's draft grazing over my skin, soft and silent. I pulled myself upward, craving the freedom of the woodland air. Just a few more hand-lengths. I could already hear the scurrying of woodland creatures, the call of night birds, the song of the insects.

I put my hand through the opening. Thorns scratched my skin but at least the air was cool and fresh. I put my other hand out after it and pulled myself out of the tunnel, ignoring the brambles biting through my clothes and into the surface of my skin.

Once out of the tunnel, I rose to my feet. The night was alive, stirring with the sound of woodland creatures. Something rustled in the bushes. A hobgoblin? A fox?

A wolf?

My shoulder ached, remembering the feeling of teeth sinking through my skin, almost reaching the bone. My foot hurt, remembering the strength of the animal's jaw.

I straightened, willing the pain to go away. I didn't have time for fear. Not even the remembrance of fear. I pulled in a long, deep breath, and ran.

My bare feet pounded against the earth. My heart pounded inside my chest. I concentrated on keeping my breath steady, moving faster and faster with each step. Leaves crunched underfoot and caught in my hair. I didn't stop. For the first time in my life I knew where I was running to. I knew where I had to go.

It had been so long ago and yet I remembered every rock, every tree and fallen log. I whirred past them, stronger with each step. Toward the manor. Toward Lucille. Toward quiet, empty halls and pale silent servants. Toward legions of grim faced soldiers and the unheard screams behind locked dungeon doors.

Toward every tangled nightmare of my past as if I had never left them.

Toward Rose.

I ran. Through bushes and nettles and ditches and puddles of mud. Around pines and oaks and willows and firs. I dodged and weaved and circled and side-stepped, running and running and running. I had to keep moving, to arrive at the manor in time to save Rose from whatever fate Lucille intended for her. I plummeted forward, one foot leaping after the other until, all at once, like a crack of thunder over the sky, I was standing in front of the manor.

The walls weren't as high as I remembered. I could see the torrents and towers of the keep poking out over them like sharp, jagged rocks in the almost dawn. The dark gray and brown shapes looked black as soot in the shadows. I hesitated for a moment, savoring the last safety of the trees, then stepped toward the wall.

There was no point in going to the gate. The guards might not recognize me but Lucille would and she knew I was coming. She had to know. What else could I do?

I moved along the shadow of the wall, searching for the crumbled spot Hans had taken me over all those years ago. I didn't have a rope but my grip had grown stronger in the years of life in the wood, my balance more sure. If the stones were spaced evenly enough, if no one had repaired them, if the stable still stood on the other side, I might manage the climb.

The wall hadn't been repaired. The slope in the structure remained where it had been since the siege before I was born. A peasant's revolt, Papa had told me, just a few years before his father had died and left the land to him. Lucille had enough wealth from her lands in the north to build the whole manor over if she wanted to. I could only imagine she had been too preoccupied with conquering other lands to bother with repairs. I could only imagine that she was so confident in the efficiency of her army and magic that she didn't believe she needed walls.

I could only imagine that she was wrong.

I lodged my foot over a stone then placed my fingers into the crack of another and began to climb. My fingers grew stiff and pale beneath the pull of my own weight. My elbows bumped and scratched against the stones. I checked each ledge for stability before pressing my weight against it but the stones protruded outward, poking into my hips and breasts as I made my way up.

The stable footholds led me to the side, away from the crumbled bit of wall. Away from the only place I knew I could climb without breaking any bones. I edged back toward the center, reaching for a stable stone with my hand. They were large near the bottom and I had to stretch my arm far.

My fingers took hold of a stone. It didn't shake. I dragged myself back toward the center, letting my feet dangle. My weight pulled at my arms beneath my shoulders. My fingers screamed at me to let go.

At last I found a ledge for my foot. I landed on it and pushed myself up. My hands relaxed only a little, glad for whatever rest they were allowed.

Something tingled across my ankle. Tiny, almost invisible feet, crawled over my skin, making their way up my leg. My foot twitched. I gripped the stones tighter, resisting the urge to shake the ants off, to reach down and smack them away. My eyes watered. The ants tingled and sidled and itched their way up my shin as I felt for the next ledge.

The stones were smaller and easier to reach towards the top of the wall. They were also looser. One dislodged at my touch. It fell past my nose, landed on my shoulder and hit me in the knee. My foot slipped and I dangled again, gripping tighter and tighter onto the stone in my other hand. There was no more feeling left in my hands. My wrist tingled, swarmed by another line of ants. Then they were everywhere, crawling over the stone and my arms and my neck and my face. I wrinkled my nose, willing them to go away but there seemed to be more of them every second.

I felt my foot along the edge of the wall, looking for a safe foothold. Every stone I touched moved. I lifted my knee, trying higher up.

There. A small one but I only needed it for a second. Just long enough to push myself up a few more inches. I could see the top of the wall already. And then I could reach it. I gripped the top edge and pulled myself up, first one knee, then the other onto the hard, bumpy surface.

I stood. The pale green of dawn traced the edge of the sky. The manor ward was quiet. Soldiers passed back and forth across the inside of the gate. Smoke rose from the kitchens. I could make out the shingles of the stable roof across from me and the dark silhouette of Lucille's iron smith lighting the furnace in the forge. Dogs barked from the kennel.

"You took your time, Snow."

My insides twisted. My soul frosted with fear. I turned toward the voice. "Lucille."

She smiled from where she stood on top of the wall. Like silk. Like fine china. Delicate and serene. "Good morning."

"Where is she?" I demanded. "Where is Rose?" My eyes strayed to a sash in her hands, pale blue, embroidered with purple and green. It was Rose's —the one she'd made because we hadn't had enough fabric left to make dresses after I'd made clothes for Otto. I'd seen her working on it for months, stitching and restitching every intricate detail.

Lucille stepped toward me. She lifted the sash. Her smile grew sweeter. The first hints of morning sun gleamed gold off of her hair, painting her face with soft shadows. A piece of silver glinted off the side of her head. Mama's silver comb. Another trophy she had stolen from my life.

I stepped forward, reaching for the sash. My fingers closed over the smooth fabric. I had admired it so much when we'd gone to town that Rose had insisted we buy it even though we could have bought twice as much of the brown fabric. The wild violets —my favorite of all Rose's flowers —were stitched in wide, neat petals with perfect care. "Where is she?" I asked again, almost choking on the words. My throat felt swollen.

Lucille jerked the sash back before I could loosen my grip on it. I stumbled into her arms as if she'd whisked me in after a dance spin. My back pressed against her stomach. I could feel her breath against my neck. She held me still, pressing into my stomach with one of her perfect, soft hands, while she pried the sash out of my fingers with the other.

I swung my elbow up toward her jaw but the motion was too late. She swung the sash over my waist, pulling it tight around my ribcage. I gasped for air, reached for her hands to pry them off, but her hold was too tight. Lucille held my arms against my back, pulling the sash tighter and tighter. I squirmed inside her grip but her hold was too strong.

My head swam as I struggled for air. Pain tightened inside my chest, growing stronger and stronger until it was almost all I could think about. The sash cut into my ribcage, bruising and then cracking the bones beneath the unnatural strength of her grip.

"I trusted Constanze last time I wanted you dead and then I trusted

Hans." Her lips pressed up against my earlobes as she spoke. Her words squirmed, unwanted, inside my ear. "I won't make that mistake again."

I tried to scream but there was no air for it. Pain in my chest. Pain in my head. Stronger and stronger every second. I could hardly move. The sun grew bright. Too bright. The world spun, twirling slower and slower until I couldn't see anything anymore. I felt my head swing forward, hanging slack from my neck. Lucille let go of me at last, and then I was falling over the edge of the wall.

I reached up with my last remnants of strength, grasping for anything that would hold me up. My fingers closed over a tangle of hair and something else. Something cold and hard that slid out of Lucille's hair along with my fingers.

But I was still falling. Down, down, down. Into darkness. Into oblivion. I couldn't breath. There was nothing to hold onto and then . . . there was nothing

ROSE

I didn't sleep. Even after the poison wore off I lay on my back, staring at the ceiling. I had never seen such intricate carvings before. I had never seen such ornate craftsmanship. Wooden creatures, strange and otherworldly, twisted together over my head. I could see the harsh pupils in their eyes and the sharp gleam of their claws.

"I love you." He had said, over and over, thrust after thrust. The word made me feel sick all over. Sicker even than the bruises and bleeding on my thighs and wrists and breasts. Sicker even than the pain in places in my mind and body that had never felt pain before.

I stared at the ceiling. I had tried to light him on fire the moment the poison had allowed me to move but my song, --my light, my magic, my innermost self –was gone. Nothing remained but a deep, hollow emptiness that seemed to reach on and on, forever into nothingness. I tried to listen to the trees. I tried to feel the thrum of the earth --to see what the creatures of the wood saw-- but all was silent. I was lost. I was alone.

A knock rapped against the door. I sat up. I picked my torn shift up off the floor and --shaking --pulled it over my head. My whole body shook as if it were afraid it would shatter into pieces with each movement. I staggered to the door and pressed against the latch of the heavy oak.

Slowly the door creaked open.

He stared at me from the corridor with his playful brown eyes and crooked smile. The corridor echoed with the sound of his breathing. I tried not to hear his heartbeat. I tried not to let my breath fall in time with his as he stepped toward me. The floor pounded with the sound of his feet over the carpet.

My heart should have been beating. I should have been afraid.

He smiled. That same ridiculous smile. His eyes glinted with danger and lust. He reached his hand out to stroke my face.

I stepped back, pushing his hand away in the same jerky, involuntary movement. The back of my hand hit the a tray I hadn't even noticed he was holding. It went crashing to the floor. Globs of thick white porridge fell out of silver bowls. Silver cups of hot milk spilled over the rug. Sausages and toasted cinnamon buns rolled across the floor. "I'm not drugged anymore." I said. My voice was clearer than I had expected it to be, cutting with the precision of a needle.

Boris's forehead wrinkled. "I saved your life. Mother was going to kill you. She was going to eat your heart. If I hadn't let Hans out of his cell to distract her she would have."

It was hard to look at him. Hard to see his smile and cheeks and nose without shutting my eyes and hoping every memory of his existence would go away. Without feeling them . . .

"You should have let her kill me." I said.

"Why?" He asked. "I love you, Rose."

Those words again. I shuddered, forcing myself to keep my eyes open, watching every hint of movement in his face and body. "Where is Snow?" I asked. "Has Lucille . . . found her yet?"

"I don't know." He said but the answer came too quickly.

"She's dead." I heard the words fall out of my mouth but I didn't feel them. My entire body went numb. Numb and cold and still.

"Rose--"

A whisk of silk drifted through the open door. Lucile stepped into the chamber. She wore no plain blue wool this morning. A long, glittering green train draped down her back, dragging against the ground like a carpet of moss. Her sleeves hung off her shoulders to reveal the pale smoothness of her neck and arms. A silver necklace with engravings to match her rings hung around her throat. "It's my turn now, Boris." She reached for my wrist.

Boris's smile twisted into a snarl. "I won't let you kill her."

"She doesn't want you, Boris." Lucille spoke his name with contempt. "She never did. Your distraction last night bought you a night with her not a lifetime. You knew that or you wouldn't have been so impatient to make use of it." She reached for my wrist again. Her fingers twisted tight around my skin, digging into my bones and bruises. She pulled me toward the door. I didn't resist.

"Mother--"

Lucille lifted her other hand. Silver rings glittered on her fingers. "Stand back. There are other girls. It is no concern of mine if they don't like you either."

She pulled me out into the hall. Boris stared after us, his lips bent into a pout, his eyes wide with hurt and hatred. I couldn't take my eyes off him.

I'd never wanted to forget any sight more.

"If you want to make yourself useful." Lucille said. "Fetch me Snow's body."

She slammed the door and his face was gone. I released a breath I hadn't known I was holding.

Lucille dragged me through a long twist of corridors. Her grip was inhumanly tight, grinding into my wrist as she glided past each door, floating like a cloud of mist. I felt swallowed by the power of the magic that engulfed her. It was stronger than anything I had ever reached for. Stronger than anything I would have dared to touch. Cold. Harsh. Unforgiving. A power that saw no alternative but its own will.

I twisted myself in her grasp as she pushed me along in front of her. "I could be carrying his child." I said. "Your grandchild." The idea sickened me but in spite of everything I wasn't ready to die yet. Was there anything I could say to make her spare me?

I craned my neck to see her expression. A shadow flickered over her face then disappeared as she forced me around the next turn. I had expected to be taken down into the dungeons but here was a flight of stairs. She pushed me onto them and I marched obediently upward. She followed. The soft swish of her train dragged after us.

"You said my Gran was fortunate to have me to love her in her old age. My child might love you in yours."

Her hold on my wrist tightened. "You think I enjoy having even Boris to remind me of my true age? My body will be young long after any child you could ever have has rotted in her grave. Why would I want to watch something so obscene."

"You want to be loved." I said. "Boris doesn't love you. Neither did his father or any of the other men you order about. They fear you. They desire you. But they do not love you."

She prodded me to move faster up the stairs. The swish of her train slithered like a snake.

"That's why you hated Gran so much. You saw how Otto –a child untouched by the contaminations of life –loved her even though she had chosen age and you had chosen youth. You knew that no matter how many admirers you had no child would ever love you. You hate children because they remind you of what they have and you don't, what you will never get back no matter how many of their hearts you devour."

We reached the top of the stairs. She flung open the door and twisted me around to face her. "I can take their youth." She said "Just as I will take yours along with every last remnant of your power."

"That's not what you want." I said. "Not really. You want the other thing they have. The only thing you can take over and over but never keep. Innocence."

Lucille's gaze remained solid, un-braised by my words. She let go of me, pushed me into the chamber, and slammed the door shut. I listened as her train slithered back down the stairs and the engulfing force of her power faded.

At last I could breathe again. I turned around. I stood in a small plain room without a bench or stool or chamber pot inside. A woman with pursed lips stood across from me.

"Greta?" I wasn't shocked. I wasn't sure I could be shocked anymore. I wasn't sure I could be anything.

Her face was as expressionless as it had been all those years we had lived together in the village. She stepped toward me and I did what I hadn't done all night long. What I hadn't done standing over Gran's grave or listening to Lucille talk about Snow's body.

I burst into tears.

SNOW

I woke with a gasp. My head ached. My chest ached. My heart pounded and pounded beneath my breast. Air. Sweet, beautiful, gorgeous air. I drew in another long, greedy breath, letting it reach into every inch of me. My head. My toes. My fingers.

"Hold still."

Whose voice was that? I knew I'd heard it before. One of the hobgoblins. The eldest, white-haired one. Glen. I remembered his silhouette weaving with his brothers' against the cave walls. Had I fallen asleep after the dancing? The earth was hard beneath me, covered in crisp, dry leaves.

I opened my eyes. The sun seared into them, bright and blazing. I squinted, trying to make out the two short figures standing over me. One was Glen, the eldest hobgoblin, grave and concerned. The other was Trouble. He was scowling. Bunched up in his hand was Rose's sash. Bits of blue and green and purple rippled in the breeze.

And then I remembered. Lucille on top of the manor wall. Her hands over my mouth, trapping the air inside. Her grip on the sash, squeezing my ribcage and lungs.

Falling. Falling toward the ground with nothing to hold onto.

I lifted myself onto my elbow, gritting my teeth at the pain in my ribs. "I'm alive?" I asked.

"Ha!" Trouble said "We save her life and she doesn't even notice. How's that for thanks? We caught you coming down. Me and him and two more of my brothers. Twisted his ankle." he pointed to Sludge, the cook, sitting on the ground a little to the side, leaning against a tree. "And just about broke my arm, you great big heavy girl. Then we had to pull this off you." He handed me Rose's sash.

I stroked the embroidered green vines, gripping the gauzy blue fabric that had nearly killed me. My breath was still short and shallow, my heart beating and beating like a battle drum. "Thank you." I managed to say.

"Well," Trouble tapped his foot impatiently. "Aren't you going to ask what we were doing here?"

I shivered slightly in the morning sun. My skin still felt hot to touch. "What about Rose?" I asked instead.

Glen shook his head. "Your prince --Otto-- said she might have been taken. We haven't found her."

I collapsed back onto the ground, closing my eyes. How could I hope to get her back when Lucille had defeated me so quickly? How could I ever have imagined that I could stand against her?

"Well how could we?" Trouble's voice was terse, constrained, as if he had to force the words to come out at all. "We had you to look after -- not that that was our idea, mind you. Your prince sent us after you. Said to help you find the --find Rose and make sure you didn't come to any harm while he gathered that army."

"You're the one who said we should--" Glen stopped talking abruptly. I opened my eyes again to see the two brothers glaring at each other.

"We were just doing what Otto told us to." Trouble insisted.

I must have fallen on the outside of the manor. We were somewhere in the wood. I could see the canopy overhead, blocking all but a few patches of the sunlight. I pulled myself up again, ignoring the pain in my chest. The leaves stirred beneath me. They crumbled beneath my weight. My hand hit something cold. Something cold and hard and small.

Mama's silver comb, ripped from Lucille's head as I fell.

I rested it in the palm of my hand and lifted it off the ground. The form of a running deer was imprinted onto the side. How long since I had last held it? Since Papa had first pressed it into my hand, telling me what a good wife my mother had been? It felt a lifetime away.

"How far are we from the manor?" I asked.

"Not far." Glen answered. "We smuggle Lad inside with the morning guard to find out what he can."

"And hopefully something to eat." Sludge muttered from beneath his tree. "Hard work, this rescuing. It's a wonder you bothered so many times with that rascal." He tilted his head toward Trouble.

Trouble glared at him. "At least we managed to rescue her without ruining her beard or destroying her coat."

"She doesn't have a beard or a coat, you idiot."

I shuffled over to a fir tree and leaned my back against the trunk. The last thing I wanted to do was wait but I had no chance of climbing the manor wall again until my heart stopped racing like a stag on the run and I could manage a decent sized breath. Perhaps Lad would be back soon with news of Rose.

Trouble handed me a skin of water. I took it gratefully and gulped it down. The skin was small but the water inside was still fresh and cool.

We waited an hour. Glen paced. Trouble grumbled. Sludge sat against his tree, whittling a stick, while I sat against mine, watching the sun rise higher and higher over the trees. I began to hum, trying to remember the weave of Rose's song, trying to paint its comfort and mystery into the still, warming forest air.

"Will you stop that noise?" Trouble asked. "As if we didn't have enough to worry about."

I sighed, fingering my mother's comb in my hand. So far, the only thing I'd been able to take back from Lucille. It was far from the most valuable thing she'd taken. Would she believe I was dead again or would she send someone to collect the body and make sure? Perhaps we should move in case her men came looking for us —but then how would Lad find his way back to us?

I lifted the comb and ran it absently through my hair. It caught in the knots, tangling into the strands. I pulled it out, then stuck it in again, stroking it through my hair until all the tangles were gone. When I had finished I stuck the comb on the top of my head, just behind my ear, so that the silver deer could be seen resting over the strands of black. So that if Lucille found me she would see that I had taken it back from her —that she couldn't keep everything she took.

The tip of the comb pricked against my scalp. The skin broke. My head tingled. It felt numb. My skin burned hot. A chill ran through me. Confused, I lifted my hand to take out the comb, but my arm, already lethargic from loss of air, didn't move.

'Help.' I tried to say 'I did something very foolish. Help me pull the comb out.' But my lips wouldn't move either. My eyelids slid shut. I leaned forward and felt myself falling again. Falling with my nose headed straight for the ground.

ROSE

Greta put her arms around me, cradling me as she never had when I was a child. I buried my face into the crook of her shoulder. She pulled tear soaked hair away from my face. Her breathing was deep, steady, and familiar like the constant pulse of her spinning wheel.

"Why are you here?" I asked at last. The words were hardly discernible through my drizzling nose and swollen throat. "Are you a prisoner too?"

"No. The queen has commanded that I cut out your heart to prove my loyalty to her." I couldn't see her face but I imagined her lips pursed in a perfect straight line. Probably the only expression she knew how to make.

"To prove your loyalty?" I pulled away, untangling myself from her embrace. "Because I lived with you as a child?"

Greta shook her head. "She knows nothing of that. These last three years i have served her carefully, all the time in terror that she would learn that I had hidden a child she had wanted dead but I had never thought to conceal the fact that Hans --the Hunter, they call him here -- is my brother. There was no reason to. He was her most trusted servant but she has learned that he betrayed her and so I am under suspicion."

"Snow." Her name hurt to say. The tears had brought with them more places to ache from. "You're here because Lucille learned that Snow was alive."

Greta nodded. "Hans fed the queen a hind's heart instead of Snow's. It wasn't the first time he'd deceived her."

"What do you mean?" Tears still clung to my cheeks and the rims of my swollen eyes.

Greta stepped back. She pursed her lips, eying me from head to toe. Like a slave master surveying his merchandise, I used to think when she looked at me like, that but now . . .

She was so still, so quiet, so practiced in betraying nothing of herself that even her eyes were hard to read. And yet, was that just the tiniest glint of . . .

It couldn't have been pride. It couldn't have been love.

"You're a princess, Rose." She said. "Did you know that? Your parents ruled the North when they were alive. Lucille killed them. She sent Hans to kill you but he brought you to me in the village instead."

I blinked, staring at her. "But Gran . . ."

Greta shook her head. "It was Hans. We lost our parents to the plague when we were both children. He learned to hunt. I learned to spin. But it wasn't enough. We were still hungry almost every night. Lucille offered him anything he wanted when she began her army. Gold. Protection. Glory.

"Hans had killed deer and rabbit and wild boar. He knew his business. He did well on the attack, killing masses of soldiers with the same detached precision he had killed so much forest game. Lucille praised his work, promising him more rewards than he could possibly imagine, then she sent him up to your nursery to bring her your heart.

"He found you playing with a candle that had fallen on the rug. You looked up at him. You didn't cry or squirm. You must have been used to seeing men with knives drawn. You reached for him with a drool covered fist, smiling.

"So he hid you in his cloak and brought Lucille a young sow's heart instead. Once she had eaten it and set up court in the northern castle he brought you to me. He didn't know Lucille would ever come here. He didn't know he would find his heart again and save another child. He didn't know Lucille would ever learn that she had been betrayed.

"Boris let him go. Last night." This time I was sure I saw it in her eyes. One last remaining twinkle, something the world hadn't taken from her yet. Pride. Love. "I don't know why. The queen tried to keep it from me but servants talk. She was going to make him watch her rip Snow's heart out before she killed him but now he's out there. Somewhere. Alive. Lucille has no idea who you are. She knows you're a powerful witch. She wants your power and whatever years of your youth she can still take but she doesn't know that you've already escaped her grasp once."

I didn't see that it mattered. She wanted me dead either way. Only .

. .

Otto. She didn't know about Otto.

"What about Gran?" I asked. Otto had said that she was my nurse in the castle.

"Lucille's sister. She wasn't in the castle when it was attacked. She searched for years before she found us. You were only just learning to speak. She offered to care for you herself but I had grown used to having you. I never married. I had no children of my own. The villagers thought I must have had a foreign lover. I let them believe that that was why you were tall and pale haired but when Hans visited —only once while you were buying bread —and told me who the new queen was I didn't like anything that drew attention to your differences, anything that might help her find you"

I shook my head. I had never heard Greta talk so much all at once. Why couldn't she have told me all this before? "You left." I said "After Gran died, you just left."

The same way Boris had. And I hadn't looked for her. I had been content to stay in the wood with Snow. The wood. Where I should have been all along.

"Hans took me here." Greta said. "He promised me you would be safe."

"I wasn't."

She shook her head. "No one keeps their promises."

I looked at the knife lying on the cold, stone floor. Long. Slender. Sharp. The door was locked. There was no way out for either of us. "What happens now?" I asked.

Greta twisted her lips into the ghost of a smile. "Lucille has promised that I will be bitten by a viper if I don't bring her your heart. It is a more painful death than I had hoped for but she has given worse."

"Don't be stupid." I said. "Then we'll both die." Lucille wasn't going to let me go just because one of her servants disobeyed her.

"What would you have me do?" Greta asked "I spin thread. I don't have the stomach my brother does. Even if I had never seen you before in my life I couldn't . . ."

"What if it were a hind? Like Hans used to fool her before?"

She shook her head. "The door is locked and even if it weren't I don't have the skills to find one before nightfall."

"I'll find one." I said. "I'll find a hind and bring her close enough for you to kill."

I clenched my fists, vaguely aware that I had once refused to use my power to help Snow hunt or for anything that would harm what I had been made guardian of. The memory flowed through me like an ache, encompassing my entire body, but it strengthened my resolve rather than weakened it. Lucille and her son had taken my home, my family, my body, even my kindness, from me, but my will was my own. I would not surrender to them. Not yet. Not ever.

I stood and strode past Greta toward the window.

"It won't fool her." Greta said. "She will check to make sure you are dead."

"It will give us time." I said. Time to find a way out. Time to get a message to Otto —or maybe even Hans. Time meant life and life meant a chance.

SNOW

I opened my eyes. My head hurt. The sun was blinding. I groaned.

"You're using up your debts fast, Snow. Are you trying to rival me as a troublemaker?"

"The comb." I said, still trying to make sense out of the patterns of lights and colors in front of my eyes. "I shouldn't have put it on."

"No, you shouldn't have."

The tingling and numbness. It must have been poisoned. My head was still throbbing. My nose ached where it had crashed into the ground. But how could Lucille have known I would take it?

"Lad is back." Glen said. "He found the witch."

"Lucille?"

"No. The other one."

"And food." Sludge added. He pulled a sausage out of a sack in front of him and sniffed it with a craftsman's curiosity.

I sat up, shaking the last of the grogginess out of my eyes. "Where? Is she . . ." I couldn't bring myself to ask it.

"She's alive." Lad stood behind his older brothers. His fingers hid inside his black beard just under his chin. He spat on the ground, contempt evident in his eyes. "The queen has her locked up. No one will say why. Her servants aren't very loose of tongue. Not to strangers anyway."

I shuddered, remembering the silent halls, remembering Constanze and the pale woman, afraid to speak, afraid look anywhere they weren't told to, afraid they would disappear.

"Where is she being kept?" I asked. "The dungeons?"

I knew every room in that manor. If I could find a way in, if I had time to look . . . but getting her out would be the real difficulty.

Lad shook his head. "I don't know where. Only that a prisoner escaped from the dungeons last night and the queen's son was seen carrying a girl with red hair up the stairs. Into his . . . into his bedchamber."

His bedchamber. My stomach felt sick. I placed my hand over it, choking back vomit.

"Find out." I demanded.

Lad looked at Glen. Glen nodded.

"We'll all go." Trouble said. "Better chance of getting out again that way."

The brothers were silent for a moment. Their clan had once had eleven members. Until Lucille.

Trouble snatched the sack of food away from Sludge and handed it to me. "We'll be back." He turned around and scurried off into the bushes. His brothers followed. Even Sludge who seemed to have forgotten that he was supposed to have a damaged ankle.

I stared after them, cursing myself for not going with them, but I would only attract attention. Even outside the manor Lucille had me trapped --forced to sit still, to wait, to hide.

I wasn't hungry but I dug into the sack of food anyway. For something to do or perhaps to fight back the legion of fury swelling up inside me. I pulled out an apple and bit into it. The juice was sweet, crisp, and just tart enough. It tasted like autumn and winter and . . . and a brittle spice that made my tongue numb.

Like Christmas.

Not again.

I opened my mouth, trying to spit the apple out, but my tongue wouldn't move. Neither would my jaw. Saliva built up in the back of my throat, blocking my breath, blocking my voice from calling out. I gagged, choked, gargled, but the apple piece lodged itself further and further into my throat. My eyes watered. My ears stung. I felt oblivion reach for me with its long seductive fingers.

ROSE

I stood, facing the window with my eyes closed.

His hands stroking my thighs, pulling them open.

No. I flung my eyes open, gasping for breath.

I looked down at my clenched fists. Open, I told them. Release. Accept. Speaking to the wood required trust. A mind without secrets. I couldn't afford to shrink away from anything.

My fists remained closed. My jaw clenched. My wrists were tight.

I breathed deep, then closed my eyes again.

His skin, soft and vulturous, clammy with sweat . . .

My fists tightened.

No. I forced my eyes to stay shut. I had other memories. Other thoughts.

Greta. The forever thumping of her spinning wheel. The smell of stew bubbling on the fire.

My body unable to move, unable to fight . . .

Gran. The bright wrinkles around her eyes as she flung my red cloak over my shoulders for the first time. The warm cackle of her laughter. The soft, haunting thrum of her song.

My hand -- numb, bleeding --as I fell toward the ground. Lucille's cold, beautiful smile.

Snow. The terrible green mess she turned pea soup into.

Boris. Saying he loved me, over and over. Telling me that Snow was in danger.

Snow, gone. Snow, found by Lucille.

Tears leaked down my face, pouring over my lips and down my chin. They tasted like salt. Like blood. My throat swelled. My breath caught in my belly. I couldn't breathe.

Snow. Standing in front of Boris's wolf form with her tiny silver knife inside the cottage.

Snow. Insisting that we rescue the accursed hobgoblin again and again and again.

Snow. Dancing in the cottage with Otto.

Snow. Standing with me in the wood at midsummer, fearless, as I lit the world on fire, promising me no one would ever keep me away from her. Her unblinking gaze. Her deep red lips. The sideways tilt of her head.

Everyone breaks their promises. I had broken mine too. I had trusted Boris.

The tears kept coming. Hot. Scalding. Like fire. Like music. Singing, thrumming from inside me, each tear a different note, each tear a different thought, a different piece of myself.

And then I heard the wood and it was singing and it was crying too. Rain water pattered against the earth, enriching the soil, painting it a dark, cinnamon brown. I felt it fall, drip by drip against oak leaves and fern branches, rolling in kisses down their surfaces, seeping down into their roots. I savored each drop, drinking in the sorrow that would never quench my emptied entrails.

Drip. Drip. Water caught in the wind. It scattered into the air, breaking into smaller particles before sprinkling over a bed of rotting leaves. It drifted down onto a shrew's fur. The shrew shook it off, scattering it over a carpet of pine needles, then scurried away, searching for somewhere to hide from the damp, clammy weather.

The rain poured harder. The ground grew soft with the rush of water. Mud drizzled off the side of the cliffs. Droplets leaked through the roof of Gran's empty cottage.

There. Brushing his nose against the brook, pushing his tongue out for a drink. A fawn. And next to him, shaking water out of her ears, telling him it was time to go, her heart --the same size as mine --thumping blood steadily through her body. His mother. A doe.

Come. I said. Come to your death so that I can live.

The doe stood still, listening. She twitched her nose, turning to look at her fawn.

Come. I said again. Harsher. More forcefully.

The doe turned toward the manor. She pressed her hooves against the ground and sprang into a run. She darted through the trees. Water pounded against her back. Wind burrowed its way through her fur. It pushed against her, spurring her to bound faster and faster through the wood. Her heart beat fast, fluttering as many life pulses as it could into the short moments it had left to beat. Her legs bent and straightened, bent and straightened, kicking against the forest floor.

Leaves broke apart beneath her hooves. Forest mice scurried into their holes to avoid being trampled. A bright green beetle scrambled out of her way. The wind brushed off of her damp fur, tangling into the straight, black, damp hair of a girl. A small, pale girl with deep red lips.

The rain stopped. The wind bubbled and boiled, dancing and tossing through the tree canopy, pushing the doe to run faster with each bound. She stopped at the manor wall just below the tower window.

I opened my eyes. "Now." My voice came out in a gurgle of laughter. I had to remind myself to breathe. "Kill her now."

Greta didn't move behind me. I turned around to face her. She stared at me.

"Hurry." I said "Before someone sees."

"Couldn't you?" Greta asked. I had never seen her look frightened before. I had never seen her look anything but solemn.

I shook my head. Greta had never killed before. She needed to look haunted if Lucille was going to believe her, even for a moment, that the heart was mine. I couldn't trust her to pretend it.

Greta stooped and lifted the knife off the ground. She held it gingerly in her hands, shaking as she looked up at me. "I'll miss." She said. "I've never thrown a knife before."

"You won't miss." I closed my eyes again, rummaging through the wind, pilfering it for what I needed.

Come. I commanded. There was no hesitance this time.

Greta threw the knife. It tumbled out the window, down, down toward the ground. A hawk swooped down. His talons clasped around the knife hilt. He held it in his grasp, plunging downward toward the doe.

The doe stood where she was. Silent. Still. The weapon pierced into her flesh. She fell, limp, onto the ground.

The hawk kept his claws clenched tight around the knife hilt. He flapped his wings and leapt back into the sky, up and up, back toward the window. He landed on the window sill, blinking his wide brown eyes.

"Take the dagger." I told Greta without opening my eyes. I felt her reach from behind to take it.

I sent the hawk back down. He landed on the doe. She was still alive when the talons cut into her chest. I felt her body whimper against the force of the cut. I felt the cool, sharp bite of the hawk's talons as they penetrated her breast. I felt the blood gush out of her veins as they were broke open, ripped away from their life-source. I felt the heart beat just once in the hawk's iron grip before the last traces of being left the doe.

The hawk pushed himself up, rising back up toward the window with the bloody piece of flesh in his grasp. I reached my hands out of the window, palms up. He hovered over them and dropped the heart.

Thick, sticky blood covered my fingers and palms and wrists. The flesh was still warm. I turned and held it out to Greta.

Greta reached for it, pale, trembling. Her fingers touched the tender surface, then she fell to her knees, retching into the straw. The stench of her bile added to the mildew reek of blood in my hands. When she was finished she looked up, wiping the corners of her mouth with the back of her hand.

"How can you smile?" She asked.

"Your brother is a hunter." I said "You've seen animals killed before."

She shook her head. "I've never seen him laugh. Not even Lucille . . ."

"We can't afford to be tender hearted, Greta." I said. "Not now. Not if we both want to live."

"I know." Greta stood. She stepped away from the mess of sick. "But why are you smiling?"

I couldn't hold back the laughter anymore. I closed my eyes, feeling the wind, feeling it tangle into a mess of straight black hair, feeling it graze over the skin of a small frail form, hungry, tired, but flushed and beating with life. Tears poured down my face, running down my cheek, dripping off my chin as I laughed. I held the deer's heart in my hand, determined not to lose the one chance I had, determined not to die.

"Snow is alive." I said.

SNOW

A pair of hands grabbed me from behind. They lifted me upright. One hand pressed into my chest. The other thumped me against the back. Once, twice, three times. The apple piece flew out of my mouth, landing on the wet leaves in front of me. I was damp all over. Had it been raining?

I gasped for air, then swallowed. I turned around to face my rescuer. His hands were familiar; large and rough, covered in scars. I saw his form through the veil of water leaking out of my eyes. Dark hair and stern, distant eyes.

"Hans." The name felt like wool scraping out of my swollen throat.

"Snow." His lips twisting into the ghost of a smile. His face and hands were dusted in fresh earth.

"How did she know?" I asked. "How did Lucille know I would eat that apple?" Lad had taken it from the kitchen. Had she known he was there all along?

Hans shrugged. "Her magic is incomprehensible to me. Sometimes I think she sees inside our souls. She must have wanted to make sure."

"She made sure three times." I said "And I'm still not dead. Unless . . . " I backed away from him. "Did she send you?"

He shook his head. "I escaped from the dungeon. Boris released me last night. He wanted a distraction. I didn't realize why until I'd already gone. If I had known why . . . I might have still gone. I don't know. I never was a saint."

"You saved me." I said. "Three times."

"But I've killed before, Snow --some younger than you were-- because Lucille commanded it."

It was true. It was him who I had seen lead the lost girl up to the tower.

"Why not me?" I asked.

"I don't know. You were . . . brave. Resilient. I saw a fighter in you."

I shook my head. "I locked myself in my room and pretended nothing had happened."

"You stayed alive. The only way you knew how. I've seen grown men lose their wits over less than the things you saw in that manor."

"Where is Rose?" I asked. "Was Rose in the manor when you left it?"

"She's alive." Hans said but the words came slowly and his tone didn't give me the comfort I had wanted. "Come with me." He took me by the arm and pulled me onto my feet. "Lucille will make sure one last time."

I staggered to keep up with Hans as he led me through the wood to a freshly dug pit. We stopped at the rim. It was well dug, deeper than it was wide. Fresh upturned dirt clumped around the edge of the dark space.

"A hunting pit." I said.

Hans nodded. "I've been working on it through the night. Lucille will send her wolf next."

Phantom aches simmered in my foot and shoulder. Her wolf. Otto had been right.

"The pit should be deep enough to hold him." Hans pulled what looked like a pair of dirt covered fire tongs out of his vest. "It wasn't easy with these but it was all I could grab on my way out of the dungeon. "

I helped him cover the pit. We stomped the piles of dirt flat then snapped branches off the surrounding trees and gathered bits of brush to cover the earth surrounding it in a prickly green carpet. I didn't like watching the sun rise high through the trees as we worked. Not with Rose still in the manor. When we were finished at last we only knew where the hole was from memory.

Something moved in the bushes. Footsteps. A low growl.

"Boris." Hans said.

More footsteps. Closer.

Hans looked up, eyeing the branches of the tree above us. He lifted his finger to his lips. I nodded in understanding.

The first tree branch wasn't hard to reach. I gripped my palms around the bark and hoisted myself up, then waited for Hans. He pulled himself up into the tree across from me just as the wolf creature stepped into view. My shoulder and foot began to ache.

The wolf creature sniffed the ground, his ears back, his eyes intent. He circled my tree first, then Hans's. He stopped, sniffing at the air.

I looked across the way at Hans. "Boris?" I mouthed, remembering the young man Papa had rescued me from having to marry so many years ago. His charming smile and village raids. I wasn't surprised to learn that he was a wolf as well as a monster.

Hans nodded.

I looked at the knife in my hand. The pain in my shoulder hadn't been this strong when the wolf had first bit his teeth into the flesh.

Boris sat beneath the tree. The fur on his skin began to thin. He twitched, writhing from side to side like a bag of bones as his body began to change.

If I sat still he would never reach me. He might be able to climb in his human form but he couldn't smell me. If I stayed where I was, if didn't move, if I didn't breathe, I would be safe.

But he already knew where we were. He'd sensed us in his wolf form.

I gripped my knife tighter. My palms itched with sweat. I had gone up against Boris before and I would have died if it hadn't been for Hans.

I glanced at Hans in the tree across from me. He didn't move. He watched Boris with the careful stillness of a hunter. We only had one shot from up here. One shot and if I missed he would run.

My heart thundered in my chest. I edged toward the far end of the branch, balancing on the long narrow space. I grabbed hold of the bark with my hand then dropped myself onto the ground.

Dry leaves scattered beneath my feet. The wind brushed over my face. I stared at Boris, standing in a tiny pool of sunlight halfway between his human and wolf forms. His bones stuck out at the sockets. His hairless snout twisted into an almost human grin.

"Not this time." I said. I turned and ran.

I felt him bound after me. The earth shook with the clamor of his paws. He released a long, chilling howl that tangled itself into my ears only a few short inches from the back of my neck. My own feet beat against the ground in an inconsistent drum beat, pushing me forward one spring after the other.

Not this time. He wasn't going to pierce my flesh again. He wasn't going to rob my consciousness and banish me to the place of nightmares. I pulsed with the rhythm of my footsteps, crumbling leaves and snapping bits of twig as I passed over them. One foot after the other.

Fifty seven. Fifty eight. I counted them as I ran. I could hear the heavy heave of his breath, getting closer and closer.

I stopped. For the sliver of a heartbeat. For the breadth of eternity.

He stepped nearer. Too near. Near enough for me to feel the scorch of his sweltering breath. Like the heated iron of Lucille's shoes.

I swiveled and changed direction through the trees, circling back the way I had come. Step after step after step. My limbs felt like air, heavy and cold, impossible to move. But I moved them, hoping I had given Hans enough time.

Boris howled again. He snarled and snapped at the back of my dress. A piece of my skirt tore off.

I ran faster. If I didn't stop I wouldn't shake with fright. If I didn't stop I couldn't realize how close I was to the clench of his teeth.

Running. That's all I had to do. That's all there was. My footsteps and his pounding after them.

Fifty eight. Fifty nine. I was almost back to where I had started. One more step and ---

My toe hit a rock. I stumbled and toppled onto the ground. My shins ached from the impact. My elbow scraped against the earth. I rolled onto my back.

Boris stood over me. His gold wolf's eyes glowed with triumph.

I shook my head, backing away on my elbows. A little to the left. Just a few more inches back.

Boris mirrored my motions. The leaves crunched beneath his paws, breaking apart into a crisp powder. And then –

He whimpered, releasing a sharp yelp as he fell into the pit. His claws brushed across my ankles as he dropped past me.

Hans stepped out from behind a tree. "Are you alright?"

I nodded, rising to me feet. "Shaken." I said "Scratched."

"Poor Snowy-white." Boris's human voice whined from inside the pit "Mother's no-longer-favorite pet the Hunter couldn't protect her from a little scratch. I think you broke my ankle."

Hans stepped toward the edge of the pit. He looked down into the gaping hole. "We're not finished with you yet, Boris."

Boris laughed. A short, whimpering bark. "Mother doesn't care what I do to you anymore Hans. I can shred you to as many pieces as I like and she'll only laugh when I bring them to her."

Hans growled. "You won't be bringing her anything from down there."

"Do you want to know, Snow, why I didn't finish you off when I found out that Hans didn't -- when I followed you back from Copshire?"

I joined Hans at the edge of the pit. Boris stood at the bottom of the darkness in his naked human form. He stood on one foot, leaning against the dirt to support a swelling ankle. Grime smudged his nose and covered the palms of his hands but the rest of his skin was pink and fresh as if he'd only just climbed out of the womb. He smiled up at me and I wondered how I had ever thought his smile was charming.

"Rose." His voice bit into the name as if it were a dark and savory pastry. "Your sweet Rosy-red-witch. Did you know that we used to jump off cliffs together in the dark while you were off hunting? And last night – well, you'll never know her like that will you?"

I clenched my hand around my knife hilt, lifting it to release into his heart. The sooner he was unable to talk the better the world would be. I gritted my teeth to keep from striking too soon. "Where is Rose?"

"Dead." Boris said. "Or will be by the time I get back to the manor with whatever's left of you." He set his swollen foot on the ground, reaching up for the rim of the pit in the same movement. His fingers closed over the earth. He was moving too fast for a clean strike. By the time I had taken aim he had already flung himself upward, gaining momentum as he changed form. His paws slammed into Hans's chest. His teeth closed over Hans's throat. They both fell to the forest floor, scattering leaves and dust.

"No." I leapt toward them. I landed on Boris's back and dug my blade into his shoulder all the way down to the hilt. He snarled, rising up onto his hind legs. The force of the motion flung me back across the pit. I landed on the other side with my leg twisted under my back.

Boris turned to face me. Hans's blood dripped from the toothed chasm of his snout. His haunches rose as he prepared to leap. I rolled to one side. He flew over the pit, landing where I had just been. His sharp claws dug into the damp earth.

I jumped to my feet. My blood raged. With anger. With pain. With fear.

Boris growled. My knife was still lodged into the back of his shoulder.

I stepped away from the pit. He shadowed the movement. His bloody teeth snapped at my shins. I stepped back.

I stepped in the other direction instead, teetering on the edge of the pit.

Boris stayed where he was, knowing he would fall if he judged the leap wrong, or perhaps merely waiting for me to fall in. I looked down into the darkness. Nine feet? Ten? Not far enough to kill but far enough to trap someone as short as me. I looked up, turning to face Boris.

He blinked, poised to pounce, waiting for the inevitable.

I closed my eyes, turned back toward the pit, and jumped.

Pain shot into my ankles as I landed. I rocked back, balancing myself on both feet. A whir of fur sank toward me from above.

One step was all there was room for. One step was all that it took.

Boris landed on three of his four feet beside me. I kicked his injured back paw, then reached for the knife in his shoulder with both hands.

He whimpered as I pulled the blade down, cutting deeper and wider into the flesh before I ripped it out. Dark, warm blood dribbled over his fur, over my wrists, and onto the cold, damp earth. I kicked him again. My foot lodged into the soft space of his belly.

It wasn't an animal whimper he released this time. It was a human cry. His fur thinned one last time as he writhed and wriggled against the ground like a worm until he was once again in his naked human form. He still had Hans's blood on his teeth and chin. His hazel eyes watered with pain. He stared up at me.

"Snowy-white," he said, his body limp, motionless. "Will you kill your Rosy's lover dead?"

I bent down close so that he could see my face in the darkness of the pit. He stared at me, his eyes pleading, poisoned with pain. I could have told him that my shoulder still hurt when it was cold. I could have told him how Rose had never cried when her Gran died but that I could tell she was heartbroken. I could have told him how much I hated him for touching her or that Hans had been the only friend I had had left from my childhood.

I could have told him how much he had hurt me, how much I wanted him dead, but he already knew. He had always known and he hadn't cared until this moment as I stood over his helpless body —nearly twice the size of mine -- with a knife.

"Yes." Was all I said and thrust the blade into his heart. Once. Twice. Three times. Just to be sure. Blood glistened off the blade and hilt. He was dead. Gone. Just like Papa.

He was nothing like Papa.

I stepped onto his body and used it to shorten the climb out of the pit.

I pulled myself up onto the ground. "Hans." I said but I knew he wouldn't answer. Boris's teeth had cut deep. He couldn't hear me. He would never hear anything again.

"Hans."

I walked around to the other side of the pit where his body lay. Blood spilled out of his throat, right across his jugular where he had shown me to kill rabbits. Chunks of flesh were missing where I could see the jagged marks of Boris's teeth.

I knelt next to him, pulling his arms and legs straight, hoping it would make him look more at peace. He stared up at me. At nothing.

Hans. Lucille's huntsman. A killer. My friend. Twice he had risked his life to give me a chance to live. This time he had lost it.

I touched my fingers to his eyelids. Still warm. His eyelashes were soft even though his skin had long since calloused to the harshness of the outdoors. My hands weren't soft anymore either. I rolled his eyes shut, closing his soul forever to the world.

He didn't look peaceful. He didn't look asleep. He just looked dead. Gone. Like Papa. Like Constanze. Like Dana and Elise. Like Rose's Gran. All because they wouldn't bow to the power of Lucille's whims.

I rose to my feet, holding my knife tight in my fist. It was time for me to find Lucille. Time for me to go home.

ROSE

I laid down in the hay with my back to the door and waited for Lucille's men to come for Greta. I listened as they scuttled up the stairs, as they rattled with the lock, and flung the door open. Greta stood in the center of the room. She didn't speak but she must have shown them the heart. Rough grunts and shouts turned to a chorus of incredulous whistles.

"Didn't think you had it in you, Gret." One of them said.

"I thought the witch would kill her." Another said. "The younger ones have more strength."

Footsteps creaked toward me, heavy against the wooden floor. I held my breath, willing my entire body to be still. Greta had helped me smear blood on my shift where my heart was meant to have been cut out of my chest. The shift was ripped open but if they turned me onto my back they would see that there was no hole in the flesh.

"It smells like death in here." Someone said.

A boot thumped against my back. Saliva swirled above me then fell in a splatter behind my neck. "Shame really." The owner of the saliva said. "She was a pretty thing. Old enough for a tumble too."

"Well then, mistress spinner, lead the way. You're the one with the trophy to show the queen." The speaker chuckled. "If the queen doesn't have you bitten with her snakes. I've got one you can have. I don't care how young they are so long as they know when to scream."

Feet shuffled again. Soft, careful steps first, steady and quiet. That was Greta. Then it was clatter after clatter of heavy, hurried steps, pounding after her. The booted man standing above me left last. He spat another puddle of saliva then turned and clattered toward the door.

He didn't lock it. Why would he? There was nothing in here but a corpse.

I forced myself to stay still, not to leap up and run for the door, not to pilfer through the wind looking for Snow again, not to scream at Lucille's soldiers to leave Greta alone, not to run at them with the knife they'd left in the hay, smothered in deer's blood.

How long would the deception give us. An hour? Two?

My heart beat wildly inside my chest. The mildew smell of Greta's sick filled my nose. Straw prickled against my skin. I didn't like holding still. It reminded me of being pinned down, unable to move, of . . .

I counted the steps as Greta led the procession of scuttling men further and further away, down, down into the heart of the manor house. Fifty. Sixty. Three hundred and twenty seven.

At last I could no longer hear them. I sat up. The door was ajar, hungry for me to pass through it, but there was one last task before I was free. I closed my eyes, listening. For every fox, every bear, every vulture, every flesh eating creature I could conjure.

Calling the doe had weakened me. Commanding the hawk had left me exhausted. But I didn't care. I wasn't going to be stopped. If the manor servants saw the carrion outside they would guess what Greta and I had done. They would tell the queen and Greta and I would both end up dead.

My head hurt. My arms and legs shook. My stomach cramped and heaved as if it were hungry and overfull at the same time. I was a wolf, sniffing the ground for his prey. I was a hawk, clamping his claws around the fragile bones of a mouse. I was a badger, separating flesh from fur. My feet touched the ground. My nose twitched. My wings touched the air. An insect landed on my ear. My teeth ground the raw flesh of a dove into a paste I could swallow.

I listened, straining to hold myself together. I was everything. I was nothing. Scattered in so many pieces. So many hungry pieces.

Come. I said. Dinner.

SNOW

The warden stared at me when he opened the gate. I remembered him. He had been Papa's warden long before Lucille had ever come to the manor. He liked to complain about the rain and that he and his wife had no children but I always thought that he was secretly glad for both. He stared at me, his mouth open, waiting for me to speak first.

I didn't.

"You shouldn't be here." He said at last.

"I live here." I said.

He stared some more. At my ripped skirt and bare feet. At the blood splattered over my bodice and still drying on my little silver knife.

"I am your queen." I said. "Let me in. Take me to Lucille."

"She . . . she's at supper."

"Then I will join her."

He stared. His brow creased in concentration, trying to decide why I was covered in blood, what assets could possibly give me the confidence to call myself queen, and which side he should gamble his loyalties on. Finally he stepped aside, motioning his hand for me to step inside. Not a bow but not a command either. He still hadn't made up his mind.

I stepped into the manor courtyard. The gate dropped closed behind me. The soldiers drilling outside the stable stopped as I walked past them. The kennel boy looked up from the swine trough. The washerwomen stopped, holding the soldiers' trousers up unpinned to the washline. The warden followed behind me, as far as he could manage while still pretending to lead me.

The manor was just as I had remembered it. The same pale stone walls and ebony doors and windows. The same gargoyles watching from the torrents. The same grave stillness of its residence. The same silence.

I stepped inside and flung my way up the first flight of stairs. My bare feet pattered against the cold, stiff stone. The warden clattered behind me, rushing to keep up.

Down the first corridor. One twist, then another. Here, where I had dined with Papa since I had been old enough to wear a gown and hold a spoon. Here, where servants had carried a small girl's heart on a platter, where Lucille's iron shoes had thudded across the carpets like the muffled cries of a battlefield, where Constanze had sent me decked out in silver and purple silks to frighten me out of eating the poisoned delicacies that Lucille had spread across the table.

Lucille sat alone at the head of the table, draped in pale green silks. Mama's silver necklaces hung against her neck and breasts. The hall smelled of liver and sage and onions. She looked at me, her spoon raised halfway to her mouth, then set the instrument down, pulling two delicate fingers away from it. "I am not prepared for guests tonight." She said. "Where is Boris?"

"Dead." I said.

Her perfect green eyes strayed to the knife in my hand. "With that?"

I gripped the knife hilt, remembering the calm of her voice as she had questioned the prisoner in the dungeon, remembering her silver smile as she had rolled Papa's eyes shut, remembering . . .

I gripped the knife hilt. I walked to the table, holding Lucille's green, smiling eyes in my gaze. I clapped the knife onto the table beneath my palm, then drew my hand away, leaving the bloodstained instrument among Lucille's crystal dishes. I took another step toward Lucille.

She stood up. Her green gown whisked like a waterfall. "What do you imagine you are doing, Snow?"

"I don't need the knife." I said.

"Dying is easier without a weapon." She agreed.

I smiled. "Perhaps. But will I stay dead?"

She stepped toward me, raising her hand out in front of her, summoning her magic.

"I know why you tried to starve me to death." I said. "I know why you tried to poison me —to make my death look like an accident- why you resorted to a secret knife in the dead of night instead of sentencing me to death the way you would have with anyone else."

She lowered her hand. "You know nothing."

"Your servants had all seen you kill before." I continued. "Most of them had killed for you themselves. Villagers who stood in your way. A whole castle full of people you hated. A small girl looking for shelter from the rain. Anyone who dared disobey your orders. They all died and no one lifted a voice to stop you. So why was my death a secret? Why did you come to kill me yourself when I climbed your wall last night? Why send only your son to fetch my body? Why not send your soldiers?"

She raised her eyebrows. "Does it matter? Dead is dead."

"Why," I asked "haven't you called anyone yet to come dispose of me?"

She smiled. Flawless. Like spider silk. Like the sharp edge of a knife. "Because I don't need them." She raised her hand again, laying her palm flat in front of her mouth. Her lips formed a ring. She blew air across the surface of her skin.

A wind picked up outside. It shook against the windowpanes. Glass rattled inside the ebony frames.

"Will your servants believe you?" I shouted over the noise. "When you tell them that this was an accident? Will the neighboring rulers believe it when they hear whispers of what has happened? Conquer one kingdom and you are a coveted ally. Conquer many and you become a threat. Are you strong enough yet to defend against all of them if they hear how greedy you have become?"

The wind howled. It moaned and screeched and then the glass inside the windowpanes shattered. Sharp slivers scattered through the air, flying toward me from every side. I closed my eyes, guarding my neck and chest against the glass with my arms. Pain sliced into my shoulder, my side, my back, my thigh, my hand. The sting of blood swelled around each wound, trickling down the surface of my skin.

"I'll take that chance." Lucille said.

I held my breath, afraid to move, afraid I would grind the glass shards deeper into my flesh. The pain prickled and scratched under my skin, itching like a rash. Blood leaked out drip by drip.

I felt Lucille moving toward me. I could imagine the calm, warm smile on her lips. "You've grown brave, Snow and more difficult to kill than I had expected, but you will never have the power I have. You will never be as beautiful. You will never be as strong."

I didn't move. My limbs and side and back ached. A wave of dizziness had already swelled through me, ebbing at the edges of my consciousness. How much longer could I remain on my feet? How could I keep the glass fragments in my side from slicing my organs once she reached me?

Then I heard her voice. Not Lucille's. It was too sweet. Too dangerous. Too tender. Too familiar. I had listened to that lullaby as I slept.

I had heard it in the dark of the wood when the shadows of the trees and the voices of the ghosts still frightened me. I had let it linger in my ears, soft and still and wild, as the forest lit itself on fire.

Rose's song. Always different. Always the same.

Alive. My heart rattled in my chest.

The power of her voice broke into particles around me, each note sweeter and more distinct than the last. I felt the pieces of glass lodged in my flesh break apart, lose their polish, and turn to sand. The sharp, heavy grains stung as they sifted out of my flesh and onto the ground with the ooze of my blood. I opened my eyes and looked up.

Rose stood in the doorway of the dining hall. A crimson stain was smeared across her unlaced bodice, ripped where her heart was. The blood had dried brown over the palms of her hands. Her fire curls were matted, cluttered with bits of straw. She smiled when my eyes met hers. A bright, quick smile that was almost a wink.

Lucille looked at Rose, then the uneaten dish on the table, smothered in gravy and onions. The silver fork lay on her silk napkin, a single bite still clinging to the prongs.

Rose stepped toward the table. She lifted the fork and slid the flesh and gravy into her mouth.

"What was it?" Lucille asked "Bear? Fox?"

Rose chewed then swallowed. "Deer."

Lucille smiled. "Did Greta think I wouldn't recognize the flavor? Did you think I would let her go before making sure?" She strode toward the shattered window. Wind swirled through the hall. She lifted her hand, motioning down into the manor ward.

Rose and I followed her. We stepped next to either of her shoulders and looked down into the ward. A plain woman in gray wool stood between two soldiers. A third soldier stood in front of her with a wooden box in his hand.

"They are waiting for my signal." Lucille lifted her hand.

The soldier with the box lifted the lid. The others took the woman's wrist and held it out with the underside of the forearm exposed. A long, slender creature slithered his way out of the box. It hissed in anger, then opened its mouth, fangs posed to strike.

Instead of biting the woman, the creature twisted around and sank its poisonous fangs into the soldier's wrist. The soldier cried out in pain. He dropped the snake and placed his mouth over the punctured flesh to drain out the poison. The viper landed on the ground, flopping like a thick coil of rope, then moved toward the manor wall. Slowly it began to slither its way up the wall toward the window of the dining hall.

I turned toward Rose. Her eyes were closed, her face unmoving, serene as if she were in a trance. I had seen that expression before —or something like it —when she had first told me that she could hear the trees. She was calling the snake.

Lucile turned around. She lifted her hand again and struck Rose across the face. Rose opened her eyes. I moved to pull Lucille away from her.

Lucille's hand swept back. It struck hard against my chin. The cuts in my side and hands and legs and shoulder stung, leaking my life away in thick red drops. My head swam. My throat was still swollen from the apple that had been lodged in it. I reeled out of balance. My cheek smashed against the hard grains of sand scattered over the ground.

Lucille didn't even tilt her head to look down at me. "Do you really imagine you can match your powers against mine?" She demanded of Rose. "You may have much of it but you lack the will and strength to wield it." She lifted her hand again. The wind billowed around us.

My hair fluttered across my eyes, obscuring my vision. Thunder rumbled in the sky. I lifted myself onto my elbow. My head spun as I fought to remain conscious.

Lightning flashed. The sky went dark. Sharp bits of hail flew in through the window, parting as they passed Lucille. Once they passed her they joined together again, speeding toward Rose with their dagger edges directed at her breasts.

Rose lifted her arm, warding off the onslaught. Her lips pressed together.

Her voice. Soft. Quiet. Pale as the wind. Warm as a candle.

The bits of ice melted away, dripping onto the ground around her in a wet slur.

I pulled myself onto my knees, edging my way back toward Rose and Lucille.

Lucille shrieked. It sounded like a hawk. Like a dragon's cry. "Let's see you sing when you are screaming." She closed her eyes. She didn't sing. She chanted. The words came out in cracking clips of sound, one syllable after the other, crunching like ice. Indistinguishable words. Noises I had never imagined a human mouth could make. Crisp. Cutting. Course.

Rose stood still. The swirling notes of her song stopped, replaced with a dry scraping in her throat. Her hand moved toward her mouth then stopped. Suddenly as if she could no longer move. Her eyes widened in fear. I had never seen her afraid before. I had never seen her eyes bleed with tears of terror. The tears crystallized into ice in the corners of her eyes as I realized what Lucille had done.

She had turned every drop of moisture in Rose's body to ice.

Rose's face twisted with pain. Her skin grew pale and red. And then she began to scream.

Loud. Shrill. Like the soul cry she had released the night she had discovered her gran's body. Like the prisoner Lucille had questioned in the dungeon. Like my heart, so, so deep down that I couldn't even reach it.

But Rose could. It shattered at the sound of her scream. I jumped to my feet, rushing at Lucille with every living particle left in my body.

My hand closed over her shoulder. My knee jammed into her thigh. My arm twisted around hers. Together we plummeted down onto the ground.

Lucille shoved me off of her. She kicked me in the shin with her iron slippers. I ignored the hard, heavy force of the impact. "Rose." I said but she couldn't hear me over the sound of her own screams. "Rose." I said again.

Lucille opened her mouth. I jammed my fist into it, cracking my bones against her teeth. No chance I would let her speak again. A thick trickle of blood ran down her chin.

Rose kept screaming. The spell had stopped but the pain was still there. She was stiff with ice.

Lucille rose to her knees, towering over me. I grabbed her wrists and pulled downward with all my strength.

"Rose." Now I was screaming too. "Rose. If you can scream you can sing. Rose, listen to me."

Lucille kicked me again. Her iron shoes dug into my thigh, grinding against the bone.

"Rose." I screamed. "Her shoes. Her iron slippers."

Lucille shook her head, chuckling, almost smiling. A whisk of her nut curls fell against her chin next to the trickle of blood. Her green eyes were almost manic. "It's too late." She said "Rose is gone. It's just me and you now and we know how that ends."

"She's alive." I said "I can hear her."

"She's screaming." Lucille purred. "There is nothing left of her but pain."

"Will her heart be worth anything to you frozen?" I asked. "What power will you find in ice crystals?"

Lucille laughed. The same warm, liquid laugh she had used for Papa's jokes. The wrinkles in her forehead smoothed out. Her green eyes twinkled. Her lips, still drizzling with blood, twisted into a smile. "The same power that is in mine."

"Then it is a useless power." I said. "Rose's power isn't like that. It's not cold and stiff and controlling. It's wild and loose and full of fire. It's alive. It's fearless and rampant and defiant. It swells and burns and listens to the earth. It sings even with pain and death dancing in circles around it and when it can't sing anymore it screams because no one can silence it. Not ice. Not pain. Not death. How could you wield power like that? All you can do is kill and take and live the longest death anyone has ever known. Your power is nothing."

Lucille's smile dropped from her face. She lifted her foot, aiming the iron sole at my head.

Something was wrong. Something had changed.

Rose had stopped screaming.

My heart stopped. "Rose." I said. "Rose."

Silence.

"Rose." I rolled my head back and forth, trying to see her, but all I could see was Lucille's still, staring eyes and gritted jaw. Why hadn't she slammed her iron shoe down on my face yet? What was that blistering smoke smell, the heat creeping into the air above me?

The screams began again. Only they weren't Rose's anymore. They were Lucille's. Her foot moved downward. I rolled to the side, swinging out of the way just as her shoes hit the ground, orange and sizzling with heat. I could smell the searing of her feet —rich and heavy like roasted sow flesh. She lifted her foot up again, dropping the other one to the ground.

Up and down her feet went, one after the other, burning to a black and blistering ooze of flesh over her bone as she screamed and screamed and screamed.

There was another sound floating behind the screams, driving them forward with a fierce haunting call. Of fear. Of pain. Of anger.

Of love.

Rose, singing.

I pulled myself onto my feet, shaking with fatigue. I turned to face her. The room swirled and swished around me. I struggled to hold myself upright.

Rose smiled through her song. She reached her hand out for mine. Her skin had retrieved its flushed tones, her eyes their fire. I turned away and stepped toward Lucille, still dancing like a broken puppet next to the window. I placed my hand on Lucille's shoulder.

One shove was all it took. One shove and she was flying downward, soaring toward the ground like a heavy piece of rock. I didn't hear her hit the courtyard. I didn't hear her soldiers' shouts as they stepped out of her way. I only heard Rose's song. I only felt Rose's hand reach around my waist, her head lean against the top of my head. She closed her eyes, concentrating, as the viper slithered across the courtyard, coiling its long body around Lucille's arms and wrists. The animal sank its fangs into her neck.

Lucille's mouth foamed. Her body shook. Her men swarmed around her, shouting and pointing and kneeling next to her. Then she stopped moving.

Rose's body slackened against mine. She released a long heavy sigh, a whisper against my forehead as her song came to an end.

I nestled the side of my head into the crook of her neck, soft and warm and safe. "I thought you were gone."

She lifted her head, pressed her lips against my temple, tightened her arms around my waist. "Never."

ROSE

I woke in a bed. The sheets were made of silk. My head hurt. My throat was dry and cracked. Every muscle ached. I stared at the ceiling a moment, trying to remember if I had ever lain in a bed before. Probably not since I had lain in the nursery of Otto's castle in the north.

My castle.

"You're awake." Otto's voice.

I rose up onto my elbows, looking around the room for Snow. My stomach swirled with sickness from the motion. Snow was lying on another bed across from me, still asleep. Her wounds had been cleaned. The bleeding had stopped but bits of black and purple had begun to spread over her skin where she had been hit.

"She was bruised badly." Otto said, sensing my concern. "A few broken bones, but we stopped the bleeding in time. She will recover."

I sank back into the bed. I closed my eyes. Had anything ever been so soft? My shift wasn't torn anymore either and the bloodstains were gone. It must have been a new one.

"We didn't know what to do for you." Otto said. "We couldn't find any wounds but you were passed out cold next to Snow."

The wounds were there. I could feel them in every ounce of my being. Invisible, magical bruises that might never heal. So much power had coursed through my being. How had I done it all? How had I dared?

"How did you get here?" I asked Otto. What I really meant was why was he here at all.

"I came to rescue you." He answered.

I opened my eyes and wrinkled my nose. "You were a bit late."

He looked like he might chuckle, then didn't. "I'm sorry." He said. Softly. Simply. "I thought I would have a better chance with an army behind me so I went to Copshire first to hire every mercenary I could coerce. If Snow had waited for me —if she had done as I'd told her —you would be dead."

I smiled in spite of all the pain. "Snow's much too smart to do as she's told."

Otto turned toward her bed. He smiled softly. Wistfully. "She is." He stared a moment longer, then turned back toward me. "But now I have an army I don't know what to do with. Two actually. Lucille's men surrendered without a fight since their queen and her heir were both dead."

"Those are Snow's." I said.

He burrowed his forehead in confusion.

"The men." I said. "They should surrender to Snow. This is her manor." Her home.

Otto nodded. "Yes, of course."

Something else he had said struck me. "Lucille's heir —Boris —he's dead?"

He nodded again. "Stabbed three times in the heart with Snow's knife."

I stared past Otto at the ornate picture frame hanging on the wall, wondering why I wasn't gladder, why I felt like crying.

I wouldn't miss him. I could never miss him after what he had done but his death did nothing to the memories still clogging up inside my head. I shook them out. As hard and as fast as I could.

"Are you alright?" Otto asked.

I shrugged. "As much as I can be after draining a life's worth of magic in a single hour."

He didn't look convinced. "Have you changed your mind?" He asked. "About coming with me to the north? I could keep you safe there. We could rule together, both of us our parents' heirs."

I shook my head. "I belong in the forest." That would never change no matter how many queens died.

He nodded, rising off the bed. "Well you have until the end of summer to decide for certain. I don't want to leave until Snow is healed."

I raised my eyebrows. Of course he didn't. Then she couldn't travel with him after he asked her to. If he hadn't already.

Otto's face flushed red. He touched the back of his neck. "Let me fetch you some water." He flashed me a quick half smile and whisked out of the chamber in quick, long strides.

I don't remember closing my eyes again but I do remember waking for a second time. The chamber was dark. Strange shadows cast from the writing table and bedposts and candelabra like dark fingers trying to curl themselves around my heart. I pulled back the thick layers of bed coverings and sat up.

Snow slept in the bed across from me. I could hear the soft, even ebbing of her breath whispering into the silence. I placed my bare feet onto the soft carpeted floor and approached her bed. She was pale from loss of blood but her eyes were closed, the lines smoothed out of her forehead. Her deep red lips were bent into the slightest smile. I had never seen her sleep so peacefully. Still, without a glint of sweat on her skin. Her nightmares were gone.

This was her world. The beds, the carpets, the candelabra. When her wounds healed she would dance at her own coronation. She would glide and twirl across the ballroom in silks and silver like the queen she always was. And I . . .

I was made for the wood. I listened for the thrum of the tree roots but heard nothing. The stone walls were thick with silence. Even the wind was stifled by their stillness. Even then. Even with the compression of the walls I would stay if . . .

But Otto had his own plans and Lucille was gone. Snow would be safe. She didn't need me. I knelt beside her and kissed her lightly on the lips. She sighed softly in her sleep but didn't wake. "Goodbye." I whispered.

I got lost twice in the long, twisting corridors looking for a way out of the manor. Every step echoed into the darkness. The soldiers watched me when I finally found my way out into the courtyard, unsure if they should try to stop me. Or perhaps they were afraid I would light them on fire or call all the beasts of the wilderness to rip their flesh off of their bones. I considered trying it but the warden let me out without a question. I passed through the archway back out into the woodland. The heavy oak door slammed shut behind me.

The moon was a sliver short of full, shedding light as it hung over the trees. I listened. The forest was silent. The animals said nothing. Wind rustled through the trees. Creatures scurried through the bushes. An owl hooted but I couldn't feel the spread of his wings in the air. I couldn't taste the long centuries the trees had lived for. Even the ghosts were gone.

Hello, I tried to say but my head began to burn. Pain struck through my center, sending it reeling into oblivion. I stepped back. Sickness swirled inside my stomach. My limbs ached. My head throbbed. There was nothing for me to reach for. My connection with the wood had broken.

Calling the woodland creatures, turning the glass shards in Snow's flesh to sand, heating Lucille's iron shoes, coaxing the viper to bite her. The power had rushed through me, almost as if I had been drowning in it. As if I had had no choice but to wield it.

I hadn't had a choice. Not so long as Snow was alive. Not so long as she had been in danger.

The wind brushed across my face, bringing with it the rotting scent of an animal carcass. The doe Greta had killed.

The doe I had killed.

I closed my eyes, not trying to speak, only to listen.

Nothing.

I waited, humming silently to myself, feeling the wind, feeling the earth beneath my bare feet.

A fire spread through my stomach. Dim, but warm. It spread through my body like a sickness. A hatred that reeked of death. Power. Unstoppable. Like Lucille's. Like the wood itself. The rhythm of my heart quickened. A dark thrill shot through me.

"Claim me." the ghosts had said and so I had. I had made them my children and sung them to sleep. I had felt their pains as my own pains but now they were gone. Perhaps they had gone to sleep at last when Lucille had died or perhaps when I had broken Lucille's ice they had been trapped so deep inside me that I could no longer hear them. Perhaps they would always be there in silent, undefinable pain.

I opened my eyes, pulling away from the burn of the forest. My head ached as it had never ached before. As if it were trapped in a wool press. As if it had been bashed in with an ax.

Power. Everywhere around me. The memory of the wood itself, sharp, brittle, ancient and terrifying. But I lacked the strength to touch it.

Or I no longer wanted to.

I looked back at the manor, sleeping silently through the night as if it were under a curse. I could go back if I wanted. I could live amongst the safe, comfortable ceremonies of ruler-ship.

I turned back toward the wood. I lifted my foot and stepped into the the dark canopies. I went home.

The leaves and twigs prickled against the soles of my feet. The summer night fondled my skin, cool and fresh and fearless. The trees stood tall and silent as I passed them, each an unsolved mystery of existence. Their leaves fluttered in the brush of the wind, whispering to me in a language I would never understand. A welcoming or a warning.

The moonlight faded as I walked. Soon I could no longer catch glimpses of the glowing orb over the canopy of branches. The bats and owls and other night creatures fluttered back to their nests. A fractured gray glow filtered into the air. Dawn.

Song birds chirruped from the trees, soaring down to the mist-covered ground to peck through the earth for worms and beetles. A sparrow looked up at me. He blinked with his wide, curious eyes. I didn't feel his eyelids sliding down. I didn't know what kind of insect he had just swallowed.

Somehow that made him more real. He was his own entity because he was a mystery. I smiled, releasing a half sigh into the cool cusp of the morning. He turned his head away from me, spread his wings, and lifted into the air. He was gone in the blink of an eye, pilfering another part of the wood for the rest of his breakfast. I didn't know where.

I looked around me. The trees glittered with the first traces of sunlight. I could hear the quiet giggle of a brook nearby.

A brook. Suddenly the oak next to me was familiar. The pine with the bent branch. The blue jay nest in the poplar. The thick rampage of hawthorn bushes. I turned, moving toward the sound of the water. My steps were slow and careful as I rolled my feet over the forest floor without disturbing the earth. I listened. For movement. For change.

There was the edge of the cliff, getting closer and closer as I stepped toward it. There was the abandoned fox den, the deer trail, the scattering of ferns, the wild roses. The sound of the water grew nearer and nearer until at last I could see the pale tracing of water rippling its way down toward the river.

And there, standing next to it, exactly where his mother had left him, was the young fawn. He turned his head toward the sound of my approach. His tail and ear lifted, alert. He was a late born fawn. Traces of round white spots were still visible on his coat, sprinkled like fading smudges of ash. He watched me. Curious. Wary.

I crouched down low so that my size was less threatening. "Good morning." I said, reaching my hand out to him, waiting for him to come to me in his own time.

He sniffed the air, then stepped back. Did he know that it was me who had killed his mother?

I plucked a handful of hawthorn berries off the nearest bush. The maroon colored berries leaked juice over my fingers. The thorns stung my hands. I held them out to the fawn.

The fawn tilted his head, considering. If he wanted to fetch such a treat himself he would have to risk scratching his nose on the thorns. He stayed where he was, deciding if I was a better or worse risk.

I kept my hand out, waiting.

We remained like that for some time. Watching each other. Waiting. Deciding. Twice the fawn moved toward me, one or two tentative steps, then stepped back, further away than he had been before. My arm grew sore. The dawn brightened into full morning.

At last he came towards me. He darted straight for me in a succession of quick leaps as if he were afraid he might change his mind. His muzzle was soft as he nestled it into my hand. His tongue was warm and rough. His ears twitched. He stepped back, watching me, waiting for more.

"There." I said "You see? I won't harm you." I plucked another handful of berries and held them out. When he finished those I gave him another. Finally I rose, wiping the berry juices off on my skirt, and stepped away.

I moved through the woods, one step after the other, striking a path toward the cottage once again. I didn't look back to see if the fawn was watching me. I didn't look to see if he had turned and darted away.

The cottage was in some disorder when I reached it. The door left open, leaves and broken china scattered over the ground, my blood dried onto the table, the bath curtain draped in a lump next to the table. I placed my hands on my hips with a sigh then set to work picking up the mess. I had just swept up the leaves and shattered china and had started working on rubbing the brown dried blood off of the table when a tiny shadow blocked the sunlight streaming through the door.

I turned with a rag lifted in one hand. The fawn placed his hooves onto the wooden floor, lifting his tail. He clattered into the cottage next to me and sniffed the cleaning bucket beneath the table.

"There now." I said. "I thought we might be friends."

I called him First Light since I had found him at dawn. I had taken his mother from him. The least I could do was keep him from starving. He slept next to the fire where Otto had slept when he was a bear. In the morning he chased insects and turned up plants while I worked in the garden, harvesting vegetables and planting the autumn crop. Then he would follow me through the wood. I picked berries for us both, found him fresh beds of grass, climbed trees, and watched the birds flutter and chirp among the branches.

I heard only the surface sounds of the forest. I didn't hear the trees thrum. I didn't feel their roots twist, reaching for the center of the earth. The willow I used to sit in never bent her branches for me again. I couldn't see what the animals saw.

The leaves began to brown as the days passed. Summer storms sifted into cold bitter winds. The trees shed their color like the bits of old snake skin piled on the ground beneath them. I traded some of Snow's woodpile for a flint to burn it with. The village children ran in the square with First Light, laughing and chasing him in circles while I made the trade. A woman in a long simple green dress sat on the edge of the well, watching me.

I held the flint in my hand as the smith headed back for his forge with the bundles of wood I had given him. The woman at the well looked familiar. She had a long thin face with a soft half smile brushed onto her thin lips. I stared, trying to decide where I had seen her before, which tradesman she was married to or if she did trade herself.

She waved. Her smile brightened.

I laughed in sudden recognition. Greta. It was Greta. Smiling. Wearing color. No wonder I hadn't recognized her. She embraced me when I approached, and insisted that I have supper with her in her house.

She was living in a different house, smaller than the one we had lived in together. Instead of a loft she had a small bed next to her spinning wheel. I sat on it while she cut up vegetables and bits of rabbit to put into a stew. First Light laid down next to the door, tucking his nose beneath his tail.

"Hans is dead." Greta said. "Killed trying to kill Lucille's son."

"I'm sorry." I said.

She dropped the bits of food into a pot over the fire. "He gave me another chance. To live. To be free. I've never had that chance before. Not since I was a child. I've always been so afraid. Of Lucille. Of loss. Now that's gone."

"You didn't want to stay in the manor? Working for Snow?"

She shook her head. "I never liked that manor. It's too big. Full of too many people. Those little men stayed though. The ill mannered ones. They're royal messengers or spies or something now."

"The ghosts are gone from the wood too." I said. And the wolf. All the monsters were gone now.

Greta turned from the pot she was stirring. "What about you?" She tilted her head, staring at me with more intensity that I would have liked. "You didn't stay at the manor?"

I shook my head.

She turned back to the stew. "That king —your brother, he said he was —will be leaving for the north soon. Before winter, he said. Just as soon as Snow is well enough to travel."

I turned toward the window, watching dusk set in over the village.

"She wanted you to stay." Greta said.

I snapped my gaze back toward Greta. "Do you want any help with that stew? Smells about ready to add the garlic."

Greta sighed. Her lips returned for only a moment to their habitual somber line. I helped her add the spices to the stew. We ate it with bread from the village. We ate in silence but it was a soft, warm silence. Not the cold, tense silence I remembered from the old nights with Greta. It had been weeks since I'd had anyone but First Light and the other woodland creatures to keep me company. I almost didn't want to leave when we had finished with the washing but night had fallen as we ate and there was no place for me to sleep.

"Come with me." I said, standing in the doorway with my cloak flung over my shoulders and a sleepy First Light at my heel. There was more than enough room for both of us in Gran's cottage. "The forest isn't as frightening as it looks."

Greta shook her head. "I don't think I'll ever step foot in there."

So First Light and I went home alone. We walked through the dark of the forest. Quiet. Still. There were no ghosts. There were no wolves. There were no hobgoblins.

I slept hard that night and late that morning. I dreampt of birds and thorns and long colored threads spinning and spinning through a forever turning wheel. I woke to the scuffling scrapes of someone mixing things up and the sour scent of yeast. I sat up, dazed, my hair full of straw.

"If your porridge is lumpy." Snow said. "It's your fault for sleeping so late that I had to make it."

I stared down at her from the loft. Her cheeks were bright from the glow of the fire. Her hair was tied in a scarf behind her head, cut neat and short behind her ears. She had a fresh linen shift and violet wool bodice on. Laced around her feet were big, black, leather boots. Not the sort of clothing a queen usually wore.

"What are you doing here?" I asked.

She wiped a flour covered finger off on her skirt then pointed to a sash laid out over the table. My sash. The one I'd embroidered for her with vines and doves but then never gave her. "You left your sash at the manor."

I turned back to look at her. She stared at me with her dark, unblinking gaze.

"I made it for you."

Her red lips twisted into a smile, coy, almost shy. "Then you left me."

"I . . ." My heart pounded. I concentrated on deep, full breaths. "Don't you have a kingdom to rule?"

She shook her head, grinning, laughing. "I abdicated. Otto rules both kingdoms now. Only I ought to have waited. He refused to let me leave the manor until I was fully healed and since I had already told him that he was my king I couldn't disobey him without causing discord among his new followers."

"But . . . your home. Didn't you want your home back?"

"Yes." she said "That's why I came here. You are my home, Rose."

I was grinning now too. And crying. I laughed. I pushed my blankets back and clattered down the ladder, almost tripping on the steps. "Here, let me check that bread for you before you burn it. There's probably nothing I can do about the porridge."

But Snow stopped me. She took me by the waist and spun me around to face her. She lifted herself onto her toes and placed one hand behind my neck.

Her lips melted against mine, soft like a whisper, strong like a storm. She tasted like the sunrise. Like dusk. Like rain. I leaned against her, thirsty for her touch. We stood together, entwined like roses on a vine, while the bread burnt as black as charcoal.

NIGHT BRIARS

Snow and Rose live together in their cozy woodland cottage, entranced by each other's love, when an invitation to King Otto's wedding sends them out of their safe haven and on a perilous journey to his castle.

Once they arrive at the castle Rose is drawn to the court life of her ancestors. The feeling of home she finds there helps her re-ignite the magic within herself that she had lost.

Meanwhile Snow seems to find dead bodies and loneliness wherever she goes. Not everyone in the castle is who they appear to be and the dangerous magic she encounters prevents her from giving voice to the dark deeds she has witnessed. Her silence drives her further and further into madness as the secrets she unearths become more and more perilous.

These different experiences begin to unravel the love Snow and Rose have for each other. When the castle's secrets rise to the surface at last the two girls must decide if being true to themselves means letting go of each other.

Based off of Grimm's Fairytales, Night Briars is a richly drawn lesbian romance that explores the nuances of what happens after "Happily Ever After".

Made in the USA
Columbia, SC
16 November 2021

49075022R00124